PENGUIN BOOKS

THE SECRET DIARY OF A

D0714475

Praise for Adrian Mole:

'Adrian Mole really is a brilliant comic creation' *The Times*

'Every sentence is witty and well thought out, and the whole has reverberations beyond itself' *The Times*

'He will be remembered some day as one of England's great diarists' *Evening Standard*

'The publishers could offer a money back guarantee if you don't laugh and be sure they wouldn't have to write a single cheque' Jeremy Paxman

'A classic. The Adrian Mole diaries are thoroughly subversive. A true hero for our time' Richard Ingrams

'The real greatness of Townsend's creation comes from the gap between aspiration and reality. Adrian Mole is one of literature's great underachievers; his tragedy is that he knows it and the sadness of this undercuts the humour and makes us laugh not until, but while, it hurts' *Daily Mail*

'Adrian Mole is one of the great comic characters of our time . . . [Townsend] never writes a sentence which doesn't ring true; she never gets Adrian's voice wrong or attributes a thought or feeling to him which strikes one as false. Whatever happens, we may be sure that new troubles will assail Adrian, that new disasters will threaten, but that he will survive them all. Like Evelyn Waugh's Captain Grimes, Adrian is "one of the immortals" and the series of his diaries the comic masterpiece of our time' *Scotsman*

Praise for *The Growing Pains of Adrian Mole*:

'The funniest, most bittersweet book you're likely to read this year' *Daily Mirror*

Praise for *True Confessions of Adrian Albert Mole*:

'Wonderfully funny and sharp as knives' *Sunday Times*

Praise for *Adrian Mole: The Wilderness Years*:

'A very, very funny book' *Sunday Times*

Praise for *Adrian Mole: The Cappuccino Years*:

'I can't remember a more relentlessly funny book' *Daily Mirror*

Praise for *Adrian Mole: The Lost Diaries*:

'Very funny indeed. A satire of our times' *Sunday Times*

Praise for *Adrian Mole and the Weapons of Mass Destruction*:

'The funniest book of the year. I can think of no more comical read' Jeremy Paxman, *Sunday Telegraph*

Praise for *Adrian Mole: The Prostrate Years*:

'Brilliant, sharp, honest, moving, an exquisite social comedy' *Daily Telegraph*

Praise for *Queen Camilla*:

'Wickedly satirical, mad, ferociously farcical, subversive. Great stuff' *Daily Mail*

Praise for *The Queen and I*:

'Absorbing, entertaining . . . the funniest thing in print since Adrian Mole' Ruth Rendell, *Daily Telegraph*

The Secret Diary of
Adrian Mole
Aged 13¾

Sue Townsend

With a Foreword by David Walliams

PENGUIN BOOKS

PENGUIN BOOKS

Published by the Penguin Group
Penguin Books Ltd, 80 Strand, London WC2R ORL, England
Penguin Group (USA), Inc., 375 Hudson Street, New York, New York 10014, USA
Penguin Group (Canada), 90 Eglinton Avenue East, Suite 700, Toronto, Ontario, Canada M4P 2Y3
(a division of Pearson Penguin Canada Inc.)
Penguin Ireland, 25 St Stephen's Green, Dublin 2, Ireland (a division of Penguin Books Ltd)
Penguin Group (Australia), 250 Camberwell Road, Camberwell, Victoria 3124, Australia
(a division of Pearson Australia Group Pty Ltd)
Penguin Books India Pvt Ltd, 11 Community Centre, Panchsheel Park, New Delhi – 110 017, India
Penguin Group (NZ), 67 Apollo Drive, Rosedale, Auckland 0632, New Zealand
(a division of Pearson New Zealand Ltd)
Penguin Books (South Africa) (Pty) Ltd, 24 Sturdee Avenue, Rosebank, Johannesburg 2196, South Africa

Penguin Books Ltd, Registered Offices: 80 Strand, London WC2R ORL, England

www.penguin.com

First published in Great Britain by Methuen 1982
Published in Mandarin Paperbacks 1983
Reprinted in Arrow Books 1998
Published in Penguin Books 2002
Reissued with a new Foreword in this edition 2012
001

Text copyright © Sue Townsend, 1982
Foreword copyright © David Walliams, 2012

The moral right of the author and of the introducer has been asserted

Printed in Great Britain by Clays Ltd, St Ives plc

A CIP catalogue record for this book is available from the British Library

ISBN: 978–1–405–93056–7

www.greenpenguin.co.uk

MIX
Paper from
responsible sources
FSC
www.fsc.org
FSC® C018179

Penguin Books is committed to a sustainable
future for our business, our readers and our planet.
This book is made from Forest Stewardship
Council™ certified paper.

For Colin
and also for Sean, Dan, Vicki and Elizabeth
with love and thanks

'Paul walked with something screwed up tight inside him . . . yet he chatted away with his mother. He would never have confessed to her how he suffered over these things and she only partly guessed.'

D. H. Lawrence *Sons and Lovers*

Foreword by David Walliams

'I blame that Adrian Mole,' said my sea-scout master Roger. 'Boys weren't obsessed with the length of their things before reading that awful book.'

Of course Roger was wrong. Boys have always been obsessed with the length of their things. Somehow, a lady called Sue Townsend understood what it was to be an adolescent boy better than any adolescent boy. That parents and teachers and responsible adults all disapproved of the book, which of course made us kids love it all the more.

I was born in 1971, and it is unthinkable that any boy I knew from school (Reigate Grammar School), or scouts (Second Tadworth Sea Scouts), or from hanging around outside the swimming pool (Merland Rise Leisure Centre) on a Saturday night hadn't read this book. Even boys who were proud to say they had never read a book in their life read this one. They had to. There was no choice. This was our bible. Perhaps not until Helen Fielding created Bridget Jones had a fictional character connected so intimately with the reader. Townsend's book was a phenomenon. It spawned a theatre show, an Ian Dury single, a number of television series (why couldn't I have played Adrian Mole, damn you, Gian Sammarco!), and of course Townsend has written seven sequels to date. J. K. Rowling's success with Harry Potter has redefined what constitutes a publishing phenomenon. I asked my publisher recently how many copies of my children's book *Mr Stink* I had sold. They replied confidently, 'It's doing really well; you sold 10,000 copies last week.'

'Wow!' I replied. 'Just out of interest, how many did J. K. Rowling sell in the last seven days?'

'A million.'

However, *The Secret Diary of Adrian Mole* was a genuine phenomenon. It has been translated into numerous languages and sold over ten million copies. It was probably the biggest phenomenon of my youth after *Star Wars*, and *Star Wars* was bigger than God.

How did this rather parochial book become so wildly popular? The answer is quite simple: it's one of the funniest books ever written. I love P. G. Wodehouse, I adore Douglas Adams, I worship Tom Sharpe, I am incredibly fond of Kingsley Amis, but Sue Townsend's books make me laugh out loud more than anyone else's. At the centre of the book you have the character of Adrian Mole: one of the most enduring British comedy characters of all time. He can take his place alongside Bertie Wooster, Toad and Mr Micawber; even Basil Fawlty and Del Boy. My sometime writing partner Matt Lucas and I would agonize over finding the right names for our characters while working on *Little Britain* or *Come Fly With Me*. When we hit on names that sounded real, yet had a slight suggestion of absurdity – Andy Pipkin, Carol Beer, Moses Beacon – we were pleased. However, in over a decade of writing together we never came up with a name as good as Adrian Mole. That name is perfect; you have a strong sense of whom he is before you have read a word of the book. Most impressive of all, Sue Townsend has created a character who is at once an archetype, and yet unique. Like all teenage boys he is obsessed with his spots, a girl (Pandora, of course) and the size of his thing. Yet he also writes poems about a tap, reads *The Female Eunuch*, and in his spare time visits a communist OAP called Bert Baxter who refuses to die before the death of capitalism.

The Secret Diary of Adrian Mole has supporting characters that are worthy of their own books. The saga of his mum and dad's unhappy marriage; his dad's advice to his son on boarding a train, 'He said I was not to buy a pork pie from the buffet car'; his grouchy grandma; his mum's Sheffield-based boyfriend Mr Lucas; his long-suffering teacher Miss Elf; all create a sense that this is not a series of great jokes but the patchwork of someone's real life. Pandora is perhaps the most memorable supporting character. She is, of course, forever slightly out of Adrian's reach. Her intellectual superiority, her beauty and her unwillingness to lose her virginity torment our hero: 'We indulged in a bit of light petting but then Pandora developed a headache and went home to rest. I was racked with sexuality but it wore off when I helped my father put manure on our rose bed.'

However, what I love most about this book is that unlike a lot of modern comedy (and yes, I am partly to blame), Townsend's writing is full of warmth. The writers she most reminds me of are Victoria Wood, Alan Bennett and Caroline Aherne. All are absolute favourites of mine, and Caroline is a particular hero and I am proud to also call her a friend. Like Townsend they can all depict ordinary people, the people they grew up with, and laugh with them rather than at them. *The Royle Family* is the most perfect example of this. Like that show, so many of Townsend's laughs are in the small details – after three days of painting his room black over his juvenile wallpaper Adrian writes, 'Third coat. Slight improvement, only Noddy's hat showing through now.'

The boredom of existence is also brilliantly captured. Take this sublime entry from Saturday 22 August: 'Went to see Rob Roy's grave. Saw it, came back.' It makes me think of Galton and Simpson's best writing for Tony Hancock. It's about nothing.

The book also captures the utter absurdity of people's observations. This next entry is worthy of vintage Alan Bennett. Commenting on a misbehaving Barry Kent on a disastrous school coach trip to London, Adrian writes in his diary, 'The sex shop are not pressing charges either because officially Barry Kent is a child. A child! Barry Kent has never been a child.'

Even historical events, such as the royal wedding of 1981 and the declaration of the Falklands War in 1982, are brought into the lives of ordinary people living in middle England, yet the profundity of the occasions are instantly pricked. Of the first event Adrian writes, 'I have seen the Royal Wedding repeats seven times on television ... Sick to death of the Royal Wedding.' On the second, this particular sequence always makes me laugh out loud: '10am. Woke my father up to tell him Argentina has invaded the Falklands. He shot out of bed because he thought the Falklands lay off the coast of Scotland. When I pointed out that they were eight thousand miles away he got back into bed and pulled the covers over his head.'

I should stop writing now and let you read it. *The Secret Diary of Adrian Mole* is now thirty years old. I have no doubt that someone else will be writing a new foreword in another thirty years. People will want to read this book for ever. The reason is simple: it's really really really funny. Life is pain, and we all need to laugh.

Winter

Thursday January 1st
*Bank Holiday in England, Ireland,
Scotland and Wales*

These are my New Year's resolutions:

1. I will help the blind across the road.
2. I will hang my trousers up.
3. I will put the sleeves back on my records.
4. I will not start smoking.
5. I will stop squeezing my spots.
6. I will be kind to the dog.
7. I will help the poor and ignorant.
8. After hearing the disgusting noises from downstairs last night, I have also vowed never to drink
   alcohol.

My father got the dog drunk on cherry brandy at
the party last night. If the RSPCA hear about it
he could get done. Eight days have gone by since
Christmas Day but my mother still hasn't worn the
green lurex apron I bought her for Christmas! She
will get bathcubes next year.

Just my luck, I've got a spot on my chin for the first
day of the New Year!

Friday January 2nd
Bank Holiday in Scotland. Full Moon

I felt rotten today. It's my mother's fault for singing 'My Way' at two o'clock in the morning at the top of the stairs. Just my luck to have a mother like her. There is a chance my parents could be alcoholics. Next year I could be in a children's home.

The dog got its own back on my father. It jumped up and knocked down his model ship, then ran into the garden with the rigging tangled in its feet. My father kept saying, 'Three months' work down the drain', over and over again.

The spot on my chin is getting bigger. It's my mother's fault for not knowing about vitamins.

Saturday January 3rd

I shall go mad through lack of sleep! My father has banned the dog from the house so it barked outside my window all night. Just my luck! My father shouted a swear-word at it. If he's not careful he will get done by the police for obscene language.

I think the spot is a boil. Just my luck to have it where everybody can see it. I pointed out to my mother that I hadn't had any vitamin C today. She said, 'Go and buy an orange, then'. This is typical.

She still hasn't worn the lurex apron.

I will be glad to get back to school.

Sunday January 4th
Second after Christmas

My father has got the flu. I'm not surprised with the diet we get. My mother went out in the rain to get him a vitamin C drink, but as I told her, 'It's too late now'. It's a miracle we don't get scurvy. My mother says she can't see anything on my chin, but this is guilt because of the diet.

The dog has run off because my mother didn't close the gate. I have broken the arm on the stereo. Nobody knows yet, and with a bit of luck my father will be ill for a long time. He is the only one who uses it apart from me. No sign of the apron.

Monday January 5th

The dog hasn't come back yet. It is peaceful without it. My mother rang the police and gave a description of the dog. She made it sound worse than it actually is: straggly hair over its eyes and all that. I really think the police have got better things to do than look for dogs, such as catching murderers. I told my mother this but she still rang them. Serve her right if she was murdered because of the dog.

My father is still lazing about in bed. He is supposed to be ill, but I noticed he is still smoking!

Nigel came round today. He has got a tan from his Christmas holiday. I think Nigel will be ill soon from the shock of the cold in England. I think Nigel's parents were wrong to take him abroad.

He hasn't got a single spot yet.

Tuesday January 6th
Epiphany. New Moon

The dog is in trouble!

It knocked a meter-reader off his bike and messed all the cards up. So now we will all end up in court I expect. A policeman said we must keep the dog under control and asked how long it had been lame. My mother said it wasn't lame, and examined it. There was a tiny model pirate trapped in its left front paw.

The dog was pleased when my mother took the pirate out and it jumped up the policeman's tunic with its muddy paws. My mother fetched a cloth from the kitchen but it had strawberry jam on it where I had wiped the knife, so the tunic was worse than ever. The policeman went then. I'm sure he swore. I could report him for that.

I will look up 'Epiphany' in my new dictionary.

Wednesday January 7th

Nigel came round on his new bike this morning. It has got a water bottle, a milometer, a speedometer, a yellow saddle, and very thin racing wheels. It's wasted on Nigel. He only goes to the shops and back on it. If

I had it, I would go all over the country and have an experience.

My spot or boil has reached its peak. Surely it can't get any bigger!

I found a word in my dictionary that describes my father. It is *malingerer.* He is still in bed guzzling vitamin C.

The dog is locked in the coal shed.

Epiphany is something to do with the three wise men. Big deal!

Thursday January 8th

Now my mother has got the flu. This means that I have to look after them both. Just my luck!

I have been up and down the stairs all day. I cooked a big dinner for them tonight: two poached eggs with beans, and tinned semolina pudding. (It's a good job I wore the green lurex apron because the poached eggs escaped out of the pan and got all over me.) I nearly said something when I saw they hadn't eaten *any* of it. They can't be that ill. I gave it to the dog in the coal shed. My grandmother is coming tomorrow morning, so I had to clean the burnt saucepans, then take the dog for a walk. It was half-past eleven before I got to bed. No wonder I am short for my age.

I have decided against medicine for a career.

Friday January 9th

It was cough, cough, cough last night. If it wasn't one it was the other. You'd think they'd show some consideration after the hard day I'd had.

My grandma came and was disgusted with the state of the house. I showed her my room which is always neat and tidy and she gave me fifty pence. I showed her all the empty drink bottles in the dustbin and she was disgusted.

My grandma let the dog out of the coal shed. She said my mother was cruel to lock it up. The dog was sick on the kitchen floor. My grandma locked it up again.

She squeezed the spot on my chin. It has made it worse. I told grandma about the green apron and grandma said that she bought my mother a one hundred per cent acrylic cardigan every Christmas and my mother had *never ever* worn one of them!

Saturday January 10th

a.m. Now the dog is ill! It keeps being sick so the vet has got to come. My father told me not to tell the vet that the dog had been locked in the coal shed for two days.

I have put a plaster over the spot to stop germs getting in it from the dog.

The vet has taken the dog away. He says he thinks

it has got an obstruction and will need an emergency operation.

My grandma has had a row with my mother and gone home. My grandma found the Christmas cardigans all cut up in the duster bag. It is disgusting when people are starving.

Mr Lucas from next door has been in to see my mother and father who are still in bed. He brought a 'get well' card and some flowers for my mother. My mother sat up in bed in a nightie that showed a lot of her chest. She talked to Mr Lucas in a yukky voice. My father pretended to be asleep.

Nigel brought his records round. He is into punk, but I don't see the point if you can't hear the words. Anyway I think I'm turning into an intellectual. It must be all the worry.

p.m. I went to see how the dog is. It has had its operation. The vet showed me a plastic bag with lots of yukky things in it. There was a lump of coal, the fir tree from the Christmas cake, and the model pirates from my father's ship. One of the pirates was waving a cutlass which must have been very painful for the dog. The dog looks a lot better. It can come home in two days, worse luck.

My father was having a row with my grandma on the phone about the empty bottles in the dustbin when I got home.

Mr Lucas was upstairs talking to my mother. When Mr Lucas went, my father went upstairs and had an argument with my mother and made her cry. My father is in a bad mood. This means he is feeling better. I made my mother a cup of tea without her asking. This made her cry as well. You can't please some people!

The spot is still there.

Sunday January 11th
First after Epiphany

Now I *know* I am an intellectual. I saw Malcolm Muggeridge on the television last night, and I understood nearly every word. It all adds up. A bad home, poor diet, not liking punk. I think I will join the library and see what happens.

It is a pity there aren't any more intellectuals living round here. Mr Lucas wears corduroy trousers, but he's an insurance man. Just my luck.

The first what after Epiphany?

Monday January 12th

The dog is back. It keeps licking its stitches, so when I am eating I sit with my back to it.

My mother got up this morning to make the dog a bed to sleep in until it's better. It is made out of a cardboard box that used to contain packets of soap powder. My father said this would make the dog sneeze and burst its stitches, and the vet would charge even more to stitch it back up again. They had a row about the box, then my father went on about Mr Lucas. Though what Mr Lucas has to do with the dog's bed is a mystery to me.

Tuesday January 13th

My father has gone back to work. Thank God! I don't know how my mother sticks him.

Mr Lucas came in this morning to see if my mother needed any help in the house. He is very kind. Mrs Lucas was next door cleaning the outside windows. The ladder didn't look very safe. I have written to Malcolm Muggeridge, c/o the BBC, asking him what to do about being an intellectual. I hope he writes back soon because I'm getting fed up being one on my own. I have written a poem, and it only took me two minutes. Even the famous poets take longer than that. It is called 'The Tap', but it isn't really about a tap, it's very deep, and about life and stuff like that.

> *The Tap, by Adrian Mole*
> The tap drips and keeps me awake,
> In the morning there will be a lake.
> For the want of a washer the carpet will spoil,
> Then for another my father will toil.
> My father could snuff it while he is at work.
> Dad, fit a washer don't be a burk!

I showed it to my mother, but she laughed. She isn't

very bright. She still hasn't washed my PE shorts, and it is school tomorrow. She is not like the mothers on television.

Wednesday January 14th

Joined the library. Got *Care of the Skin, Origin of Species*, and a book by a woman my mother is always going on about. It is called *Pride and Prejudice*, by a woman called Jane Austen. I could tell the librarian was impressed. Perhaps she is an intellectual like me. She didn't look at my spot, so perhaps it is getting smaller. About time!

Mr Lucas was in the kitchen drinking coffee with my mother. The room was full of smoke. They were laughing, but when I went in, they stopped.

Mrs Lucas was next door cleaning the drains. She looked as if she was in a bad mood. I think Mr and Mrs Lucas have got an unhappy marriage. Poor Mr Lucas!

None of the teachers at school have noticed that I am an intellectual. They will be sorry when I am famous. There is a new girl in our class. She sits next to me in Geography. She is all right. Her name is Pandora, but she likes being called 'Box'. Don't ask me why. I might fall in love with her. It's time I fell in love, after all I am 13³/₄ years old.

Thursday January 15th

Pandora has got hair the colour of treacle, and it's long like girls' hair should be. She has quite a good figure. I saw her playing netball and her chest was wobbling. I felt a bit funny. I think this is it!

The dog has had its stitches out. It bit the vet, but I expect he's used to it. (The vet I mean; I know the dog is.)

My father found out about the arm on the stereo. I told a lie. I said the dog jumped up and broke it. My father said he will wait until the dog is completely cured of its operation then kick it. I hope this is a joke.

Mr Lucas was in the kitchen again when I got home from school. My mother is better now, so why he keeps coming round is a mystery to me. Mrs Lucas was planting trees in the dark. I read a bit of *Pride and Prejudice*, but it was very old-fashioned. I think Jane Austen should write something a bit more modern.

The dog has got the same colour eyes as Pandora. I only noticed because my mother cut the dog's hair. It looks worse than ever. Mr Lucas and my mother were laughing at the dog's new haircut which is not very nice, because dogs can't answer back, just like the Royal Family.

I am going to bed early to think about Pandora and do my back-stretching exercises. I haven't grown for two weeks. If this carries on I will be a midget.

I will go to the doctor's on Saturday if the spot is still there. I can't live like this with everybody staring.

Friday January 16th

Mr Lucas came round and offered to take my mother shopping in the car. They dropped me off at school. I was glad to get out of the car what with all the laughing and cigarette smoke. We saw Mrs Lucas on the way. She was carrying big bags of shopping. My mother waved, but Mrs Lucas couldn't wave back.

It was Geography today so I sat next to Pandora for a whole hour. She looks better every day. I told her about her eyes being the same as the dog's. She asked what kind of dog it was. I told her it was a mongrel.

I lent Pandora my blue felt-tip pen to colour round the British Isles.

I think she appreciates these small attentions.

I started *Origin of Species* today, but it's not as good as the television series. *Care of the Skin* is dead good. I have left it open on the pages about vitamins. I hope my mother takes the hint. I have left it on the kitchen table near the ashtray, so she is bound to see it.

I have made an appointment about the spot. It has turned purple.

Saturday January 17th

I was woken up early this morning. Mrs Lucas is concreting the front of their house and the concrete lorry had to keep its engine running while she shovelled the concrete round before it set. Mr Lucas made her a cup of tea. He really is kind.

Nigel came round to see if I wanted to go to the pictures but I told him I couldn't, because I was going to the doctor's about the spot. He said he couldn't see a spot, but he was just being polite because the spot is massive today.

Dr Taylor must be one of those overworked GPs you are always reading about. He didn't examine the spot, he just said I mustn't worry and was everything all right at home. I told him about my bad home life and my poor diet, but he said I was well nourished and to go home and count my blessings. So much for the National Health Service.

I will get a paper-round and go private.

Sunday January 18th
Second after Epiphany. Oxford Hilary Term starts

Mrs Lucas and my mother have had a row over the dog. Somehow it escaped from the house and trampled on Mrs Lucas's wet concrete. My father offered to have the dog put down, but my mother started to cry so he said he wouldn't. All the neighbours were out in the street washing their cars and listening. Sometimes I really hate that dog!

I remembered my resolution about helping the poor and ignorant today, so I took some of my old *Beano* annuals to a quite poor family who have moved into the next street. I know they are poor because they have only got a black and white telly. A boy answered the door. I explained why I had come. He looked at the annuals and said, 'I've read 'em', and slammed the door in my face. So much for helping the poor!

Monday January 19th

I have joined a group at school called the Good Samaritans. We go out into the community helping and stuff like that. We miss Maths on Monday afternoons.

Today we had a talk on the sort of things we will be doing. I have been put in the old age pensioners' group. Nigel has got a dead yukky job looking after kids in a playgroup. He is as sick as a parrot.

I can't wait for next Monday. I will get a cassette so I can tape all the old fogies' stories about the war and stuff. I hope I get one with a good memory.

The dog is back at the vet's. It has got concrete stuck on its paws. No wonder it was making such a row on the stairs last night. Pandora smiled at me in school dinner today, but I was choking on a piece of gristle so I couldn't smile back. Just my luck!

Tuesday January 20th
Full Moon

My mother is looking for a job!

Now I could end up a delinquent roaming the streets and all that. And what will I do during the holidays?

I expect I will have to sit in a launderette all day to keep warm. I will be a latchkey kid, whatever that is. And who will look after the dog? And what will I have to eat all day? I will be forced to eat crisps and sweets until my skin is ruined and my teeth fall out. I think my mother is being very selfish. She won't be any good in a job anyway. She isn't very bright and she drinks too much at Christmas.

I rang my grandma up and told her, and she says I could stay at her house in the holidays, and go to the Evergreens' meetings in the afternoons and stuff like that. I wish I hadn't rung now. The Samaritans met today during break. The old people were shared out. I got an old man called Bert Baxter. He is eighty-nine so I don't suppose I'll have him for long. I'm going round to see him tomorrow. I hope he hasn't got a dog. I'm fed up with dogs. They are either at the vet's or standing in front of the television.

Wednesday January 21st

Mr and Mrs Lucas are getting a divorce! They are the first down our road. My mother went next door to comfort Mr Lucas. He must have been very upset because she was still there when my father came home from work. Mrs Lucas has gone somewhere in a taxi. I think she has left for ever because she has taken her socket set with her. Poor Mr Lucas, now he will have to do his own washing and stuff.

My father cooked the tea tonight. We had boil-in-the-bag curry and rice, it was the only thing left in the freezer apart from a bag of green stuff which has lost its label. My father made a joke about sending it to the public health inspector. My mother didn't laugh. Perhaps she was thinking about poor Mr Lucas left on his own.

I went to see old Mr Baxter after tea. My father dropped me off on his way to play badminton. Mr Baxter's house is hard to see from the road. It has got a massive overgrown privet hedge all round it. When I knocked on the door a dog started barking and growling and jumping up at the letter-box. I heard the sound of bottles being knocked over and a man swearing before I ran off. I hope I got the wrong number.

I saw Nigel on the way home. He told me Pandora's father is a milkman! I have gone off her a bit.

Nobody was in when I got home so I fed the dog, looked at my spots and went to bed.

Thursday January 22nd

It is a dirty lie about Pandora's father being a milkman! He is an accountant at the dairy. Pandora says she will duff Nigel up if he goes round committing libel. I am in love with her again.

Nigel has asked me to go to a disco at the youth club tomorrow night; it is being held to raise funds for a new packet of ping-pong balls. I don't know if I will go because Nigel is a punk at weekends. His mother lets him be one providing he wears a string vest under his bondage T-shirt.

My mother has got an interview for a job. She is practising her typing and not doing any cooking. So what will it be like if she *gets* the job? My father should put his foot down before we are a broken home.

Friday January 23rd

That is the last time I go to a disco. Everybody there was a punk except me and Rick Lemon, the youth leader. Nigel was showing off all night. He ended up putting a safety pin through his ear. My father had to take him to the hospital in our car. Nigel's parents haven't got a car because his father's got a steel plate in his head and his mother is only four feet eleven inches tall. It's not surprising Nigel has turned out bad really, with a maniac and a midget for parents.

I still haven't heard from Malcolm Muggeridge. Perhaps he is in a bad mood. Intellectuals like him and me often have bad moods. Ordinary people don't understand us and say we are sulking, but we're not.

Pandora has been to see Nigel in hospital. He has got a bit of blood poisoning from the safety pin. Pandora thinks Nigel is dead brave. I think he is dead stupid.

I have had a headache all day because of my mother's rotten typing, but I'm not complaining. I must go to sleep now. I've got to go and see Bert Baxter tomorrow at his house. It was the right number WORSE LUCK!

Saturday January 24th

Today was the most terrible day of my life. My mother has got a job doing her rotten typing in an insurance office! She starts on Monday! Mr Lucas works at the same place. He is going to give her a lift every day.

And my father is in a bad mood – he thinks his big-end is going.

But worst of all, Bert Baxter is not a nice old age pensioner! He drinks and smokes and has an alsatian dog called Sabre. Sabre was locked in the kitchen while I was cutting the massive hedge, but he didn't stop growling once.

But even worse than that! Pandora is going out with Nigel!!!!! I think I will never get over this shock.

Sunday January 25th
Third after Epiphany

10 a.m. I am ill with all the worry, too weak to write much. Nobody has noticed I haven't eaten any breakfast.

2 p.m. Had two junior aspirins at midday and rallied a bit. Perhaps when I am famous and my diary is discovered people will understand the torment of being a 13¾-year-old undiscovered intellectual.

6 p.m. Pandora! My lost love!

Now I will never stroke your treacle hair! (Although my blue felt-tip is still at your disposal.)

8 p.m. Pandora! Pandora! Pandora!

10 p.m. Why? Why? Why?

Midnight. Had a crab-paste sandwich and a satsuma (for the good of my skin). Feel a bit better. I hope Nigel falls off his bike and is squashed flat by a lorry. I will never speak to him again. He knew I was in love with Pandora! If I'd had a racing bike for Christmas instead of a lousy digital stereo alarm clock, none of this would have happened.

Monday January 26th

I had to leave my sick-bed to visit Bert Baxter before school. It took me ages to get there, what with feeling weak and having to stop for a rest every now and again, but with the help of an old lady who had a long black moustache I made it to the front door. Bert Baxter was in bed but he threw the key down and I let myself in. Sabre was locked in the bathroom; he was growling and sounded as if he was ripping up towels or something.

Bert Baxter was lying in a filthy-looking bed smoking a cigarette, there was a horrible smell in the room, I think it came from Bert Baxter himself. The bed sheets looked as though they were covered in blood, but Bert said that was caused by the beetroot sandwiches he always eats last thing at night. It was the most disgusting room I have ever seen (and I'm no stranger to squalor). Bert Baxter gave me ten pence and asked me to get him the *Morning Star* from the newsagent's. So he is a communist as well as everything else! Sabre usually fetches the paper but he is being kept in as a punishment for chewing the sink.

The man in the newsagent's asked me to give Bert Baxter his bill (he owes for his papers, £31.97), but when I did Bert Baxter said, 'Smarmy four-eyed git', and laughed and ripped the bill up. I was late for school so I had to go to the school secretary's office and have my name put in the late book. That's the gratitude I get for being a Good Samaritan! I didn't miss Maths either! Saw Pandora and Nigel standing close together in the dinner queue but chose to ignore them.

Mr Lucas has taken to his bed because of being deserted so my mother is taking care of him when she finishes work. She is the only person he will see. So when will she find time to look after me and my father?

My father is sulking. I think he must be jealous because Mr Lucas doesn't want to see *him*.

Midnight. Goodnight Pandora my treacle-haired love.

XXXXXXXXX

Tuesday January 27th

Art was dead good today. I painted a lonely boy standing on a bridge. The boy had just lost his first love to his ex-best friend. The ex-best friend was struggling in the torrential river. The boy was watching his ex-best friend drown. The ex-best friend looked a bit like Nigel. The boy looked a bit like me. Ms Fossington-Gore said my picture 'had depth', so did the river. Ha! Ha! Ha!

Wednesday January 28th
Last Quarter

I woke up with a bit of a cold this morning. I asked my mother for a note to excuse me from Games. She said she refused to namby-pamby me a day longer! How would she like to run about on a muddy field in the freezing drizzle, dressed only in PE shorts and a singlet? When I was in the school sports day three-legged race last year she came to watch me, *and* she had her fur coat on *and* she put a blanket round her legs, *and* it was only June! Anyway my mother is sorry now, we had rugger and my PE stuff was so full of mud that it has clogged up the drain hose on the washing machine.

The vet rang up to demand that we come and fetch the dog back from his surgery. It has been there nine days. My father says it will have to stay there until he gets paid tomorrow. The vet only takes cash and my father hasn't got any.

Pandora! Why?

Thursday January 29th

The stupid dog is back. I am not taking it for a walk until its hair grows back on its shaved paws. My father looked pale when he came home from the vet's, he kept saying 'It's money down the drain', and he said that from now on the dog can only be fed on leftovers from his plate.

This means the dog will soon starve.

Friday January 30th

That filthy commie Bert Baxter has phoned the school to complain that I left the hedge-clippers out in the rain! He claims that they have gone all rusty. He wants compensation. I told Mr Scruton, the headmaster, that they were already rusty but I could tell he didn't believe me. He gave me a lecture on how hard it was for old people to make ends meet. He has ordered me to go to Bert Baxter's and clean and sharpen the hedge-clippers. I wanted to tell the headmaster all about horrible Bert Baxter but there is something about Mr Scruton that makes my mind go blank. I think it's the way his eyes pop out when he is in a temper.

On the way to Bert Baxter's I saw my mother and Mr Lucas coming out of a betting shop together. I waved and shouted but I don't think they could have seen me. I'm glad Mr Lucas is feeling better.

Bert Baxter didn't answer the door. Perhaps he is dead.

Pandora! You are still on my mind, baby.

Saturday January 31st

It is nearly February and I have got nobody to send a Valentine's Day card to.

Sunday February 1st
Fourth after Epiphany

There was a lot of shouting downstairs late last night. The kitchen waste-bin was knocked over and the back door kept being slammed. I wish my parents would be a bit more thoughtful. I have been through an emotional time and I need my sleep. Still I don't expect them to understand what it is like being in love. They have been married for fourteen-and-a-half years.

Went to Bert Baxter's this afternoon but thank God he has gone to Skegness with the Evergreens. Sabre looked out of the living-room window. I gave him the 'V' sign. I hope he doesn't remember.

Monday February 2nd
Presentation

Mrs Lucas is back! I saw her pulling trees and bushes out of the earth and putting them in the back of a van, then she put all the gardening tools in and drove off. The van had 'Women's Refuge' painted on the side. Mr Lucas came over to our house to talk to my mother, I went down to say 'hello' to him, but he was too upset to notice me. I asked my mother if she would get home early from work tonight, I'm fed up with waiting for my tea. She didn't.

Nigel got thrown out of school dinners today for swearing at the toad-in-the-hole, he said it was 'all bleeding hole and no toad'. I think Mrs Leech was quite right to throw him out, after all the first-years were present! We third-years must set an example. Pandora has got up a petition to protest about the toad-in-the-hole. I will not sign it.

It was Good Samaritans today. So I was forced to go round to Bert Baxter's. I have missed the Algebra test! Ha! Ha! Ha! Bert gave me a stick of broken Skegness rock and said he was sorry he rang the school to complain abut the hedge-clippers. He said he was lonely and wanted to hear a human voice. If I was the loneliest person in the world I wouldn't phone up our school. I would ring the speaking clock; that talks to you every ten seconds.

Tuesday February 3rd

My mother has not done any proper housework for days now. All she does is go to work, comfort Mr Lucas and read and smoke. The big-end has gone on my father's car. I had to show him where to catch a bus into town. A man of forty not knowing where the bus stop is! My father looked such a scruff-bag that I was ashamed to be seen with him. I was glad when the bus came. I shouted through the window that he couldn't sit downstairs and smoke but he just waved and lit up a cigarette. There is a fifty pounds' fine for doing that! If I was in charge of the buses I would fine smokers a thousand pounds *and* make them eat twenty Woodbines.

My mother is reading *The Female Eunuch*, by Germaine Greer. My mother says it is the sort of book that changes your life. It hasn't changed mine, but I only glanced through it. It is full of dirty words.

Wednesday February 4th
New Moon

I had my first wet dream! So my mother was right about *The Female Eunuch*. It has changed my life.

The spot has got smaller.

Thursday February 5th

My mother has bought some of those overalls that painters and decorators wear. You can see her knickers through them. I hope she doesn't wear them in the street.

She is having her ears pierced tomorrow. I think she is turning into a spendthrift. Nigel's mother is a spendthrift. They are always getting letters about having their electricity cut off and all because Nigel's mother buys a pair of high heels every week.

I would like to know where the Family Allowance goes, by rights it should be mine. I will ask my mother tomorrow.

Friday February 6th
The Queen's Accession, 1952

It is lousy having a working mother. She rushes in with big bags of shopping, cooks the tea then rushes around tarting herself up. But she is still not doing any tidying up before comforting Mr Lucas. There has been a slice of bacon between the cooker and the fridge for three days to my knowledge!

I asked her about my Family Allowance today, she laughed and said she used it for buying gin and cigarettes. If the Social Services hear about it she will get done!

Saturday February 7th

My mother and father have been shouting at each other non-stop for hours. It started because of the bacon down the side of the fridge and carried on into how much my father's car is costing to repair. I went up to my room and put my Abba records on. My father had the nerve to crash my door open and ask me to turn the volume down. I did. When he got downstairs I turned it up again.

Nobody cooked any dinner so I went to the Chinese chip shop and bought a carton of chips and a sachet of soy sauce. I sat in the bus shelter and ate them, then walked about feeling sad. Came home. Fed dog. Read a bit of *Female Eunuch*. Felt a bit funny. Went to sleep.

Sunday February 8th
Fifth after Epiphany

My father came into my bedroom this morning, he said he wanted a chat. He looked at my Kevin Keegan scrapbook, screwed the knob of my wardrobe door back on with his Swiss army knife, and asked me about school. Then he said he was sorry about yesterday and the shouting, he said my mother and him are 'going through a bad patch'. He asked me if I had anything to say. I said he owed me thirty-two pence for the Chinese chips and soy sauce. He gave me a pound. So I made a profit of sixty-eight pence.

Monday February 9th

There was a removal lorry outside Mr Lucas's house this morning. Mrs Lucas and some other women were carrying furniture from the house and stacking it on the pavement. Mr Lucas was looking out from his bedroom window. He looked a bit frightened. Mrs Lucas was laughing and pointing up to Mr Lucas and all the other women started laughing and singing 'Why was he born so beautiful?'

My mother phoned Mr Lucas up and asked him if he was all right. Mr Lucas said he wasn't going to work today because he had to guard the stereo and records from his wife. My father helped Mrs Lucas put the gas stove in the removal van, then he and my mother walked to the bus stop together. I walked behind them because my mother was wearing long dangly earrings and my father's trouser turn-ups had come down. They started to quarrel about something so I crossed over the road and went to school the long way round.

Bert Baxter was OK today. He told me about the First World War. He said his life was saved by a Bible he always carried in his breast pocket. He showed me the Bible, it was printed in 1956. I think Bert is going a bit senile.

Pandora! The memory of you is a constant torment!

Tuesday February 10th

Mr Lucas is staying with us until he gets some new furniture.

My father has gone to Matlock to try to sell electric storage heaters to a big hotel.

Our gas boiler has packed in. It is freezing cold.

Wednesday February 11th
First Quarter

My father rang up from Matlock to say he has lost his Barclaycard and can't get home tonight, so Mr Lucas and my mother were up all night trying to mend the boiler. I went down at ten o'clock to see if I could help but the kitchen door was jammed. Mr Lucas said he couldn't open it just at that moment because he was at a crucial stage with the boiler and my mother was helping him and she had her hands full.

Thursday February 12th
Lincoln's Birthday

I found my mother dyeing her hair in the bathroom tonight. This has come as a complete shock to me. For thirteen and three-quarter years I have thought I had a mother with red hair, now I find out that it is really light brown. My mother asked me not to tell my father.

What a state their marriage must be in! I wonder if my father knows that she wears a padded bra? She doesn't hang them on the line to dry, but I have seen them shoved down the side of the airing cupboard. I wonder what other secrets my mother has got?

Friday February 13th

It was an unlucky day for me all right!

Pandora doesn't sit next to me in Geography any more. Barry Kent does. He kept copying my work and blowing bubblegum in my ears. I told Miss Elf but she is scared of Barry Kent as well, so she didn't say anything to him.

Pandora looked luscious today, she was wearing a split skirt which showed her legs. She has got a scab on one of her knees. She was wearing Nigel's football scarf round her wrist, but Miss Elf saw it and told her to take it off. Miss Elf is not scared of Pandora. I have sent her a Valentine's Day card (Pandora, not Miss Elf).

Saturday February 14th
St Valentine's Day

I only got one Valentine's Day card. It was in my mother's handwriting so it doesn't count. My mother had a massive card delivered, it was so big that a GPO van had to bring it to the door. She went all red when she opened the envelope and saw the card. It was dead good. There was a big satin elephant holding a bunch of plastic flowers in its trunk and a bubble coming out of its mouth saying 'Hi, Honey Bun! I ain't never gonna forget you!' There was no name written inside, just drawings of hearts with 'Pauline' written inside them. My father's card was very small and had a bunch of purple flowers on the front. My father had written on the inside 'Let's try again'.

Here is the poem I wrote inside Pandora's card.

> Pandora!
> I adore ya.
> I implore ye
> Don't ignore me.

I wrote it left-handed so that she wouldn't know it was from me.

Sunday February 15th
Septuagesima

Mr Lucas moved back to his empty house last night. I expect he got fed up with all the rowing over the elephant Valentine's Day card. I told my father that my mother can't help it if a man secretly admires her. My father gave a nasty laugh and said 'You've got a lot to learn, son'.

I cleared off to my grandma's at dinner-time. She

cooked me a proper Sunday dinner with gravy and individual Yorkshire puddings. She is never too busy to make real custard either.

I took the dog with me and we all went for a walk in the afternoon to settle our dinners.

My grandma hasn't spoken to my mother since the row about the cardigans. Grandma says she 'won't set foot in that house again!' Grandma asked me if I believed in life after death. I said I didn't and grandma told me that she had joined the Spiritualist church and has heard my grandad talking about his rhubarb. My grandad has been dead for four years!!! She is going on Wednesday night to try to get in touch with him again and she wants me to go with her. She says I have got an aura around me.

The dog choked on a chicken bone but we held it upside down and banged it hard, and the bone fell out. I've left the dog at grandma's to recover from its ordeal.

Looked up 'Septuagesima' in my pocket dictionary. It didn't have it. Will look in the school dictionary, tomorrow.

Lay awake for ages thinking about God, Life and Death and Pandora.

Monday February 16th
Washington's Birthday Observance

A letter from the BBC!!!!! A white oblong envelope with BBC in red fat letters. My name and address on the front! Could it be that they wanted my poems? Alas, no. But a letter from a bloke called John Tydeman, here is what he wrote:

Dear Adrian Mole,

Thank you for the poems which you sent to the BBC and which somehow landed up on my desk. I read them with interest and, taking into account your tender years, I must confess that they do show some promise. However they are not of sufficient quality for us to consider including them in any of our current poetry programmes. Have you thought of offering them to your School Magazine or to your local Parish Magazine? (If you have one.)

If, in future, you wish to submit any of your work to the BBC may I suggest you get it typed out and retain, also, a copy for yourself. The BBC does not normally consider submissions in handwritten manuscript form and, despite the neatness of presentation, I did have some difficulty in making out *all* of the words – particularly at the end of one poem entitled 'The Tap' where there was a rather nasty blotch which had caused the ink to run. (A teastain or a tear-stain? A case of 'Your Tap runneth over'!)

Since you wish to follow a literary career I suggest you will need to develop a thick skin in order to accept many of the inevitable future rejections you may receive with good grace and the minimum of personal pain.

With my best wishes to you for future literary efforts – and, above all, Good Luck!

Yours sincerely,

John Tydeman

P.S. I enclose a poem by a certain John Mole which appeared in this week's *Times Literary Supplement*. Is he a relation? It is very good.

My mother and father were really impressed. I kept getting it out and reading it at school. I was hoping one of the teachers would ask to read it but none of them did.

Bert Baxter read it while I was doing his rotten washing up. He said they were 'all a load of drug addicts in the BBC'! His brother-in-law's uncle once lived next door to a tea lady at Broadcasting House, so Bert knows all about the BBC.

Pandora got seventeen Valentine's Day cards. Nigel got seven. Even Barry Kent whom everybody hates got three! I just smiled when everybody asked me how many I got. Anyway I bet I am the only person in the school to get a letter from the BBC.

Tuesday February 17th

Barry Kent said he would do me over unless I gave him twenty-five pence every day. I told him that he was wasting his time demanding money with menaces from me. I never have any spare money. My mother puts my pocket money straight into my building-society account and gives me fifteen pence a day for a Mars bar. Barry Kent said I would have to give him my dinner money! I told him that my father pays it by cheque since it went up to sixty pence a day, but

Barry Kent hit me in the goolies and walked off saying 'There's more where that came from'.

I have put my name down for a paper round.

Wednesday February 18th
Full Moon

Woke up with a pain in my goolies. Told my mother. She wanted to look but I didn't want her to so she said I would have to soldier on. She wouldn't give me a note excusing me from Games, so I had to stumble around in the mud again. Barry Kent trod on my head in the scrum. Mr Jones saw him and sent him off for an early shower.

I wish I could have a non-painful illness so I could be excused Games. Something like a weak heart would be all right.

Fetched the dog from grandma's, she has given it a shampoo and set. It smells like the perfume counter in Woolworth's.

I went to the Spiritualist meeting with my grandma, it was full of dead old people. One madman stood up and said he had a radio inside his head which told him what to do. Nobody took any notice of him, so he sat down again. A woman called Alice Tonks started grunting and rolling her eyes about and talking to somebody called Arthur Mayfield, but my grandad kept quiet. My grandma was a bit sad so when we got home I made her a cup of Horlicks. She gave me fifty pence and I walked home with the dog.

Started reading *Animal Farm*, by George Orwell. I think I might like to be a vet when I grow up.

Thursday February 19th
Prince Andrew born, 1960

It's all right for Prince Andrew, he is protected by bodyguards. He doesn't have Barry Kent nicking money off him. Fifty pence gone just like that! I wish I knew karate, I would chop Barry Kent in his windpipe.

It is quiet at home, my parents are not speaking to each other.

Friday February 20th

Barry Kent told Miss Elf to 'get stuffed' in Geography today so she sent him to Mr Scruton to be punished. I hope he gets fifty lashes. I am going to make friends with Craig Thomas. He is one of the biggest third-years. I bought him a Mars bar in break today. I pretended I felt sick and didn't feel like eating it myself. He said, 'Ta Moley'. That is the first time he has spoken to me. If I play my cards right I could be in his gang. Then Barry Kent wouldn't dare touch me again.

My mother is reading another sex book, it is called *The Second Sex*, by a frog writer called Simone De Beauvoir. She left it on the coffee table in the living room where anybody could have seen it, even my grandma!

Saturday February 21st

Had a dead good dream that Sabre was brutally savaging Barry Kent. Mr Scruton and Miss Elf were watching. Pandora was there, she was wearing her split skirt. She put her arms round me and said, 'I am of the second sex'. Then I woke up to find I had had my second W. D. I have to put my pyjamas in the washing machine so my mother doesn't find out.

Had a good look at my face in the bathroom mirror today. I have got five spots as well as the one on my chin. I have got a few hairs on my lip. It looks as if I shall have to start shaving soon.

Went to the garage with my father, he expected to get the car back today but it still isn't ready. All the bits are on the work-bench. My father's eyes filled up with tears. I was ashamed of him. We walked to Sainsbury's. My father bought tins of salmon, crab and shrimps and a black forest cake and some dead yukky white cheese covered in grape pips. My mother was dead mad at him when we got home because he had forgotten the bread, butter and toilet paper. She says he can't be trusted to go on his own again. My father cheered up a bit.

Sunday February 22nd
Sexagesima

My father has gone fishing with the dog. Mr Lucas came for dinner and stayed for tea. He ate three slices of the black forest cake. We played Monopoly. Mr Lucas was banker. My mother kept going into jail. I won because I was the only one concentrating properly. My father came in the front door and Mr Lucas went out of the back door. My father said he had been looking forward to the black forest cake all day. There was none left. My father said he had not had a bite to eat or a bite on his fishing line all day. My mother gave him grape-pip cheese on Ry-king for his supper. He threw it at the wall and said he wasn't a ******* mouse he was a ******* man and my mother said it was a long time since he had done any *******! I was sent out of the room then. It is a terrible thing to hear your own mother swearing. I blame it on all those books she has been reading. She hasn't ironed my school uniform yet, I hope she remembers.

I let the dog sleep in my room tonight, it doesn't like quarrelling.

Monday February 23rd

Got a letter from Mr Cherry the newsagent to say I can start a paper round tomorrow. Worse luck!

Bert Baxter is worried about Sabre because he is off

his food and not trying to bite anybody. He asked me to take him to the PDSA for a check-up. I said I would take him tomorrow if his condition hadn't improved.

I'm fed up with washing up for Bert. He seems to live off fried eggs, it is no joke trying to wash up in cold water without any washing-up liquid. Also there is never a dry tea towel. In fact there are never any tea towels and Sabre has ripped up all the bath towels so I don't know how Bert can even have a wash! I think I'll see if I can get Bert a home help.

I have got to concentrate on getting my GCEs if I want to be a vet.

Tuesday February 24th
St Matthias

Got up at six o'clock for my paper round. I have got Elm Tree Avenue. It is dead posh. All the papers they read are very heavy: *The Times*, the *Daily Telegraph* and the *Guardian*. Just my luck!

Bert said Sabre is better, he tried to bite the milkman.

Wednesday February 25th

Bed early tonight because of my paper round. Delivered twenty-five *Punches* as well as the papers.

Thursday February 26th

The papers got mixed up today. Elm Tree Avenue got the *Sun* and the *Mirror* and Corporation Row got the heavy papers.

I don't know why everybody went so mad. You'd think they would enjoy reading a different paper for a change.

Friday February 27th
Last Quarter

Early this morning I saw Pandora walking down the drive of 69 Elm Tree Avenue. She had a riding hat and jodphurs on so she couldn't have been on her way to school. I didn't let her see me. I don't want her to know that I am doing a menial job.

So now I know where Pandora lives! I had a good look at the house. It is much bigger than ours. It has got rolled-up wooden blinds at all the windows, and the rooms look like jungles because of all the green plants. I looked through the letterbox and saw the big ginger cat eating something on the kitchen table. They have the *Guardian, Punch, Private Eye,* and *New Society.* Pandora reads *Jackie,* the comic for girls; she is not an intellectual, like me. But I don't suppose Malcolm Muggeridge's wife is either.

Saturday February 28th

Pandora has got a little fat horse called 'Blossom'. She feeds it and makes it jump over barrels every morning before school. I know because I hid behind her father's Volvo and then followed her to a field next to the disused railway line. I hid behind a scrap car in the corner of the field and watched her. She looked dead good in her riding stuff, her chest was wobbling like mad. She will need to wear a bra soon. My heart was beating so loudly in my throat that I felt like a stereo loudspeaker, so I left before she heard me.

People complained because the papers were late. I had a *Guardian* left over in my paper bag so I took it home to read. It was full of spelling mistakes. It is disgusting when you think of how many people who can spell are out of work.

Sunday March 1st
Quinquagesima. St David's Day

I took some sugar to Blossom before I did my paper round. It brought me closer to Pandora somehow.

Have strained my back because of carrying all the Sunday supplements. Took the leftover *Sunday People* home as a present to my mother but she said it was only fit for lining the dustbin. Got my two pounds and six pence for six mornings, it is slave labour! *And* I have to give Barry Kent half of it. Mr Cherry said he had a complaint from number 69 Elm Tree Avenue, that they didn't get a *Guardian* yesterday. Mr Cherry sent a *Daily Express* round with his apologies, but Pandora's father brought it back to the shop and said he 'would rather go without'.

Didn't bother reading the papers today, I am fed up with papers. Had chow mein and beansprouts for Sunday dinner.

Mr Lucas came round when my father had gone to visit grandma. He was wearing a plastic daffodil in his sports jacket.

My spots have completely gone. It must be the early morning air.

Monday March 2nd

My mother has just come into my room and said she had something awful to tell me. I sat up in bed and put a dead serious expression on my face just in case she'd got six months to live or she'd been caught shoplifting or something. She fiddled with the curtains, dropped cigarette ash all over my Concorde model and started mumbling on about 'adult relationships' and 'life being complicated' and how she must 'find herself'. She said she was fond of me. Fond!!! And would hate to hurt me. And then she said that for some women marriage was like being in prison. Then she went out.

Marriage is nothing like being in prison! Women are let out every day to go to the shops and stuff, and quite a lot go to work. I think my mother is being a bit melodramatic.

Finished *Animal Farm*. It is dead symbolic. I cried when Boxer was taken to the vet's. From now on I shall treat pigs with the contempt they deserve. I am boycotting pork of all kinds.

Tuesday March 3rd
Shrove Tuesday

I gave Barry Kent his protection money today. I don't see how there can be a God. If there was surely he wouldn't let people like Barry Kent walk about menacing intellectuals? Why are bigger youths unpleasant to smaller youths? Perhaps their brains are easily worn out with all the extra work they have to do making bigger bones and stuff, or it could be that the big youths have got brain damage because of all the sport they play, or perhaps big youths just *like* menacing and fighting. When I go to university I may study the problem.

I will have my thesis published and I will send a copy to Barry Kent. Perhaps by then he will have learnt to read.

My mother had forgotten that today was pancake day. I reminded her at 11 p.m. I'm sure she burnt them deliberately. I will be fourteen in one month's time.

Wednesday March 4th
Ash Wednesday

Had a nasty shock this morning. Took my empty paper sack back to Mr Cherry's newsagent's and saw Mr Lucas looking at those magazines on the top shelf. I stood behind the Mills and Boon rack and distinctly saw him choose *Big and Bouncy*, pay for it and leave the shop with it hidden inside his coat. *Big and Bouncy* is extremely indecent. It is full of disgusting pictures. My mother should be informed.

Thursday March 5th

My father got his car back from the garage today. He was cleaning it and gloating over it for a whole two hours. I noticed that the stick-on waving hand I bought him for Christmas was missing from the rear window. I told him he ought to complain to the garage but he said he didn't want to make a fuss. We went to my grandma's to test-drive the car. She gave us a cup of Bovril and a piece of yukky seedcake. She didn't ask how my mother was, she said my father was looking thin and pale and needed 'feeding up'.

She told me that Bert Baxter had been thrown out of the Evergreens because of his bad behaviour at Skegness. The coach was waiting for two hours for him at the coach station. A search party was sent out to look in the pubs, then Bert came back, drunk but alone and another search party was sent out to look for the first search party. In the end the police had to be sent for and they took hours to round up all the pensioners and get them in the coach.

My grandma said the journey back was a nightmare. All the pensioners kept falling out (with each other not out of the coach). Bert Baxter was reciting a dirty poem about an Eskimo and Mrs Harriman had a funny turn and had to have her corsets loosened.

Grandma said two pensioners had passed on since the outing, she blamed Bert Baxter and said 'He as good as murdered them', but I think it was more likely that the cold wind at Skegness killed them off. I said, 'Bert Baxter is not so bad when you get to know him'. She said she didn't understand why the Good Lord took my grandad and left scum like Baxter. Then she pulled her lips tight and dabbled her eyes with a handkerchief, so we left.

My mother was out when we got home, she has joined some women's group.

Heard my father say 'goodnight', to the car. He must be cracking up!

Friday March 6th
New Moon

Mr Cherry is very pleased with my work and he has raised my wages by two and a half pence an hour. He also offered me the Corporation Row evening round, but I declined his offer. Corporation Row is where the council put all the bad tenants. Barry Kent lives at number 13.

Mr Cherry gave me two back copies of *Big and Bouncy*. He told me not tell my mother. As if I would! I have put them under my mattress. Intellectuals like me are allowed to be interested in sex. It is ordinary people like Mr Lucas who should be ashamed of themselves.

Phoned Social Services today and asked about a home help for Bert Baxter. I told a lie and said I was his grandson. They are sending a social worker to see him on Monday.

Used my father's library tickets to get *War and Peace* out. I have lost my own.

Took dog to meet Blossom. They got on well.

Saturday March 7th

After paper round went back to bed and stayed there all morning reading *Big and Bouncy*. *Felt* like I have never *felt* before.

Went to Sainsbury's with my mother and father but the women in there reminded me of *Big and Bouncy*, even the ones over thirty! My mother said I looked hot and bothered and sent me back to the multi-storey car park to keep the dog company.

The dog already had company, it was barking and whining so loudly that a crowd of people were standing around saying 'the poor thing' and 'how cruel to leave it tied up in such a fashion'. The dog had twisted its collar on the gear lever and its eyes were bulging out of its head. When it saw me it tried to jump up and nearly killed itself.

I tried to explain to the people that I was going to be a vet when I grew up, but they wouldn't listen and started to say things about the RSPCA. The car was locked so I was forced to break the little window open and unlock the door by putting my hand through. The dog went mad with joy when I untangled him, so the people went away. But my father didn't go mad with joy when he saw the damage, he went mad with rage. He threw the Sainsbury's bags down, broke the eggs, squashed the cakes and drove home too fast. Nobody said anything on the way home, and only the dog was smiling.

Finished *War and Peace*. It was quite good.

Sunday March 8th
First in Lent

My mother has gone to a woman's workshop on assertiveness training. Men aren't allowed. I asked my father what 'assertiveness training' is. He said 'God knows, but whatever it is, it's bad news for me'.

We had boil-in-the-bag cod in butter sauce and oven-cooked chips for Sunday dinner, followed by tinned peaches and Dream-topping. My father opened a bottle of white wine and let me have some. I don't know much about wine but it seemed a pleasant enough vintage. We watched a film on television, then my mother came home and started bossing us around. She said, 'The worm has turned', and 'Things are going to be different around here', and things like that. Then she went into the kitchen and started making a chart dividing all the housework into three. I pointed out to her that I already had a paper round to do, an old age pensioner to look after and a dog to feed, as well as my school work, but she didn't listen, she put the chart on the wall and said 'We start tomorrow'.

Monday March 9th
Commonwealth Day

Cleaned toilet, washed basin and bath before doing my paper round. Came home, made breakfast, put washing in machine, went to school. Gave Barry Kent his menaces money, went to Bert Baxter's, waited for social worker who didn't come, had school dinner. Had Domestic Science – made apple crumble. Came home. Vacuumed hall, lounge, and breakfast room. Peeled potatoes, chopped up cabbage, cut finger, rinsed blood off cabbage. Put chops under grill, looked in cookery book for a recipe for gravy. Made gravy. Strained lumps out with a colander. Set table, served dinner, washed up. Put burnt saucepans in to soak. Got washing out of machine; everything blue, including white underwear and handkerchiefs. Hung washing on clothes-horse. Fed dog. Ironed PE kit, cleaned shoes. Did homework. Took dog for a walk, had bath. Cleaned bath. Made three cups of tea. Washed cups up. Went to bed. Just my luck to have an assertive mother!

Tuesday March 10th
Prince Edward born, 1964

Why couldn't I have been born Prince Edward and Prince Edward been born Adrian Mole? I am treated like a serf.

Wednesday March 11th

Dragged myself to school after doing paper round and housework. My mother wouldn't give me a note excusing me from Games so I left my PE kit at home. I just couldn't face running about in the cold wind.

That sadist Mr Jones made me run all the way home to fetch my PE kit. The dog must have followed me out of the house because when I got to the school gate it was there before me. I tried to shut the dog out but it squeezed through the railings and followed me into the playground. I ran into the changing rooms and left the dog outside but I could hear its loud bark echoing around the school. I tried to sneak into the playing fields but the dog saw me and followed behind, then it saw the football and joined in the lesson! The dog is dead good at football, even Mr Jones was laughing until the dog punctured the ball.

Mr Scruton, the pop-eyed headmaster, saw

everything from his window. He ordered me to take the dog home. I told him I would miss my sitting for school dinners but he said it would teach me not to bring pets to school.

Mrs Leech, the kitchen supervisor, did a very kind thing. She put my curry and rice, spotted dick and custard into the oven to keep warm. Mrs Leech doesn't like Mr Scruton so she gave me a large marrow-bone to take home for the dog.

Thursday March 12th

Woke up this morning to find my face covered in huge red spots. My mother said they were caused by nerves but I am still convinced that my diet is inadequate. We have been eating a lot of boil-in-the-bag stuff lately. Perhaps I am allergic to plastic. My mother rang Dr Gray's receptionist to make an appointment, but the earliest he can see me is next Monday! For all he knows I could have lassa fever and be spreading it all around the district! I told my mother to say that I was an emergency case but she said I was 'over-reacting as usual'. She said a few spots didn't mean I was dying. I couldn't believe it when she said she was going to work as usual. Surely her child should come before her job?

I rang my grandma and she came round in a taxi and took me to her house and put me to bed. I am there now. It is very clean and peaceful. I am wearing my dead grandad's pyjamas. I have just had a bowl of barley and beef soup. It is my first proper nourishment for weeks.

I expect there will be a row when my mother comes home and finds that I have gone. But frankly, my dear diary, I don't give a damn.

Friday March 13th
Moon's First Quarter

The emergency doctor came to my grandma's last night at 11.30 p.m. He diagnosed that I am suffering from *acne vulgaris*. He said it was so common that it is regarded as a normal state of adolescence. He thought it was highly unlikely that I have got lassa fever because I have not been to Africa this year. He told grandma to take the disinfected sheets off the doors and windows. Grandma said she would like a second opinion. That was when the doctor lost his temper. He shouted in a very loud voice, 'The lad has only got a few teenage spots, for Christ's sake!'

Grandma said she would complain to the Medical Council but the doctor just laughed and went downstairs and slammed the door. My father came round before he went to work and brought my Social Studies homework and the dog. He said that if I was not out of bed when he got home at lunchtime he would thrash me to within an inch of my life.

He took my grandma into the kitchen and had a loud talk with her. I heard him saying, 'Things are very bad between me and Pauline, and all we are arguing over now is who *doesn't* get custody of Adrian'. Surely my father made a mistake. He must have meant who *did* get custody of me.

So the worst has happened, my skin has gone to pot and my parents are splitting up.

Saturday March 14th

It is official. They are getting a divorce! Neither of them wants to leave the house so the spare room is being turned into a bedsitter for my father. This could have a very bad effect on me. It could prevent me from being a vet.

My mother gave me five pounds this morning and told me not to tell my father. I bought some bio-spot cream for my skin and the new Abba L P.

I rang Mr Cherry and said I had personal problems and would be unable to work for a few weeks. Mr Cherry said that he knew that my parents were divorcing because my father had cancelled my mother's *Cosmopolitan*.

My father gave me five pounds and told me not to tell my mother. I spent some of it on buying some purple paper and envelopes so that the BBC will be impressed and read my poems. The rest of it will have to go on Barry Kent and his menaces money. I don't think anybody in the world can be as unhappy as me. If I didn't have my poetry I would be a raving loonie by now.

Went out for a sad walk and took Pandora's horse

two pounds of cooking apples. Thought of a poem about Blossom. Wrote it down when I got back to the house where I live.

> *Blossom, by Adrian Mole, aged nearly fourteen*
> Little Brown Horse
> Eating apples in a field,
> Perhaps one day
> My heart will be healed.
> I stroke the places Pandora has sat
> Wearing her jodphurs and riding hat.
> Goodbye, brown horse.
> I turn and retreat,
> The rain and mud are wetting my feet.

I have sent it to the BBC. I marked the envelope 'Urgent'.

Sunday March 15th
Second in Lent

The house is very quiet. My father sits in the spare room smoking and my mother sits in the bedroom smoking. They are not eating much.

Mr Lucas has phoned my mother three times. All she says to him is 'not yet, it's too early'. Perhaps he has asked her to go to the pub for a drink and take her mind off her troubles.

My father has put the stereo in his bedroom. He is playing his Jim Reeves records and staring out of the window. I took him a cup of tea and he said 'Thanks, son' in a choked-up voice.

My mother was looking at old letters in my father's handwriting when I took her tea in; she said, 'Adrian, what must you think of us?' I said that Rick Lemon, the youth leader, thinks divorce is society's fault. My mother said, 'Bugger society'.

I washed and ironed my school uniform ready for school tomorrow. I am getting quite good at housework.

My spots are so horrific that I can't bear to write about them. I will be the laughing stock at school.

I am reading *The Man in the Iron Mask*. I know exactly how he feels.

Monday March 16th

Went to school. Found it closed. In my anguish I had forgotten that I am on holiday. Didn't want to go home, so went to see Bert Baxter instead. He said the social worker had been to see him and had promised to get Sabre a new kennel but he can't have a home help. (Bert, not Sabre.)

There must have been a full week's washing up in the sink again. Bert says he saves it for me because I make a good job of it. While I washed up I told Bert about my parents getting a divorce. He said he didn't hold with divorce. He said he was married for thirty-five miserable years so why should anybody else get away with it? He told me that he has got four children and that none of them come to see him. Two of them are in Australia so they can't be blamed, but I think the other two should be ashamed of themselves. Bert showed me a photograph of his dead wife, it was taken in the days before they had plastic surgery. Bert told me that he was a hostler when he got married (a hostler is somebody doing things with horses) and didn't really notice that his wife looked like a horse until he left to work on the railways. I asked him if he would like to see a horse again. He said he would, so I took him to see Blossom.

It took us ages to get there. Bert walks dead slow and he kept having to sit down on garden walls, but we got there eventually. Bert said that Blossom was not a horse, she was a girl pony. He kept patting her and saying 'who's a beauty then, eh?' Then Blossom went for a run about so we sat down on the scrap car, and Bert had a Woodbine and I had a Mars bar. Then we walked back to Bert's house. I went to the shops and bought a packet of Vesta chow mein and a butterscotch Instant Whip for our dinner, so Bert ate a decent meal for once. We watched *Pebble Mill at One*, then Bert showed me his old horse brushes and photographs of the big house where he worked when he was a boy. He said he was made into a communist when he was there, but he fell asleep before he could tell me why.

Came home, nobody was in so I played my Abba records at the highest volume until the deaf woman next door banged on the wall.

Tuesday March 17th
St Patrick's Day. Bank Holiday in N. Ireland and Rep. of Ireland

Looked at *Big and Bouncy*. Measured my 'thing'. It was eleven centimetres.

Mr O'Leary who lives across the road from us was drunk at ten o'clock in the morning! He got thrown out of the butcher's for singing.

Wednesday March 18th

My mother and father are both speaking to solicitors. I expect they are fighting over who gets custody of me. I will be a tug-of-love child, and my picture will be in the newspapers. I hope my spots clear up before then.

Thursday March 19th

Mr Lucas has put his house up for sale. My mother says the asking price is thirty thousand pounds!!

What will he do with all that money?

My mother says he will buy another bigger house. How stupid can you get?

If I had thirty thousand pounds I would wander the world having experiences.

I wouldn't take any real money with me because I

have read that most foreigners are thieves. Instead I would have three thousand pounds' worth of traveller's cheques sewn into my trousers. Before I set off, I would:

a) Send Pandora three dozen red roses.
b) Pay a mercenary fifty pounds to duff Barry Kent up.
c) Buy the best racing bike in the world and ride it past Nigel's house.
d) Order a massive crate of expensive dog food so that the dog is properly fed while I'm away.
e) Buy a housekeeper for Bert Baxter.
f) Offer my mother and father a thousand pounds (*each*) to stay together.

When I came back from the world I would be tall, brown and full of ironical experiences and Pandora would cry into her pillow at night because of the chance she missed to be Mrs Pandora Mole. I would qualify to be a vet in record time then I would buy a farmhouse. I would convert one room into a study so that I could have somewhere quiet to be intellectual in.

I wouldn't waste thirty thousand pounds on buying a semi-detached house!

Friday March 20th
First day of Spring. Full Moon

It is the first day of spring. The council have chopped all the elms down in Elm Tree Avenue.

Saturday March 21st

My parents are eating different things at different times, so I usually have six meals a day because I don't want to hurt anyone's feelings.

The television is in my room now because they couldn't decide who it belongs to. I can lie in bed and watch the late-night horror.

I am starting to get a bit suspicious about my mother's feelings towards Mr Lucas. I found a note she had from him; it says: 'Pauline how much longer? For God's sake come away with me. Yours forever, Bimbo.'

Although it was signed 'Bimbo' I know it was from Mr Lucas because it was written on the back of his red electricity bill.

My father should be informed. I have put the note under my mattress next to the *Big and Bouncy* magazines.

Sunday March 22nd
Third in Lent. British Summer Time begins

It is my grandma's birthday today; she is seventy-six and looks it. I took her a card and a pot plant; it is called Leopard Lily, its foreign name is *Dieffenbachia*. It had a plastic label stuck in the soil which said, 'The sap in this plant is poisonous so take care'. My grandma asked me who chose the plant. I told her my mother did.

My grandma is quite pleased that my parents are getting a divorce! She said that she always thought that my mother had a wanton streak in her and that now she had been proved right.

I didn't like to hear my mother being spoken of in such a way so I came home. I pretended to grandma that I had promised to meet a friend. But I haven't really got a friend any more, it must be because I'm an intellectual. I expect people are in awe of me. Looked in my dictionary to find out what 'wanton' means. It is not very nice!

Monday March 23rd

Back to school, worse luck! We had Domestic Science today. We did baked potatoes in the oven with cheese filling. My potatoes were bigger than anyone else's so they weren't properly cooked by the time the lesson ended, so I finished them off at Bert Baxter's. He wanted to see Blossom again which was a bit of a drag because he takes so long to walk anywhere. But we went, anything is better than doing Maths at school.

Bert took his horse brushes with him and gave Blossom a good clean, she was shining like a conker by the time he'd finished. Bert got out of breath so he sat on the scrap car and had a Woodbine, then we walked back to Bert's house.

Sabre is in a better temper since he got his new kennel and Bert's house is in a better condition as a result of Sabre being outside. Bert told me that the social worker thought he ought to go into an old people's home where he can be properly looked after. Bert doesn't want to. He told a lie to the social worker, he said his grandson came in every day and looked after him. The social worker is going to check up so I could be in trouble for impersonation!!! I don't know how much more worry I can take.

Tuesday March 24th

Late last night I saw my mother and Mr Lucas going out in Mr Lucas's car. They went somewhere special because my mother was wearing a boiler suit with sequins. She did look a bit wanton. Mr Lucas was wearing his best suit and he had a lot of gold jewellery on. For an old person he certainly knows how to dress.

If my father took more care of his appearance, none of this would have happened. It stands to reason that any woman would prefer a man to wear a suit and a lot of gold jewellery to one like my father who hardly ever shaves and wears old clothes and no jewellery.

I am going to stay awake and find out what time my mother comes home.

Midnight. Mother still not home.

2 a.m. No sign of my mother.

Wednesday March 25th
Annunciation of B. V. Mary

Fell asleep, so don't know what time my mother got home. My father said she had gone to the insurance firm's Christmas dinner and dance. In March! Come off it dad! I was not born yesterday! We had swimming in Games today. The water was freezing cold and so were the changing cubicles. I will try to get athlete's foot so that I don't have to go next week.

Thursday March 26th

Barry Kent has been done by the police for riding a bike without a rear light. I hope he gets sent to a Detention Centre. A short sharp shock will do him good.

Friday March 27th

Pandora and Nigel have split up! It is all round the school. This is the best news I have had for ages.

I am reading *Madame Bovary*, by another frog writer.

Saturday March 28th
Last Quarter

Nigel has just left, he is heartbroken. I tried to comfort him. I said that there are plenty more pebbles on the beach and fish in the sea. But he was much too upset to listen.

I told him about my suspicions about my mother and Mr Lucas and he said that it had been going on for a long while. Everybody knew except me and my father!!

We had a long talk about racing bikes, then Nigel went home to think about Pandora.

It is Mother's Day tomorrow. I am in two minds about whether to buy her something or not. I have only got sixty-eight pence.

Sunday March 29th
Fourth in Lent. Mothering Sunday

My father gave me three pounds last night. He said, 'Get your mother something decent, son, it could be the last time'. I certainly wasn't going all the way into town for her, so I went to Mr Cherry's and bought a box of Black Magic, and a card saying 'To a wonderful mother'.

Card manufacturers must think that all mothers are wonderful because every single card has 'wonderful' written on it somewhere. I felt like crossing 'wonderful' out and putting 'wanton' in its place, but I didn't. I signed it 'from your son, Adrian'. I gave it to her this morning. She said, 'Adrian, you shouldn't have'. She was right, I shouldn't have.

Must stop now. My mother has arranged what she called 'a civilized meeting'. Mr Lucas is going to be there. Naturally *I* am not invited! I am going to listen at the door.

Monday March 30th

A terrible thing happened last night. My father and Mr Lucas had a fight in the *front* garden, the whole street came outside to watch! My mother tried to separate them but they both told her to 'keep out of it'. Mr O'Leary tried to help my father, he kept shouting 'Give the smarmy bugger one for me, George'. Mrs O'Leary was shouting horrible things at my mother. By the sounds of things she had been watching my mother's movements since Christmas. The civilized meeting broke up at about five o'clock when my father found out how long my mother and Mr Lucas had been in love.

They had another civilized meeting at about seven o'clock, but when my mother disclosed that she was leaving for Sheffield with Mr Lucas my father became uncivilized and started fighting. Mr Lucas ran into the garden but my father rugby-tackled him by the laurel bush and the fight broke out again. It was quite exciting really. I had a good view from my bedroom window.

Mrs O'Leary said, "'Tis the child I feel sorry for', and all the people looked up and saw me, so I looked especially sad. I expect the experience will give me a trauma at some stage in the future. I'm all right at the moment, but you never know.

Tuesday March 31st

My mother has gone to Sheffield with Mr Lucas. She had to drive because Mr Lucas couldn't see out of his black eyes. I have informed the school secretary of my mother's desertion. She was very kind and gave me a form to give to my father; it is for free school dinners. We are now a single-parent family.

Nigel has asked Barry Kent to stop menacing me for a few weeks. Barry Kent said he would think about it.

Spring

Wednesday April 1st
All Fools' Day

Nigel rang up this morning and pretended he was an undertaker and asked when he was to pick up the body. My father answered the phone. Honestly! He has got no sense of humour.

I had a good laugh telling girls that their petticoats were showing when they weren't. Barry Kent brought a packet of itching powder into the Art lesson, he put some down Ms Fossington-Gore's flying boots. She is another one without any sense of humour. Barry Kent put some down my back. It wasn't funny. I had to go to the matron and have it removed.

The house is looking extremely squalid because my father is not doing any housework. The dog is pining for my mother.

I was born exactly thirteen years and three hundred and sixty-four days ago.

Thursday April 2nd

I am fourteen today! Got a track suit and a football from my father. (He is completely insensitive to my needs.) *A Boy's Book of Carpentry* from my grandma Mole. (No comment.) One pound inside a card from my grandad Sugden. (Last of the big spenders.) Best of all was ten pounds from my mother and five pounds from Mr Lucas. (Conscience money.)

Nigel sent a joke card; it said on the front, 'Who's sexy, charming, intelligent and handsome?' Inside it said, 'Well it certainly ain't you buddy!!!' Nigel wrote 'No offence mate'. He put ten pence inside the envelope.

Bert Baxter sent a card to the school because he doesn't know where I live. His handwriting is dead good, I think it is called 'brass plate'. His card had a picture of an alsatian on the front. Inside Bert had written, 'Best wishes from Bert and Sabre. P.S. Drain blocked up'. Inside the card there was a book token for ten shillings. It expired in December 1958, but it was a kind thought.

So at last I am fourteen! Had a good look at myself in the mirror tonight and I think I can detect a certain maturity. (Apart from the rotten spots.)

Friday April 3rd

Got full marks in the Geography test today. Yes! I am proud to report that I got twenty out of twenty! I was also complimented on the neat presentation of my work. There is nothing I don't know about the Norwegian leather industry. Barry Kent seems to take delight in being ignorant. When Miss Elf asked him where Norway was in relation to Britain he said, 'First cousin twice removed'. It hurts me to relate that even Pandora laughed with the rest of the class. Only Miss Elf and I remained composed. Unblocked Bert Baxter's drain, it was full of old bones and tea leaves. I told Bert that he really ought to use tea-bags. After all this is the twentieth century! Bert said that he would give them a try. I told him that my mother has run away with an insurance man, he said 'Was it an Act of God?' Then he laughed until his eyes watered.

Saturday April 4th
New Moon

Me and my father cleaned the house up today. We had no choice: my grandma is coming for tea tomorrow. We went to Sainsbury's in the afternoon. My father chose a trolley that was impossible to steer. It also squeaked as if somebody was torturing mice. I was ashamed to be heard with it. My father chose food that is bad for you. I had to put my foot down and insist that he bought some fresh fruit and salad. When we got to the check-out he couldn't find his banker's card, the cashier wouldn't take a cheque without it, so the supervisor had to come and stop the argument. I had to lend my father some of my birthday money. So he owes me eight pounds thirty-eight and a half pence. I made him write an IOU on the back of the till roll.

But I must say that I take my hat off to Sainsbury's, they seem to attract a better class of person. I saw a vicar choosing toilet paper; he chose a four-roll pack of purple three-ply. He must have money to burn! He could have bought some shiny white and given the difference to the poor. What a hypocrite!

Sunday April 5th
Passion Sunday

Nigel came round this morning. He is still mad about Pandora. I tried to take his mind off her by talking about the Norwegian leather industry but he couldn't get interested somehow.

I made my father get up at 1 p.m. I don't see why he should lie stinking in bed all day when I am up and about. He got up and went outside to clean the car. He found one of my mother's earrings down the side of the back seat and he just sat there staring at it. He said, 'Adrian, do you miss your mother?' I replied, 'Of course I do, but life must go on'. He then said, 'I don't see why'. I took this to mean that he was suicidal, so

I immediately went upstairs and removed anything harmful from the bathroom.

After we had eaten our frozen roast-beef dinner and I was washing up, he shouted from the bathroom for his razor. I lied and shouted back that I didn't know where it was. I then removed every knife and sharp instrument from the kitchen drawer. He tried to get his battery razor to work but the batteries had leaked and gone all green.

I like to think I am broad-minded but the language my father used was beyond the pale, and all because he couldn't have a shave! Tea was a bit of a drag. My grandma kept saying horrible things about my mother and my father kept rambling on about how much he missed her. Nobody even noticed I was in the room! The dog got more attention than me!

My grandma told my father off for growing a beard. She said, 'You may think it amusing to look like a communist, George, but I don't'. She said that even in the trenches at Ypres my grandad had shaved every day. Sometimes he had to stop rats from eating his shaving soap. She said that my grandad was even shaved by the undertaker when lying in his coffin, so if the dead could shave there was no excuse for the living. My father tried to explain, but grandma didn't stop talking once so it was a bit difficult.

We were both glad when she went home.

Looked at *Big and Bouncy*. It is Passion Sunday after all!

Monday April 6th

Had a postcard from my mother. It said 'they' were staying with friends until they found a flat. She said I could go and stay for a weekend when they were fixed up.

I didn't show it to my father.

Tuesday April 7th

My precious Pandora is going out with Craig Thomas. That's the last time you get a Mars bar from me, Thomas!

Barry Kent is in trouble for drawing a nude woman in Art. Ms Fossington-Gore said that it wasn't so much the subject matter but his ignorance of basic biological facts that was so upsetting. I did a good drawing of the Incredible Hulk smashing Craig Thomas to bits. Ms Fossington-Gore said it was a 'powerful statement of monolithic oppression'.

Phone call from my mother. Her voice sounded funny as if she had a cold. She kept saying, 'You'll understand one day, Adrian'. There was a slurping sound in the background. I expect it was that Lucas creep kissing her neck. I have seen them do it on the films.

Wednesday April 8th

My father wouldn't give me a note excusing me from Games so I spent nearly all morning dressed in pyjamas diving into a swimming pool and picking up a brick from the bottom. I had a bath when I came home but I still smell of chlorine. I just don't see the point of the above lesson. When I am grown up I am hardly going to walk along a river bank in my pyjamas am I? And who would be stupid enough to dive into a river for a boring old brick? Bricks are lying around all over the place!

Thursday April 9th

My father and me had a good talk last night. He asked me who I would prefer to live with, him or my mother? I said both. He told me he had made friends with a woman at work, she is called Doreen Slater. He said he would like me to meet her one day. Here we go again; so much for the suicidal, heartbroken, deserted husband!

Friday April 10th

Rang my grandmother to tell her about Doreen Slater. My grandma didn't sound too pleased, she said it was a common-sounding name and I am inclined to agree with her.

Got *Waiting for Godot* out of the library. Disappointed to find that it was a play. Still, I will give it a go. I have been neglecting my brain lately.

Nigel asked me if I wanted to stay the weekend. His parents are going to a wedding in Croydon. My father said I could. He looked quite pleased. I am going round to Nigel's in the morning.

I broke up for the Easter holidays today. Must make sure my brain keeps active.

Saturday April 11th
First Quarter

Nigel is dead lucky. His house is absolutely fantastic! Everything is modern. I don't know what he must think of our house, some of our furniture is over a hundred years old!

His bedroom is massive and he has got a stereo, a *colour* television, a tapedeck, a Scalextric track, an electric guitar and amplifier. Spotlights over his bed. Black walls and a white carpet and a racing car continental quilt. He has got loads of back issues of *Big and Bouncy*, so we looked through them, then Nigel had a cold shower while I cooked the soup and cut the French loaf. We had a good laugh at *Waiting for Godot*. Nigel had hysterics when I said that Vladimir and Estragon sounded like contraception pills.

I had a go on Nigel's racing bike. I now want one

more than anything in the world. If I had to choose between Pandora and a racing bike, I would choose the bike. Sorry, Pandora, but that's how things are.

We went to the chip shop and had the works. Fish, chips, pickled onions, gherkins, sloppy peas. Nothing was too expensive for Nigel, he gets loads of pocket money. We walked round for a bit then we came back and watched *The Bug-Eyed Monster Strikes Back* on the television. I said the bug-eyed monster reminded me of Mr Scruton the headmaster. Nigel had hysterics again. I think I have got quite a talent to amuse people. I might change my mind about becoming a vet and try writing situation comedy for television.

When the film finished Nigel said, 'How about a nightcap?' He went to the bar in the corner of the lounge and he poured us both a stiff whisky and soda. I hadn't actually tasted whisky before and I never will again. How people can drink it for pleasure I don't know. If it was in a medicine bottle they would pour it down the sink!

Don't remember going to bed, but I must have done because I am sitting up in Nigel's parents' bed writing my diary.

Sunday April 12th
Palm Sunday

This weekend with Nigel has really opened my eyes! Without knowing it I have been living in poverty for the past fourteen years. I have had to put up with inferior accommodation, lousy food and paltry pocket money. If my father can't provide a decent standard of living for me on his present salary, then he will just have to start looking for another job. He is always complaining about having to flog electric storage heaters anyway. Nigel's father has worked like a slave to create a modern environment for *his* family. Perhaps if *my* father had built a formica cocktail bar in the corner of *our* lounge my mother would still be living with us. But oh no. My father actually boasts about our hundred-year-old furniture.

Yes! Instead of being ashamed of our antiques, he is proud of the clapped-out old rubbish.

My father should take lessons from Great Literature. Madame Bovary ran away from that idiot Doctor Bovary because he couldn't supply her needs.

Monday April 13th

Had a note from Mr Cherry asking me when I can resume my paper round. I sent a note back to say that due to my mother's desertion I am still in a mental state. This is true. I wore odd socks yesterday without knowing it. One was red and one was green. I must pull myself together. I could end up in a lunatic asylum.

Tuesday April 14th

Had a postcard from my mother. She has found a flat and she wants me to visit her and Lucas as soon as possible.

Why can't my mother write a letter like any normal person? Why should the postman be able to read my confidential business? Her new address is 79A, President Carter Walk, Sheffield.

I asked my father if I could go; he said, 'Yes, providing she sends the train fare'. So I have written a letter asking her to send eleven pounds eighty.

Wednesday April 15th

Went to the youth club with Nigel. It was dead good. We played ping-pong until the balls cracked. Then we had a go on the football table. I beat Nigel fifty goals to thirteen. Nigel went into a sulk and said that he only lost because his goalkeeper's legs were stuck on with Sellotape but he was wrong. It was my superior skill that did it.

A gang of punks passed unkind comments about my flared trousers but Rick Lemon, the youth leader, stepped in and led a discussion on personal taste. We all agreed it should be up to the individual to dress how he or she likes. All the same I think I will ask my father if I can have a new pair of trousers. Not many fourteen-year-olds wear flared trousers today, and I don't wish to be conspicuous.

Barry Kent tried to get in the fire-doors to avoid paying his five-pence subs. But Rick Lemon pushed him back outside into the rain. I was very pleased. I owe Barry Kent two pounds' menaces money.

Thursday April 16th

Got a birthday card from my Auntie Susan, two weeks late! She always forgets the right day. My father said that she's under a lot of pressure because of her job, but I can't see it myself. I'd have thought that being a prison wardress was dead cushy, it is only locking and unlocking doors after all. She has sent a present via the GPO so with luck I should get it by Christmas. Ha! Ha!

Friday April 17th
Good Friday

Poor Jesus, it must have been dead awful for him. I wouldn't have had the guts to do it myself.

The dog has mauled the hot-cross buns; it doesn't respect any traditions.

Saturday April 18th

Got parcel from Auntie Susan. It is an embroidered toothbrush holder and it was made by one of the prisoners! She is called Grace Pool. Auntie Susan said that I should write and thank her! It is bad enough that my father's sister works in Holloway Prison. But now I am expected to start writing to the prisoners! Grace Pool could be a murderess or anything!

Still waiting for the eleven pounds eighty pence. It doesn't seem as if my mother is desperate to see me.

Sunday April 19th
Easter Sunday

Today is the day that Jesus escaped from the cave. I expect that Houdini got the idea from him.

My father forgot to go to the bank on Friday so we are penniless. I had to take the pop bottles back to the shop to buy myself an Easter egg. Watched film, then had a fantastic tea at grandma's. She made a cake covered in little fluffy chicks. Some of the fluff got into my father's mouth, he had to have his back thumped hard. He always manages to spoil things. He has got no Social Decorum at all. Went to see Bert Baxter after tea. He was pleased to see me and I felt a bit rotten because I have neglected him lately. He gave me a pile of comics. They are called the *Eagle* and they have got great pictures. I read them until 3 a.m. this morning. Us intellectuals keep anti-social hours. It does us good.

Monday April 20th
Bank Holiday in UK (except Scotland)

My father is in a rage because the bank is still shut. He has run out of cigarettes. It will do him good. No sign of the eleven pounds eighty pence.

Wrote to Grace Pool. She is in 'D' Wing. I put:

Dear Miss Pool,

Thank you for making the toothbrush holder. It is charming.

Yours, with kind regards, Adrian

Tuesday April 21st

My father was first in the queue at the bank this morning. When he got inside the cashier said he couldn't have any money because he hadn't got any left. My father demanded to see the manager. I was dead ashamed so I sat behind a plastic plant and waited until the shouting had stopped. Mr Niggard, the head bloke, came out and calmed my father down. He said he would arrange a temporary overdraft. My father looked dead pathetic, he kept saying, 'It was that bloody vet's bill'. Mr Niggard looked as if he understood. Perhaps he has got a mad dog as well. We can't be the only ones, can we?

The eleven pounds, etc., came by second post so I am going to Sheffield tomorrow morning. I've never been on a train on my own before. I am certainly stretching my wings lately.

Wednesday April 22nd

My father gave me a lift to the station. He also gave me a bit of advice about the journey; he said I was not to buy a pork pie from the buffet car.

I stood in the train with my head out of the window and my father stood on the platform. He kept looking at his watch. I couldn't think of anything to say and neither could he. In the end I said, 'Don't forget to feed the dog, will you?' My father gave a nasty laugh, then the train started to move so I waved and went to look for a non-smoking seat. All the filthy smokers were crammed together choking and coughing. They were a rough-looking, noisy lot so I hurried through their small carriage holding my breath. The non-smoking carriages seemed to have a quieter type of person in them. I found a window seat opposite an old lady. I had wanted to look at the landscape or read my book but the old bat started on about her daughter's hysterectomy and telling me things I didn't want to hear. She just about sent me barmy! It was nag, nag, nag. But thank God she got off at Chesterfield. She left her *Woman's Own* behind so I had a good laugh at the Problem Page, read the story, and then the train slowed down for Sheffield. My mother started crying when she saw me. It was a bit embarrassing but quite nice at the same time. We got a taxi from the station, Sheffield looks OK, just like home really. I didn't see any knife and fork factories. I expect Margaret Thatcher has closed them all down.

Lucas was out flogging insurance so I had my mother all to myself until eight o'clock. The flat is dead grotty, it is modern but small. You can hear the neighbours coughing. My mother is used to better things. I am dead tired, so will stop.

I hope my father is being kind to the dog. I wish my mother would come home, I had forgotten how nice she is.

Thursday April 23rd
St George's Day

Me and mum went shopping today. We bought a Habitat lampshade for her bedroom and a new pair of trousers for me. They are dead good, really tight.

We had a Chinese Businessman's Lunch and then went to see a Monty Python film all about the life of Jesus. It was dead daring, I felt guilty laughing.

Lucas was at the flat when we got back. He had got the dinner ready but I said I wasn't hungry and I went to my room. It would choke me to eat anything that creep had touched! Later on I phoned my father from a call-box; I just had time to shout, 'Don't forget to feed the dog', before the pips went.

Retired to bed early because of all the slopping Lucas was doing. He calls my mother 'Paulie' when he knows very well that her name is Pauline.

Friday April 24th

Helped my mother to paint her kitchen. She is doing it brown and cream, it looks awful, just like the toilets at school. Lucas bought me a penknife. He is trying to bribe me into liking him again. Hard luck, Lucas! Us Moles never forget. We are just like the Mafia, once you cross us we bear a grudge all our lives. He has stolen a wife and mother so he will have to pay the price! It is a shame because the penknife is full of gadgets that would be useful to me in my everyday life.

Saturday April 25th

Lucas doesn't work on Saturdays so I had to put up with his lechery all day. He is constantly touching my mother's hand or kissing her or putting his arm round her shoulders, I don't know how she stands it, it would drive me mad.

Lucas drove us out into the countryside this after-noon, it was hilly and high up. I got cold so I sat in the car and watched my mother and Lucas making an exhibition of themselves. Thank God, no members of the public were around. It is not a pretty sight to see old people running up hills laughing.

Came back, had a bath, thought about the dog, went to sleep.

Home tomorrow.

3 a.m. Just had a dream about stabbing Lucas with the toothpick on my penknife. Best dream I've had for ages.

Sunday April 26th

2.10 p.m. So my little sojourn in Sheffield is drawing to a close. I am catching the 7.10 p.m. train which only leaves five hours to do my packing. My father was right. I didn't need two suitcases of clothes. Still it is better to be safe than sorry, I always say. I shan't be sorry to leave this sordid flat with the coughing neighbours, though naturally I have some regrets about my mother's stubbornness in refusing to come home with me.

I told her that the dog was pining to death for her but she rang my father up and like a fool he told her that the dog had just eaten a whole tin of Pedigree Chum and a bowl of Winalot.

I told her about my father and Doreen Slater, hoping to send her mad with jealousy, but she just laughed and said, 'Oh is Doreen still making the rounds?' I have done my best to get her back, but must admit defeat.

11 p.m. Journey back a nightmare, non-smoking compartments all full, forced to share carriage with pipes, cigars and cigarettes. Queued for twenty minutes for a cup of coffee in the buffet. Just got to the counter when the grille came down and the man put up a sign saying: 'Closed due to signal failure'! Got back to seat, found a soldier in my place. Found another seat, but had to endure maniac sitting opposite telling me he had a radio inside his head controlled by Fidel Castro.

My father met me at the station, the dog jumped up to meet me, missed, and nearly fell in front of the 9.23 p.m. Birmingham express.

My father said he had had Doreen Slater for tea. By the state of the house I should think he'd had her for breakfast, dinner and tea! I have never seen the woman, but from the evidence she left behind I know she has got bright red hair, wears orange lipstick and sleeps on the left side of the bed.

What a homecoming!

My father said Doreen had ironed my school clothes ready for the morning. What did he expect? Thanks?

Monday April 27th

Mrs Bull taught us to wash up in Domestic Science. Talk about teaching your grandmother to suck eggs! I must be one of the best washer-uppers in the world! Barry Kent broke an unbreakable plate so Mrs Bull sent him out of the room. I saw him smoking quite openly in the corridor. He has certainly got a nerve! I felt it was my duty to report him to Mrs Bull. I did this purely out of concern for Barry Kent's health. He was taken to pop-eye Scruton and his Benson and Hedges were confiscated. Nigel said he saw Mr Scruton smoking them in the staff room at dinner-time, but surely this can't be true?

Pandora and Craig Thomas are creating a scandal by flaunting their sexuality in the playground. Miss Elf had to knock on the staff-room window and ask them to stop kissing.

Tuesday April 28th

Mr Scruton made a speech in assembly this morning. It was about the country's lack of morals, but really he was talking about Pandora and Craig Thomas. The speech didn't do any good because while we were singing 'There is a Green Hill Far Away', I distinctly saw glances of a passionate nature pass between them.

Wednesday April 29th

My father is worried, electric storage heaters are not selling well. My father says this proves that consumers are not as stupid as everyone thinks. I'm fed up with him mooning about the house at night. I have advised him to join a club or get a hobby but he is determined to feel sorry for himself. The only time he laughs is when those advertisements for electric storage heaters are shown on television. Then he laughs himself silly.

Thursday April 30th

I was seriously menaced at school today. Barry Kent threw my snaplock executive brief-case on to the rugby pitch. I have got to find two pounds quickly before he starts throwing *me* on to the rugby pitch. It's no good asking my father for money, he is in despair because of all the red bills.

Friday May 1st

Grandma rang early this morning to say 'Cast ne'er a clout till May be out'. I haven't got the faintest idea what she was going on about. All I know is that it has something to do with vests.

I am pleased to report that Barry Kent and his gang have been banned from the Off The Streets youth club. (But this means that they are now *on* the streets, worse luck.) They filled a French letter with water and threw it at a bunch of girls and made them scream. Pandora burst the thing with a badge pin and Rick Lemon came out of his office and slipped in the water. Rick was dead mad, he got dirty marks all over his yellow trousers. Pandora helped Rick to throw the gang out, she looked dead fierce. I expect she will win the medal for 'Most helpful member of the year'.

Saturday May 2nd

Had a letter from Grace Pool! This is what it said:

Dear Adrian,

Thank you for your charming letter of thanks. It fair brightened up my day. The girls are all joshing me about my suitor. I am due for parole on June 15th, would it be possible to come and see you? Your Auntie Susan is one of the best screws in here, that's why I obliged and made the toothbrush holder. See you on the fifteenth then.

Yours with fond regards,

Grace Pool

P.S. I was falsely convicted of arson but that is all in the past now.

My God! What shall I do?

Sunday May 3rd
Second after Easter

There is nothing left in the freezer, nothing in the pantry and only slimming bread in the bread bin. I don't know what my father does with all the money. I was forced to go round to grandma's before I died from malnutrition. At four o'clock I had one of those rare moments of happiness that I will remember all my life. I was sitting in front of grandma's electric coal fire eating dripping toast and reading the *News of the World*. There was a good play on Radio Four about torturing in concentration camps. Grandma was asleep and the dog was being quiet. All at once I felt this dead good feeling. Perhaps I am turning religious.

I think I have got it in me to be a Saint of some kind.

Phoned Auntie Susan but she is on duty in Holloway. Left a message with her friend Gloria, asking Auntie Susan to ring me urgently.

Monday May 4th
Bank Holiday in UK. New Moon

Auntie Susan rang to say that Grace Pool has had her parole cancelled because she set fire to the embroidery workshop and destroyed a gross of toothbrush holders.

Their loss is my gain!

Tuesday May 5th

Saw our postman on the way to school, he said that my mother is coming to visit me on Saturday. I've a good mind to report him to the Postmaster General for reading a person's private postcard!

My father had also read my postcard by the time I got home from school. He looked pleased and started

cleaning rubbish out of the lounge, then he rang
Doreen Slater and said he would have to 'take a rain
check on Saturday's flick'. Grown ups are always telling
adolescents to speak clearly then they go and talk a lot
of gibberish themselves. Doreen Slater shouted down
the phone. My father shouted back that he 'didn't
want a long-term relationship', he had 'made that clear
from the start', and that 'nobody could replace his
Pauline'. Doreen Slater went shrieking on and on until
my father slammed the phone down. The phone kept
ringing until my father took the phone off the hook. He
went mad doing housework until 2 a.m. this morning,
and it's only Tuesday! What will he be like on Saturday
morning? The poor fool is convinced that my mother
is coming back for good.

Wednesday May 6th

I am proud to report that I have been made a school-
dinner monitor. My duties are to stand at the side of
the pig bin and make sure that my fellow pupils scrape
their plates properly.

Thursday May 7th

Bert Baxter rang the school to ask me to call round
urgently. Mr Scruton told me off, he said the school
telephone was not for the convenience of the pupils.
Get stuffed, Scruton, you pop-eyed git!!! Bert was in

a terrible state. He had lost his false teeth. He has had them since 1946, they have got sentimental value for him because they used to belong to his father. I looked everywhere for them, but couldn't find them.

I went to the shops and bought him a tin of soup and a butterscotch Instant Whip. It was all he could manage at the moment. I have promised to go round tomorrow and look again. Sabre was happy for once; he was chewing something in his kennel.

My father is still cleaning the house up. Even Nigel commented on how clean the kitchen floor looked. I wish my father wouldn't wear the apron though, he looks like a poofter in it.

Friday May 8th

Found Bert's teeth in Sabre's kennel. Bert rinsed them under the tap and put them back in his mouth! This is the most revolting thing I have ever seen.

My father has got bunches of flowers to welcome my mother home. They are all over the house stinking the place out.

Mr Lucas's house has been sold at last. I saw the estate agent's minion putting the board up. I hope the new people are respectable. I am reading *The Mill on the Floss*, by a bloke called George Eliot.

Saturday May 9th

I was woken up at 8.30 by a loud banging on the front door. It was an Electricity Board official. I was amazed to hear that he had come to turn off our electricity! My father owes £95.79p. I told the official that we needed electricity for life's essentials like the television and stereo, but he said that people like us are sapping the country's strength. He went to the meter cupboard, did something with tools, and the second hand on the kitchen clock stopped. It was dead symbolic. My father came in from fetching the *Daily Express*. He was whistling and looking dead cheerful. He even asked the official if he would like a cup of tea! The official said, 'No thank you', and hurried up the path and got into his little blue van. My father switched the electric kettle on. I was forced to tell him.

Naturally I got the blame! My father said I should have refused entry. I told him that he should have put all the bill money away each week like grandma does. But he just went berserk. My mother turned up with Lucas! It was just like old times with everybody shouting at once. I took the dog to the shops and bought five boxes of candles. Mr Lucas lent me the money.

When I got back I stood in the hall and heard my mother say, 'No wonder you can't pay the bills, George; just look at all these flowers. They must have cost a fortune'. She said it very kindly. Mr Lucas said he would lend my father a 'ton' but my father was very dignified and said, 'All I want from you, Lucas, is my wife'. My mother complimented my father on how nicely he was keeping the house. My father just looked sad and old. I felt dead sorry for him.

I was sent outside while they talked about who was getting custody of me, the arguing went on for ages. In fact until it was time to light the candles.

Lucas spilt candle-wax over his new suede shoes. It was the only cheerful incident in a tragic day.

When my mother and Lucas had gone off in a taxi I went to bed with the dog. I heard my father talking to Doreen Slater on the phone, then the front door slammed and I looked out of my window to see him driving off in the car. The back seat was full of flowers.

Sunday May 10th
Third after Easter. Mother's Day, USA and Canada.
Moon's First Quarter

Didn't get up until half-past four this afternoon. I think I am suffering from depression. Nothing happened at all today, apart from a hail storm around six o'clock.

Monday May 11th

Bert Baxter offered to lend us a paraffin heater. Our gas central heating won't work without electricity. I thanked him but refused his kind offer. I have read that they are easily knocked over and our dog would no doubt cause a towering inferno.

If it gets out that our electricity has been cut off, I will cut my throat. The shame would be too much to bear.

Tuesday May 12th

Had a long talk with Mr Vann the Careers teacher today. He said that if I want to be a vet I will have to do Physics, Chemistry and Biology for O level. He said that Art, Woodwork and Domestic Science won't do much good.

I am at the Crossroads in my life. The wrong decision now could result in a tragic loss to the veterinary world. I am hopeless at science. I asked Mr Vann which O levels you need to write situation comedy for television. Mr Vann said that you don't need qualifications at all, you just need to be a moron.

Wednesday May 13th

Had an in-depth talk about O levels with my father, he advised me to only do the subjects that I am good at. He said that vets spend half their working life with their hands up cows' bums, and the other half injecting spoiled fat dogs. So I am rethinking my future career prospects.

I wouldn't mind being a sponge-diver, but I don't think there is much call for them in England.

Thursday May 14th

Miss Sproxton told me off because my English essay was covered in drops of candle-wax. I explained that I had caught my overcoat sleeve on the candle whilst doing my homework. Her eyes filled with tears and she said I was 'a dear brave lad', and she gave me a merit mark.

After supper of cream crackers and tuna fish, played cards in the candlelight. It was dead good. My father cut the ends off our gloves, we looked like two criminals on the run.

I am reading *Hard Times*, by Charles Dickens.

Friday May 15th

My grandmother has just made a surprise visit. She caught us huddled round our new Camping-gaz stove eating cold beans out of a tin. My father was reading *Playboy* under cover of the candlelight and I was reading *Hard Times* by my key-ring torch. We were quite contented. My father had just said that it was a 'good training for when civilization collapses' when grandma burst in and started having hysterics. She has forced us to go to her house so I am there now sleeping in my dead grandad's bed. My father is sleeping downstairs on two armchairs pushed together. Grandma has written a Giro cheque for the electricity money, she is furious because she wanted the money for restocking her freezer. She buys two dead cows a year.

Saturday May 16th

Helped grandma with the weekend shopping. She was dead fierce in the grocer's; she watched the scales like a hawk watching a fieldmouse. Then she pounced and accused the shop assistant of giving her underweight bacon. The shop assistant was dead scared of her and put another slice on.

Our arms were dead tired by the time we'd staggered up the hill carrying big bags of shopping. I don't know how my grandma does it when she's alone. I think the council ought to put escalators on hills; they would save money in the long run, old people wouldn't go about collapsing all over the place. My father paid the electricity bill at the post office today, but it will be at least a week before the computer gives permission for our electricity to be reconnected.

Sunday May 17th

My grandma made us get up early and go to church with her. My father was made to comb his hair and wear one of his dead father's ties. Grandma held both our arms and looked proud to be with us. The church service was dead boring. The vicar looked like the oldest man alive and spoke in a feeble sort of voice. My father kept standing up when we were supposed to sit down and vice versa. I copied what grandma did, she is always right. My father sang too loudly, everyone looked at him. I shook the vicar's hand when we were allowed outside. It was like touching dead leaves.

After dinner we listened to my grandma's records of Al Jolson, then grandma went upstairs for a sleep and my father and me washed up. My father broke a forty-one-year-old milk jug! He had to go out for a drink to recover from the shock. I went to see Bert Baxter but he wasn't in, so I went to see Blossom instead. She was very pleased to see me. It must be dead boring standing in a field all day long. No wonder she welcomes visitors.

Monday May 18th

Grandma is not speaking to my father because of the milk jug. Can't wait to get home where things like milk jugs don't matter.

Tuesday May 19th
Full Moon

My father is in trouble for staying out late last night. Honestly! He is the same age as the milk jug so surely he can come in what time he likes!

Told my father about being menaced today. I was forced to because Barry Kent seriously damaged my school blazer and tore the school badge off. My father is going to speak to Barry Kent tomorrow *and* he is going to get all the menaces money back off him, so it looks like I could be rich!

Wednesday May 20th

Barry Kent denied all knowledge of menacing me and laughed when my father asked him to repay the money. My father went to see his father and had a serious argument and threatened to call the police. I think my father is dead brave. Barry Kent's father looks like a big ape and has got more hair on the back of his hands than my father has got on his entire head.

The police have said that they can't do anything without proof so I am going to ask Nigel to give them a sworn statement that he has seen me handing menaces money over.

Thursday May 21st

Barry Kent duffed me up in the cloakroom today. He hung me on one of the coathooks. He called me a 'coppers' nark' and other things too bad to write down. My grandma found out about the menacing (my father didn't want her to know on account of her diabetes). She listened to it all then she put her hat on, thinned her lips and went out. She was gone one hour and seven minutes, she came in, took her coat off, fluffed her hair out, took £27.18 from the anti-mugger belt round her waist. She said, 'He won't bother you again, Adrian, but if he does, let me know'. Then she got the tea ready. Pilchards, tomatoes and ginger cake. I bought her a box of diabetic chocolates from the chemist's as a token of my esteem.

Friday May 22nd

It is all round the school that an old lady of seventy-six frightened Barry Kent and his dad into returning my menaces money. Barry Kent daren't show his face. His gang are electing a new leader.

Saturday May 23rd

Home again, the electricity has been reconnected. All the plants are dead. Red bills on the doormat.

Sunday May 24th
Rogation Sunday

I have decided to paint my room black; it is a colour I like. I can't live a moment longer with Noddy wallpaper. At my age it is positively indecent to wake up to Big Ears and all the rest of the Toyland idiots running around the walls. My father says I can use any colour I like so long as I buy the paint and do it myself.

Monday May 25th

I have decided to be a poet. My father said that there isn't a suitable career structure for poets and no pensions and other boring things, but I am quite decided. He tried to interest me in becoming a computer operator, but I said, 'I need to put my soul into my work and it is well known that computers haven't got a soul'. My father said, 'The Americans are working on it'. But I can't wait that long.

Bought two tins of black vinyl silk-finish paint and a half-inch brush. Started painting as soon as I got home from the DIY centre. Noddy keeps showing through the black paint. Looks like it'll need two coats. Just my luck!

Tuesday May 26th
Moon's Last Quarter

Now put on two coats of black paint! Noddy still showing through! Black paw-marks over landing and stairs. Can't get paint off hands. Hairs falling out of brush. Fed up with whole thing. Room looks dark and gloomy. Father hasn't lifted a finger to help. Black paint everywhere.

Wednesday May 27th
Third coat. Slight improvement, only Noddy's hat showing through now.

Thursday May 28th
Ascension Day

Went over Noddy's hat with kid's paintbrush and last of black paint, but bloody hat bells are still showing through!

Friday May 29th

Went over hat bells with black felt-tip pen, did sixty-nine tonight, only a hundred and twenty-four to go.

Saturday May 30th

Finished last bell at 11.25 p.m. Know just how Rembrandt must have felt after painting the Sistine Chapel in Venice.

2 a.m. The paint is dry but it must have been faulty because it is all streaky, and here and there you can see Gollywog's striped trousers and Mr Plod's nose. Thank God the bloody bells don't show through! My father has just been in to tell me to go to sleep, he said my room reminded him of a Salvador Dali painting. He said it was a surrealist nightmare, but he is only jealous because he has got yukky roses on his bedroom walls.

Sunday May 31st
Sunday after Ascension

I bought a joss stick from Mr Singh's shop. I lit it in my room to try and get rid of the paint smell. My father came into my room and threw the joss stick out of the window, he said he 'wouldn't have me messing with drugs'! I tried to explain but my father was too angry to listen. I stayed in my room for a few hours but the black walls seemed to be closing in on me so I went to see Bert Baxter. Couldn't make him hear, so I came home and watched religion on the television. Had tea, did Geography homework, went to bed. Dog won't stay in room any more; it whimpers to be let out.

Monday June 1st
Bank Holiday in the Rep. of Ireland

My father had a letter that made his face go white: he has been made redundant from his job! He will be on the dole! How can we live on the pittance that the government will give us? The dog will have to go! It costs thirty-five pence a day for dog food, not counting Winalot. I am now a single-parent child whose father is on the dole! Social Security will be buying my shoes!

I didn't go to school today, I rang the school secretary and told her that my father is mentally ill and needs looking after. She sounded dead worried and asked if he was violent. I said that he hadn't shown any signs of being violent, but if he started I would call the doctor. I made my father lots of hot, sweet drinks for shock, he kept going on about electric storage heaters and saying that he would spill the beans to the media.

He rang Doreen Slater up and she came round straightaway, she had a horrible little kid called Maxwell with her. It was quite a shock to see Doreen Slater for the first time. Why my father wanted to have carnal knowledge of her I can't imagine. She is as thin as a stick insect. She has got no bust and no bum.

She is just straight all the way up and down, including her nose and mouth and hair. She put her arms round my father as soon as she came into the house. Maxwell started to cry, the dog started to bark, so I went back to my black room and counted how many things were now showing through the paint: a hundred and seventeen!

Doreen left at 1.30 p.m. to take Maxwell to play-school. She did some shopping for us then cooked a sloppy sort of meal made of spaghetti and cheese. She is a one-parent family; Maxwell was born out of wedlock. She told me about herself when we were washing up. She would be quite nice if she were a bit fatter.

Tuesday June 2nd
New Moon

Doreen and Maxwell stayed the night. Maxwell was supposed to sleep on the sofa, but he cried so much that he ended up sleeping in the double bed between my father and Doreen, so my father was unable to extend his carnal knowledge of Doreen. He was as sick as a pig, but not as sick as Maxwell was. Ha! Ha! Ha!

Wednesday June 3rd

Went to school today, couldn't concentrate, kept thinking about the stick insect. She has got lovely white teeth (straight of course). She made some jam tarts for when I came home from school. She is not stingy with the jam like some women are.

My father is smoking and drinking heavily, but he has been made temporarily impotent according to

Doreen. This is something I do not wish to know! Doreen talks to me as if I were another adult instead of her lover's son aged fourteen and two months and one day.

Thursday June 4th

Doreen answered the phone to my mother first thing this morning. My mother asked to speak to me. She demanded to know what Doreen was doing in the house. I told her that my father was having a breakdown and that Doreen Slater was looking after him. I told her about his redundancy. I said he was drinking heavily, smoking too much and generally letting himself go. Then I went to school. I was feeling rebellious, so I wore red socks. It is strictly forbidden but I don't care any more.

Friday June 5th

Miss Sproxton spotted my red socks in assembly! The old bag reported me to pop-eyed Scruton. He had me in his office and gave me a lecture on the dangers of being a nonconformist. Then he sent me home to change into regulation black socks. My father was in bed when I got home; he was having his impotence cured. I watched *Play School* with Maxwell until he came downstairs. I told him about the sock saga.

He instantly turned into a raving loonie! He phoned

the school and dragged Scruton out of a caretakers' strike-meeting. He kept shouting down the phone; he said, 'My wife's left me, I've been made redundant, I'm in charge of an idiot boy,' – Maxwell, I presume – 'and you're victimizing my son because of the colour of his socks!' Scruton said if I came to school in black socks everything would be forgotten but my father said I would wear whatever colour socks I liked. Scruton said he was anxious to maintain standards. My father said that the England World Cup team in 1966 did not wear black socks, nor did Sir Edmund Hillary in 1953. Scruton seemed to go quiet then. My father put the phone down. He said, 'Round one to me'.

This could well get into the papers: 'Black socks row at school'. My mother might read about it and come home.

Saturday June 6th

Oh Joy! Oh Rapture! Pandora is organizing a sock protest! She came round to my house today! Yes! She actually stood on our front porch and told me that she admired the stand I was taking! I would have asked her in, but the house is in a squalid state so I didn't. She is going round the school with a petition on Monday morning. She said I was a freedom fighter for the rights of the individual. She wants me to go round to her house tomorrow morning. A committee is being set up, and I am the principal speaker! She wanted to see the red socks but I told her they were in the wash.

Doreen Slater and Maxwell went home today. My grandma is coming round tonight, so all traces of them have got to be wiped out.

Sunday June 7th
Whit Sunday

Grandma found Maxwell's dummy in my father's bed. I lied and said that the dog must have brought it in off the street. It was a nasty moment. I am not a good liar, my face goes bright red and my grandma has got eyes like Superman's, they seem to bore right through you. To divert her I told her about the red-sock row, but she said rules were made to be kept.

Pandora and the committee were waiting for me in the big lounge of her house. Pandora is Chairperson, Nigel is Secretary and Pandora's friend Claire Neilson is Treasurer. Craig Thomas and his brother Brett are just ordinary supporters. I am not allowed to hold high office because I am the victim.

Pandora's parents were in the wooden kitchen doing *The Sunday Times* crossword. They seem to get on quite well together.

They brought a tray of coffee and health biscuits into the lounge for us. Pandora introduced me to her parents. They said they admired the stand that I was taking. They were both members of the Labour Party and they went on about the Tolpuddle Martyrs. They asked me if the fact that I had chosen to protest in *red* socks had any significance. I lied and said I had chosen red because it was a symbol of revolution, then I blushed revolutionary red. I am turning into quite a liar recently.

Pandora's mother said I could call her Tania. Surely that is a Russian name? Her father said I could call him Ivan. He is very nice, he gave me a book to read; it is called *The Ragged Trousered Philanthropists*. I haven't looked through it yet but I'm quite interested in stamp collecting so I will read it tonight.

Washed red socks, put them on radiator to dry ready for the morning.

Monday June 8th

Woke up, dressed, put red socks on before underpants or vest. Father stood at the door and wished me luck. Felt like a hero. Met Pandora and rest of committee at corner of our road; all of us were wearing red socks. Pandora's were lurex. She has certainly got guts! We sang 'We shall not be moved' all the way to school. I felt a bit scared when we went through the gates but Pandora rallied us with shouts of encouragement.

Pop-eyed Scruton must have been tipped off because he was waiting in the fourth-year cloakroom. He was standing very still with his arms folded, staring with poached egg eyes. He didn't speak, he just nodded upstairs. All the red socks trooped upstairs. My heart was beating dead loud. He went silently into his office and sat at his desk and started tapping his teeth with a school pen. We just stood there.

He smiled in a horrible way then rang the bell on his desk. His secretary came in, he said, 'Sit down and take a letter, Mrs Claricoates'. The letter was to our parents, it said:

Dear Mr and Mrs . . . .,

It is my sad duty to inform you that your son/daughter has deliberately flaunted one of the rules of this school. I take an extremely serious view of this contravention. I am therefore suspending your son/daughter for a period of one week. Young people today often lack sufficient moral guidance in the home, therefore I feel that it is my duty to take a firm stand in my school. If you wish to discuss the matter further with me do not hesitate to ring my secretary for an appointment.

Your faithfully,
R. G. Scruton
Headmaster

Pandora started to say something about her O levels suffering but Scruton roared at her to shut up! Even Mrs Claricoates jumped. Scruton said that we could wait until the letters had been typed, duplicated and signed and then we had better 'hot foot it out of school'. We waited outside Scruton's office. Pandora was crying (because she was angry and frustrated, she said). I put my arm round her a bit. Mrs Claricoates gave us our letters. She smiled very kindly, it can't be very easy working for a despot.

We went round to Pandora's house but it was locked, so I said everyone could come round to my house. It was quite tidy for once, apart from the dog hairs. My father raged about the letter. He is supposed to be a Conservative but he is not being very conservative at the moment.

I can't help wishing that I had worn black socks on Friday.

Tuesday June 9th
Moon's First Quarter

My father saw Scruton today and told him that if he didn't allow me back to school in whatever colour socks I like he would protest to his MP. Mr Scruton asked my father who his MP was. My father didn't know.

Wednesday June 10th

Pandora and I are in love! It is official! She told Claire Neilson, who told Nigel, who told me.

I told Nigel to tell Claire to tell Pandora that I return her love. I am over the moon with joy and rapture. I can overlook the fact that Pandora smokes five Benson and Hedges a day and has her own lighter. When you are in love such things cease to matter.

Thursday June 11th

Spent all day with my love. Can't write much, my hands are still trembling.

Friday June 12th

Had a message from the school to say that Bert Baxter wanted to see me urgently. Went round with Pandora (we are inseparable). Bert is ill. He looked awful, Pandora made his bed up with clean sheets (she didn't seem to mind the smell) and I phoned the doctor. I described Bert's symptoms. Funny breathing, white face, sweating.

We tried to clean the bedroom up a bit, Bert kept saying stupid things that didn't make sense. Pandora said that he was delirious. She held his hand until the doctor came. Dr Patel was quite kind, he said that Bert needed oxygen. He gave me a number to ring for an ambulance, it seemed to take ages to come. I thought about how I had neglected Bert lately and I felt a real rat fink. The ambulancemen took Bert downstairs on a stretcher. They got stuck on the corner of the stairs and knocked a lot of empty beetroot jars over. Pandora and me cleared a path through the rubbish in the downstairs hall and they steered him through. He was wrapped in a big, fluffy red blanket before he went outside. Then they shut him up in the ambulance and he was sirened away. I had a big lump in my throat and my eyes were watering. It must have been caused by the dust.

Bert's house is very dusty.

Saturday June 13th

Bert is in intensive care, he can't have visitors. I ring up every four hours to find out how he is. I pretend to be a relative. The nurses say things like 'He is stable'.

Sabre is staying with us. Our dog is staying at grandma's because it is scared of alsatians.

I hope Bert doesn't die. Apart from liking him, I have got nothing to wear to a funeral.

Still madly in love with P.

Sunday June 14th
Trinity Sunday

Went to see Bert, he has got tubes all over him. I took him a jar of beetroot for when he is better. The nurse put it in his locker. I took some 'get well' cards, one from Pandora and me, one from my grandma, one from my father and one from Sabre.

Bert was asleep so I didn't stay long.

Monday June 15th

The Red Sock Committee has voted to give way to Scruton for the time being. We wear red socks underneath our black socks. This makes our shoes tight but we don't mind because a principle is involved.

Bert has made a slight improvement. He is awake more. I'll go round and see him tomorrow.

Tuesday June 16th

Bert has only got a few tubes left inside him now. He was awake when I went into his room. He didn't recognize me at first because I was wearing a mask and gown. He thought I was a doctor. He said, 'Get these bleedin' tubes out of my private parts, I ain't an underground system'. Then he saw it was me and asked how Sabre was. We had a long talk about Sabre's behaviour problems, then the nurse came in and told me I had to go. Bert asked me to tell his daughters that he is on his death bed; he gave me half-a-crown for the phone calls! Two of them live in Australia! He said the numbers are written down in the back of his old army pay-book.

My father says that half-a-crown is roughly worth twelve and a half pence. I am keeping the half-a-crown. It has a nice chunky feel about it and it will no doubt be a collector's item one day.

Wednesday June 17th
Full Moon

Pandora and me searched Bert's house looking for his army pay-book. Pandora found a pile of brown and cream postcards that were very indecent. They were signed '*avec tout mon amour chéri, Lola*'. I felt a bit funny after looking through them, so did Pandora. We exchanged our first really passionate kiss. I felt like doing a French kiss but I don't know how it's done so I had to settle for an ordinary English one.

No sign of the pay-book.

Thursday June 18th

Bert is now tubeless. He is being moved into an ordinary ward tomorrow. I told him about not finding the army pay-book, he said it doesn't matter now he knows he's not dying.

Pandora came with me tonight. She got on well with Bert; they talked about Blossom. Bert passed on a few tips about grooming ponies. Then Pandora went out to arrange the flowers she'd brought and Bert asked me if I'd had my 'leg over' yet. Sometimes he is just a dirty old man who doesn't deserve visitors.

Friday June 19th

Bert is on a big ward full of men with broken legs and bandaged chests. He looks a lot better now that he has got his teeth in. Some of the men whistled at Pandora when she walked down the ward. I wish she wasn't taller than me. Bert is in trouble with the ward sister for getting beetroot juice on the hospital sheets. He is supposed to be on a fluid diet.

Saturday June 20th

I hope Bert can come home soon. My father is fed up with Sabre and my grandma is sick to death of our dog.

Bert's consultant has told him to give up smoking but Bert says at eighty-nine years old it is hardly worth it. He has asked me to buy him twenty Woodbines and a box of matches. What shall I do?

Sunday June 21st
First after Trinity. Father's Day

Couldn't sleep last night for worrying about the Woodbines. After much heart-searching decided not to grant Bert's wish. Then went to the hospital to find that Bert had bought his stinking fags from the hospital trolley!

Just measured my thing. It has grown one centimetre. I might be needing it soon.

Monday June 22nd

Woke up with sore throat, couldn't swallow, tried to shout downstairs but could only manage a croak. Tried to attract my father's attention by banging on my bedroom floor with school shoe but my father shouted, 'Stop that bloody banging'. Eventually I sent the dog downstairs with a message tucked inside its collar. I waited for ages, then I heard the dog barking in the street. It hadn't delivered the message! I was close to despair. I had to get up to go to the toilet but how I got there I don't know; it is all a hazy blur. I stood at the top of the stairs and croaked as loud as I could but my father had his Alma Cogan records on so I was forced to go downstairs and tell him I was ill. My father looked in my mouth and said, 'Christ Almighty, Adrian, your tonsils look like Polaris missiles! What are you doing down here? Get back into bed at once, you fool'. He took my temperature: it was 112° Fahrenheit. By rights I should be dead.

It is now five minutes to midnight, the doctor is coming in the morning. I just pray that I can last out until then. Should the worst happen, I hereby leave all my worldly goods to Pandora Braithwaite of 69 Elm Tree Avenue. I think I am of sound mind. It is very hard to tell when you've got a temperature of 112° Fahrenheit.

Tuesday June 23rd

I have got tonsillitis. It is official. I am on antibiotics. Pandora sits by my bed reading aloud to me. I wish she wouldn't, every word is like a rock dropping on my head.

Wednesday June 24th

A 'get well' card from my mother. Inside a five-pound note. I asked my father to spend it on five bottles of Lucozade.

Thursday June 25th
Moon's Last Quarter

I have delirious dreams about Lady Diana Spencer; I hope I am better in time for the wedding. Temperature is still 112° Fahrenheit.

My father can't cope with Sabre, so Pandora has taken him home with her. (Sabre, not my father.)

Friday June 26th

Doctor said our thermometer is faulty. I feel slightly better.

Got up for twenty minutes today. Watched *Play*

School; it was Carol Leader's turn, she is my favourite presenter.

Pandora brought me a 'get well' card. She made it herself with felt-tip pens. She signed it: 'Forever yours, Pan.'

I wanted to kiss her but my lips are still cracked.

Saturday June 27th

Why hasn't my mother been to see me?

Sunday June 28th
Second after Trinity

My mother has just left to catch the train for Sheffield. I am worn out with all the emotion. I am having a relapse.

Monday June 29th

Pandora went to see Bert Baxter. She said the nurses are getting fed up with him because he won't stay in bed or do anything he is told to do. He is being discharged on Thursday.

I long for the peace and quiet of a hospital ward. I would be a perfect patient.

Pandora's father has put Sabre into kennels, it is

costing him three pounds a day, but Pandora's father says that it is worth every penny.

Tuesday June 30th

I am entering a period of convalescence. I will have to take things very easily if I am to regain my former vigour.

Summer

Wednesday July 1st
Dominion Day, Canada. New Moon

The truant officer came round this afternoon; he caught me sitting in a deckchair in the front garden. He didn't believe I was ill! He is reporting me to the school! The fact that I was sipping Lucozade whilst wearing pyjamas, dressing gown and slippers seemed to have escaped him. I offered to show him my yukky tonsils but he backed away and trod on the dog's paw. The dog has got a low pain threshold so it went a bit berserk. My father came out and separated them but things could get nasty for us.

Thursday July 2nd

The doctor said I can go back to school tomorrow, depending on how I feel. You can depend that I won't feel up to it.

Friday July 3rd

A brown-skinned family are moving into Mr Lucas's old house! I sat in my deckchair and had a good view of their furniture being carried out of the removal van. The brown-skinned ladies kept taking massive cooking pots into the house so it looks as if they are a large family. My father said that it was 'the beginning of the end of our street'. Pandora is in the Anti-Nazi League. She said she thinks that my father is a possible racist.

I am reading *Uncle Tom's Cabin*.

Saturday July 4th
Independence Day, USA

The street is full of brown-skinned people arriving or departing in cars, vans and mini-buses. They keep trooping in and out of Mr Lucas's old house. My father says they have probably got three families to each room.

Pandora and I are going round to welcome them to our district. We are determined to show that not all white people are racist fanatics.

Bert Baxter is still in hospital.

Sunday July 5th
Third after Trinity

Stayed in bed until 6 p.m. There was no point in getting up. Pandora has gone to a gymkhana.

Monday July 6th

Mrs O'Leary is trying to organize a street party for the Royal Wedding. The only people to put their names down so far are the Singh family.

Tuesday July 7th

Bert Baxter has escaped from hospital. He telephoned the National Council for Civil Liberties and they told him he could sign himself out, so he did. He is in our spare room. My father is going up the wall.

Pandora, Bert and I have put our names down for the street party. Bert is looking much better now that he can smoke as many Woodbines as he likes.

Pandora's father has been round to talk to my father about what to do about Bert and Sabre. They both got drunk and started arguing about politics. Bert banged on the floor and asked them to keep their voices down.

Wednesday July 8th

My father is near to despair because of Bert's snoring. It doesn't bother me, I put Blu-tack in my ears.

Went to school today. I have decided to take Domestic Science, Art, Woodwork and English O levels. I am doing Geography, Maths and History for CSE.

Pandora is taking nine O levels. But she has had more advantages than me. She has been a member of the library since she was three.

Thursday July 9th

School breaks up for eight weeks tomorrow. Pandora is going to Tunisia soon. How I will survive without my love is anybody's guess. We have tried French kissing but neither of us liked it, so we have gone back to the English.

My skin is dead good. I think it must be a combination of being in love and Lucozade.

Friday July 10th

It was magic at school today. All the teachers were in good moods. A rumour went round that pop-eyed Scruton was seen laughing but I didn't believe it myself.

Barry Kent climbed up the flagpole and flew a pair

of his mother's knickers in the breeze. Pandora said it was probably the first airing they had had for years.

Sean O'Leary is nineteen today. He has invited me to his birthday party. It is only over the road so I won't have far to go.

I am writing up my diary now just in case I have one too many. People seem to get drunk just stepping over the O'Learys' threshold.

Saturday July 11th

First proper hangover. Aged fourteen years, five months and nine days. Pandora put me to bed. She gave me a fireman's lift up the stairs.

Sunday July 12th
Fourth after Trinity

My father took me, Pandora and Bert to the Wagtails boarding kennels this morning. Mrs Kane, the proprietor, has refused to keep Sabre any longer. It was very touching to see Bert and Sabre reunited. Mrs Kane is a hard woman, she got very nasty when my father refused to pay Sabre's boarding fees, she kept smoothing her black moustache with her horny fingers and using unladylike language.

Bert said he won't be parted from Sabre again. He said that Sabre is his only friend in the world! After all *I* have done for him!! If it wasn't for me he would be a corpse by now, and Sabre would be an orphan living with the RSPCA.

Monday July 13th

Bert has been talking to Mrs Singh! He speaks fluent Hindi! He says she has found some indecent magazines under the lino in the bathroom. An heirloom from that creep Lucas!

Mr Singh is outraged. He has written to the estate agents to complain that his house has been defiled.

Bert showed me one of the magazines. They are not indecent in my opinion, but then I am a man of the world. I have put it under my mattress with the *Big and Bouncy*s. It is called *Amateur Photographer*.

Tuesday July 14th

Bert's social worker came round tonight. She is called Katie Bell. She talked to Bert in a stupid way. She said that Bert had been offered a place in the Alderman Cooper Sunshine Home. Bert told her that he didn't want to go. Katie Bell said that he has got to go. Even my father said that he felt sorry for Bert. But not sorry enough to invite Bert to live with us permanently I noticed!

Poor Bert, what will happen to him?

Wednesday July 15th

Bert has moved in with the Singhs. Mr Singh fetched Sabre's kennel so it is official. Bert looks dead happy. His favourite food is curry.

Pandora has allowed me to touch her bust. I promised not to tell anyone, but there was nothing to tell really. I couldn't tell where her bust began through all the layers of underclothes, dress, cardigan and anorak.

I am reading *Sex, The Facts*, by Dr A. P. G. Haig.

Thursday July 16th

11 a.m. My father got his redundancy cheque today. He did cowboy whoops up and down the hall. He has asked Doreen Slater to go out with him to celebrate. Guess who Maxwell's baby sitter is going to be? Yes, dear diary, you guessed right! It is I!

11 p.m. Maxwell has only just gone to sleep, Pandora rang up at nine-thirty and asked how I was doing. I couldn't hear her properly because Maxwell was screaming so loudly. Pandora said I should try putting vodka in some hot milk and forcing it down his vile throat. I have just done it. And it worked.

He is not a bad kid when he is asleep.

Friday July 17th
Full Moon

My precious love leaves these shores tomorrow. I am going to the airport to see her off. I hope her plane won't suffer from metal fatigue. I have just checked the world map to see where Tunisia is, and I am most relieved to see that Pandora won't have to fly through the Bermuda triangle.

If anything happened to my love I would never smile again.

I have bought her a book to read during the flight. It is called *Crash!*, by a bloke called William Goldenstein, III. It is very good on what to do if the worst happens.

Saturday July 18th

Pandora read the *Crash!* book in the coach on the way to the airport. When her flight was called she had slight hysterics and her father had to carry her up the steps. I waved to the plane until it had retreated into a large cloud, then I sadly got on a coach and came back home. How I will get through the next fortnight I don't know. Goodnight, my Tunisian beauty.

Sunday July 19th
Fifth after Trinity

Stayed in bed and looked at Tunisia on the map.

Monday July 20th

Not had a postcard from my love yet.

Tuesday July 21st

Bert came round this morning. He said that Tunisia is full of hazards.

Wednesday July 22nd

Why haven't I had a postcard yet? What can have happened?

Thursday July 23rd

Asked our postman about communications between Tunisia and England. He said that they were 'diabolical'; he said that the Tunisian GPO depends on camels.

Friday July 24th
Moon's Last Quarter

Went to see Mr Singh. He said that Tunisia is very unhygienic. Everybody but me seems to be familiar with Tunisia!

Saturday July 25th

PANDORA! PANDORA! PANDORA!

> Oh! my love,
> My heart is yearning,
> My mouth is dry,
> My soul is burning.
> You're in Tunisia,
> I am here.
> Remember me and shed a tear.
> Come back tanned and brown and healthy.
> You're lucky that your dad is wealthy.

She will be back in six days.

Sunday July 26th
Sixth after Trinity

Went for tea at grandma's. I was sad and withdrawn because of Pandora's sojourn in Tunisia. Grandma asked if I was constipated. I nearly said something, but what's the use of trying to explain *love* to a woman of seventy-six who thinks the word is obscene?

Monday July 27th

A camel postcard! It said:

Dearest,
    Economic conditions here are quite dreadful. I was going to buy you a present but instead I gave all my money to a beggar. You have such a generous heart Adrian that I feel sure you will understand.
All my love into infinity.
    For ever,
    Pandora

X

Fancy giving my present money to a filthy, idle beggar! Even our postman was disgusted.

Tuesday July 28th

It's a wonder I have the strength to hold my pen! I have been on the go all day with preparations for the Royal Wedding street party. Mrs O'Leary came over and asked if I would help with the bunting. I said 'I feel it is my patriotic duty'. Mrs O'Leary said that if I climbed the ladder she would pass the bunting up to me. I was all right for the first four or five rungs but then I made the mistake of looking down and I had a vertigo attack, so Mrs O'Leary did all the climbing. I couldn't help noticing Mrs O'Leary's knickers. They are surprisingly sexy for someone who goes to church every day and twice on Sundays. Black lace! With red-satin ribbons! I got the feeling that Mrs O'Leary knew that I was looking at her knickers because she asked me to call her Caitlin. I was glad when Mr O'Leary came to take over from me. Mr and Mrs Singh have hung a huge Union Jack out of their front bedroom window. Bert told me that it was one he stole when he was in the army.

Our house is letting the street down. All my father has done is pin a Charles and Diana tea towel to the front door.

My father and I watched the Royal Wedding firework display on television. All I can say is that I tried to enjoy it but failed. My father said it was one way of burning money. He is still bitter about being out of work.

I hope the Prince remembers to remove the price ticket off the bottom of his shoes; my father didn't at his wedding. Everyone in the church read the ticket. It said: '9½ reject, 10 shillings'.

Wednesday July 29th

ROYAL WEDDING DAY!!!!!

How proud I am to be English!

Foreigners must be as sick as pigs!

We truly lead the world when it comes to pageantry! I must admit to having tears in my eyes when I saw all the cockneys who had stood since dawn, cheering heartily all the rich, well-dressed, famous people going by in carriages and Rolls-Royces.

Grandma and Bert Baxter came to our house to watch the wedding because we have got a twenty-four-inch colour. They got on all right at first but then Bert remembered he was a communist and started saying anti-royalist things like 'the idle rich' and 'parasites', so grandma sent him back to the Singhs' colour portable.

Prince Charles looked quite handsome in spite of his ears. His brother is dead good-looking; it's a shame they couldn't have swapped heads just for the day. Lady Diana melted my heartstrings in her dirty white dress. She even helped an old man up the aisle. I thought it was very kind of her considering it was her wedding day. Loads of dead famous people were there. Nancy Reagan, Spike Milligan, Mark Phillips, etc., etc. The Queen looked a bit jealous. I expect it was because people weren't looking at *her* for a change.

The Prince had remembered to take the price ticket off his shoes. So that was one worry off my mind.

When the Prince and Di exchanged rings my grandma started to cry. She hadn't brought her handkerchief so I went upstairs to get the spare toilet roll. When I came downstairs they were married. So I missed the Historic moment of their marriage!

I made a cup of tea during all the boring musical interval, but I was back in time to see that Kiwi woman singing. She has certainly got a good pair of lungs on her.

Grandma and I were just settling down to watch the happy couple's triumphant ride back to the palace when there was a loud banging on the front door. We ignored it so my father was forced to get out of bed and open the door. Bert and Mr and Mrs Singh and all the little Singhs came in asking for sanctuary. Their telly had broken down! My grandma tightened her lips, she is not keen on black, brown, yellow, Irish, Jewish or foreign people. My father let them all in, then took grandma home in the car. The Singhs and Bert gathered round the television talking in Hindi.

Mrs Singh handed round some little cornish pasties. I ate one of them and had to drink a gallon of water. I thought my mouth had caught fire! They were not cornish pasties.

We watched television until the happy couple left Victoria station on a very strange-looking train. Bert said it was only strange-looking because it was clean.

Mrs O'Leary came in and asked if she could borrow our old chairs for the street party. In my father's absence I agreed and helped to carry them out on to the pavement. Our street looked dead weird without cars and with flags and bunting flapping about.

Mrs O'Leary and Mrs Singh swept the street clean. Then we all helped to put the tables and chairs out into the middle of the road. The women did all the work, the men stood around on the pavement drinking too much and making jokes about Royal Nuptials.

Mr Singh put his stereo speakers out of his lounge windows and we listened to a Des O'Connor LP whilst we set the tables with sandwiches, jam tarts, sausage rolls and sausages on sticks. Then everyone in our street was given a funny hat by Mrs O'Leary and we sat down to eat. At the end of the tea Mr Singh made a speech about how great it was to be British. Everyone cheered and sang 'Land of Hope and Glory'. But only Mr Singh knew all the words. Then my father came back with four party packs of light ale and two dozen paper cups, and soon everyone was acting in an undignified manner.

Mr O'Leary tried to teach Mrs Singh an Irish jig but he kept getting tangled up in her sari. I put my Abba LP on and turned the volume up high and soon even the old people of forty and over were dancing! When the street lamps came on Sean O'Leary climbed up and put red, white and blue crepe paper over the bulbs to help the atmosphere and I fetched our remaining candles and put them on the tables. Our street looked quite Bohemian.

Bert told some lies about the war, my father told jokes. The party went on until one o'clock in the morning!

Normally they get a petition up if you clear your throat after eleven o'clock at night!

I didn't dance, I was an amused, cynical observer. Besides my feet were aching.

Thursday July 30th

I have seen the Royal Wedding repeats seven times on television.

Friday July 31st
New Moon

Sick to death of Royal Wedding.

Pandora, the beggar's friend, is coming home tomorrow.

Saturday August 1st

Postcard from my mother, she wants me to go on holiday with her and creep Lucas. They are going to Scotland. I hope they enjoy themselves.

Pandora's flight has been delayed because of a baggage-handlers' strike in Tunis.

Sunday August 2nd
Seventh after Trinity

The baggage-handlers are still on strike and Pandora's father has had his American Express card stolen by a beggar!

Pandora said that her mother has been bitten by a camel but is recovering in the Ladies' toilet at Tunis airport. It was wonderful to hear Pandora's voice on the telephone, we talked to each other for over half an hour. How clever it was of her to arrange a reverse-charge call from Tunisia!

Monday August 3rd
Bank Holiday in Scotland and Rep. of Ireland

The Tunisian baggage-handlers have agreed to go to arbitration. Pandora says that with luck she'll be home by Thursday.

Tuesday August 4th

The Tunisian baggage-handlers can see light at the end of the tunnel.

Pandora is surviving on packets of dates and Polo mints.

Wednesday August 5th

The Tunisian baggage-handlers are now handling baggage. *Pandora home FRIDAY EVENING!*

Thursday August 6th

My father refused a reverse-charges call from Tunisia. Our lines of communication have been cut.

Friday August 7th
Moon's First Quarter

I rang Tunisia whilst my father was in the bath. He shouted down to ask whom I was phoning. I told a lie. I said I was phoning the speaking clock.

Pandora's flight left safely. She should be home around midnight.

Saturday August 8th

At 7 a.m. Pandora rang from St Pancras station. She said that due to electrification of the track at Flitwick she would be delayed.

I got dressed and went down to the station, got a platform ticket, waited on platform two for six cold, lonely hours. Went home to find a note from Pandora. This is what it said:

Adrian,
   I confess to feeling heartbroken at your apparent coldness concerning my arrival. I felt sure that we would have an emotional reunion on platform three. But it was not to be.
   Adieu,
   Pandora

Went to Pandora's house. Explained. Had an emotional reunion behind her father's tool shed.

Sunday August 9th
Eighth after Trinity

Touched Pandora's bust again. This time I think I felt something soft. My thing keeps growing and shrinking, it seems to have a life of its own. I can't control it.

Monday August 10th

Pandora and I went to the swimming baths this morning. Pandora looked superb in her white string bikini. She has gone the same colour as Mrs Singh. I didn't trust my thing to behave so I sat in the spectators' gallery and watched Pandora diving off the highest diving board. Got back to my house. Showed her my black room. Lit a joss stick. Put Abba LP on, sneaked a bottle of Sanatogen upstairs. We indulged in a bit of light petting but then Pandora developed a headache and went home to rest.

I was racked with sexuality but it wore off when I helped my father put manure on our rose bed.

Tuesday August 11th

Got another postcard from my mother.

Dear Aidy,

You've no idea how much I long to see you. The mothering bond is as strong as ever. I know you feel threatened by my involvement with Bimbo, but really Aidy there is no need. Bimbo fulfils my sexual needs. No more, no less. So, Aidy, grow up and come to Scotland.

Lots of love,

Pauline (mother)

P.S. We leave on the fifteenth. Catch 8.22 train to Sheffield.

The postman said that if my mother was his wife he would give her a good thrashing. He doesn't know my mother. If anybody laid a finger on *her* she would beat them to pulp.

Wednesday August 12th

Pandora thinks a trial separation will do us good. She says our light to medium petting will turn quite heavy soon. I must admit that the strain is having a detrimental effect on my health. I have got no energy and my sleep is constantly interrupted with dreams about Pandora's white bikini and Mrs O'Leary's knickers.

I might go to Scotland after all.

Thursday August 13th

My father has decided to go to Skegness on the fifteenth. He has booked a four-berth caravan. He is taking Doreen and Maxwell with him! He expects me to go!

If I go people will automatically assume that Doreen is my mother and Maxwell is my brother!

I am going to Scotland.

Friday August 14th

Had tragic last night with Pandora. We have both sworn to be true. I have done all my packing. The dog has been taken round to grandma's with fourteen tins of Pedigree Chum and a giant sack of Winalot.

I am taking *Escape from Childhood*, by John Holt, to read on the train.

Saturday August 15th
Full Moon

My father, Stick Insect and Maxwell House saw me off at the station. My father didn't mind a bit that I chose to go to Scotland instead of Skegness. In fact he looked dead cheerful. The train journey was terrible. I had to stand all the way to Sheffield. I spoke to a lady in a wheelchair who was in the guard's van. She was very nice, she said that the only good thing about being handicapped was that you always got a seat in trains. Even if it *was* in the guard's van.

My mother and creep Lucas met me at Sheffield. My mother looked dead thin and has started dressing in clothes that are too young for her. Lucas creep was wearing jeans! His belly was hanging over his belt. I pretended to be asleep until we got to Scotland.

Lucas mauled my mother about even whilst he was driving.

We are at a place called Loch Lubnaig. I am in bed in a log cabin. My mother and Lucas have gone to the village to try to buy cigarettes. At least that is their story.

Sunday August 16th
Ninth after Trinity

There is a loch in front of the cabin and a pine forest and a mountain behind the cabin. There is nothing to do. It is dead boring.

Monday August 17th

Did some washing in a log cabin launderette. Spoke to an American tourist called Hamish Mancini; he is the same age as me. His mother is on her honeymoon for the fourth time.

Tuesday August 18th

Rained all day.

Wednesday August 19th

Sent postcards. Phoned Pandora, reversed charges. Her father refused to accept them.

Thursday August 20th

Played cards with Hamish Mancini. His mother and stepfather and my mother and her lover have gone to see a waterfall in the car. Big deal!

Friday August 21st

Walked two and a half miles into Callander to buy Mars bar. Played on Space Invaders. Came back, had tea. Phoned Pandora from log cabin phone box. Reversed charges. She still loves me. I still love her. Went to bed.

Saturday August 22nd
Moon's Last Quarter

Went to see Rob Roy's grave. Saw it, came back.

Sunday August 23rd
Tenth after Trinity

My mother has made friends with a couple called Mr and Mrs Ball. They have gone off to Stirling Castle. Mrs Ball has got a daughter who is a writer. I asked her how her daughter qualified to be one. Mrs Ball said that her daughter was dropped on her head as a child and has been 'a bit queer' ever since.

It is Mrs Ball's birthday so they all came back to our log cabin to celebrate. I complained about the noise at 1 a.m., 2 a.m., 3 a.m., and 4 a.m. At 5 a.m. they decided to climb the mountain! I pointed out to them that they were blind drunk, too old, unqualified, unfit and lacking in any survival techniques, had no first-aid kit, weren't wearing stout boots, and had no compass, map or sustaining hot drinks.

My protest fell on deaf ears. They all climbed the mountain, came down and were cooking eggs and bacon by 11.30 a.m.

As I write Mr and Mrs Ball are canoeing on the loch. They must be on drugs.

Monday August 24th

Went to Edinburgh. Saw the castle, the toy museum, the art gallery. Bought a haggis. Came back to log cabin, read *Glencoe*, by John Prebble. We are going there tomorrow.

Tuesday August 25th

The massacre of Glencoe took place on February 13th 1692. On February 14, John Hill wrote to the Earl of Tweeddale, 'I have ruined Glencoe'.

He was dead right, there is nothing there. Glasgow tomorrow.

Wednesday August 26th

We drove through Glasgow at 11 a.m. in the morning yet I counted twenty-seven drunks in one mile! All the shops except the DIY shops had grilles at the windows. Off-licences had rolls of barbed wire and broken glass on their roofs. We had a walk round for a bit, then my mother nagged Lucas creep into taking her to the Glasgow art gallery. I intended to sit in the car and read *Glencoe*, but because of all the drunks staggering around I reluctantly followed them inside.

How glad I am that I did! I might have gone through life without having an important cultural experience!

Today I saw Salvador Dali's painting of the Crucifixion!!! *The real one!* Not a reproduction!

They have hung it at the end of a corridor so that it changes as you get nearer to it. When you are finally standing up close to it you feel like a midget. It is absolutely fantastic!

Huge! With dead good colours and Jesus looks like a real bloke. I bought six postcards of it from the museum but of course it is not the same as the real thing.

One day I will take Pandora to see it. Perhaps on our honeymoon.

Thursday August 27th

Oban today. Bumped into Mr and Mrs Swallow who live in the next street to me. Everyone kept saying, 'It's a small world isn't it?' Mrs Swallow asked creep Lucas how his wife was. Lucas told her that his wife had left him for another woman. Then everyone blushed and said what a small world it was and parted company. My mother went mad at Lucas. She said 'Do you have to tell everyone?' and 'How do you think I feel living with a lesbian's estranged husband?' Lucas whined on for a bit but then my mother started looking like my grandma. So he kept quiet.

Friday August 28th

Fort William today. Ben Nevis was another disappointment. I couldn't tell where it began or stopped. The other mountains and hills clutter it up. Lucas fell in the burn (Scottish for 'little river') but unfortunately it was too shallow to drown in.

Saturday August 29th
Full Moon

Went for a walk around the loch with Hamish Mancini. He told me that he thinks his mother is heading for her fourth divorce. He is going home tonight; he has got an appointment with his analyst in New York on Monday morning.

I have finished my packing and I am waiting for my mother and creep Lucas to come back from their furtive love-making somewhere in the pine forest.

We leave at dawn.

Sunday August 30th
Eleventh after Trinity

I made Lucas stop for souvenirs at Gretna Green. I bought Pandora a pebble shaped like an otter, Bert a tam-o'-shanter, the dog a tartan bow for its neck, grandma a box of tartan fudge, Stick Insect tartan biscuits, Maxwell a tartan sweet dummy. I bought my father a tartan tea towel.

I bought myself a tartan scribbling pad. I am determined to become a writer.

Here is an extract from 'My thoughts on Scotland' written on the M6 at 120 mph:

The hallowed mist rolls away leaving Scotland's majestic peaks revealed in all their majesty. A shape in the translucent sky reveals itself to be an eagle, that majestic bird of prey. Talons clawing, it lands on a loch, rippling the quiet majesty of the turbulent waters. The eagle pauses only to dip its majestic beak into the aqua before spreading its majestic wings and flying away to its magisterial nest high in the barren, arid, grassless hills.

The Highland cattle. Majestic horned beast of the glens lowers its brown eyed shaggy haired majestic head as it ruminates on the mysteries of Glencoe.

There are a couple too many 'majestics'. But I think it reads rather well. I will send it to the BBC when it's finished. Got home at 6 p.m. Too tired to write more.

Monday August 31st
Bank Holiday in UK (except Scotland)

Everyone is broke. The banks are closed and my father can't remember the secret code on his plastic money-card. He had the nerve to borrow five pounds from Bert Baxter. Fancy asking an old age pensioner for money! It lacks dignity.

Pandora and I are now insanely in love! The separation only served to fuel our passion. Our hormones are stirred every time we meet. Pandora slept with the otter pebble in her hand last night. How I wish the otter pebble could have been me.

Tuesday September 1st

Mr Singh has had to return to India to look after his aged parents, so Bert has been told that he will have to move back into his dirty old house! Mr Singh says that he cannot trust his womenfolk to be alone in the house with Bert. How stupid can you get? Bert doesn't mind too much; he said that it is 'quite a compliment'.

Pandora and I are going to clean Bert's house and help him move back. He owes the council two hundred and ninety-four pounds in rent arrears. He has got to pay the arrears off at fifty pence a week, so it is a certainty that Bert will die in debt.

Wednesday September 2nd

Pandora and I went to look at Bert's house today. It is a truly awesome sight. If Bert took all his empty beer bottles back to the off-licence he might get enough money on the empties to pay off his rent arrears.

Thursday September 3rd

My father helped us to move all of the furniture out of the ground floor of Bert's house, the woodworms came out to sunbathe. When we lifted the carpets we discovered that Bert had been walking about on a layer of dirt, old newspapers, hairpins, marbles and decomposed mice for years. We hung the carpets on the washing line and beat them all afternoon, but the dust billowed out non-stop. Pandora got excited at about 5 p.m., she claimed she could see a pattern emerging on one carpet, but closer examination showed it to be squashed fairy cake. We are going back tomorrow with Pandora's mother's carpet-shampooer. Pandora said it has been tested by *Which?*, but I bet it has never had to clean a filthy hovel like Bert Baxter's before.

Friday September 4th

I have just witnessed a miracle! This morning Bert's carpets were dark grey in colour. Now one is a red Axminster and the other is a blue Wilton. The carpets are hanging on the clothes line to dry. We have scraped all the floors clean and washed the furniture down with a fungicide disinfectant. Pandora took the curtains down but they fell to pieces before she could get them to the sink. Bert has been sitting in a deckchair criticizing and complaining. He can't see what's wrong with living in a dirty house.

What *is* wrong with living in a dirty house?

Saturday September 5th

My father took Bert's bottles to the off-licence this morning. The boot, back seat and floor of the car were filled with them. The car stank of brown ale. He ran out of petrol on the way and called the AA. The AA man was most uncivil, he said it wasn't the Automobile Association my father needed, it was Alcoholics Anonymous!

Sunday September 6th
Twelfth after Trinity. Moon's First Quarter

Bert's house looks great. Everything is dead clean and shiny. We have moved his bed into the lounge so that he can watch television in bed. Pandora's mother has done very artistic arrangements with flowers, and Pandora's father has made an alsatian flap in the back door so that Bert doesn't keep having to get up to answer the door to Sabre.

Bert is moving back tomorrow.

Monday September 7th
Labor Day, USA and Canada

An airmail letter from Hamish Mancini.

Hi Aid!

Howya doin'? I hope the situation Pandora-wise is ongoing! She sounds kinda zappy! Scotland blew my mind! It was so far out as to be nuked! You're a great human being, Aid. I guess I was kinda traumatized when we rapped but Dr Eagelburger (my shrink) is doing great things with my libido. Mom's really wiped out right now, turns out number four is a TV and has a better collection of Calvin Kleins than she do! Don't you think the fall is a drag? Son-of-a-bitch leaves everywhere!

See you, Buddy!!!

Hamish

I showed it to Pandora, my father and Bert but nobody understands it. Bert doesn't like Americans because it took them too long to come into the war or something.

Bert now in his clean house. He hasn't said thank-you, but he seems happy.

Tuesday September 8th

Lousy stinking school on Thursday. I tried my old uniform on but I have outgrown it so badly that my father is being forced to buy me a new one tomorrow.

He is going up the wall but I can't help it if my body is in a growth period can I? I am only five centimetres shorter than Pandora now. My thing remains static at twelve centimetres.

Wednesday September 9th

Grandma phoned, she has found out about Doreen and Maxwell going to Skegness. She is never speaking to my father again.

Here is my shopping list:

Blazer	£29.99
2 pairs grey trousers	£23.98
2 white shirts	£11.98
2 grey pullovers	£7.98
3 pairs black socks	£2.37

1 pair PE shorts	£4.99
1 PE vest	£3.99
1 track suit	£11.99
1 pair training shoes	£7.99
1 pair football boots and studs	£11.99
1 pair football socks	£2.99
Football shorts	£4.99
Football shirt	£7.99
Adidas sports bag	£4.99
1 pair black shoes	£15.99
1 calculator	£6.99
Pen and pencil set	£3.99
Geometry set	£2.99

My father can easily spare a hundred pounds. His redundancy payment must have been huge, so why he is lying on his bed moaning I don't know. He is just a mean skinflint! He hasn't paid with *real* money anyway! He used his American Express card.

Pandora admired me in my new uniform. She says she thinks I stand a good chance of being made a prefect.

Thursday September 10th

A proud start to the new term. I am a prefect! My first duty is as late duty prefect. I have to wait by the gap in the railings and take the name of anyone sneaking late into school. Pandora is also a prefect. She is in charge of silence in the dinner queue.

My new timetable was given to me today by my new form tutor, Mr Dock. It includes my O level and CSE lessons, and it is compulsory to do Maths, English, PE and Comparative Religion. But they do give you a choice of Cultural and Creative subjects. So I have chosen Media Studies (dead easy, just reading newspapers and watching telly) and Parentcraft (just learning about sex, I hope). Mr Dock also teaches English Literature, so we are bound to get on, by now I am surely the best-read kid in the school. I will be able to help him out if he gets stuck.

Asked my father for five pounds fifty for school trip to the British Museum. He went berserk and said, 'What happened to free education?' I told him that I didn't know.

Friday September 11th

Had a long talk with Mr Dock. I explained that I was a one-parent-family child with an unemployed, bad-tempered father. Mr Dock said he wouldn't care if I was the offspring of a black, lesbian, one-legged mother and an Arab, leprous, hump-backed-dwarf father so long as my essays were lucid, intelligent and unpretentious. So much for pastoral care!

Saturday September 12th

Wrote lucid, intelligent and unpretentious essay about Scottish wildlife in the morning. In afternoon did shopping in Sainsbury's with my father. Saw Rick Lemon dithering at the fruit counter; he said selecting fruit was an 'overtly political act'. He rejected South African apples, French golden delicious apples, Israeli oranges, Tunisian dates, and American grapefruits. In the end he selected English rhubarb, 'Although,' he said, 'the shape is phallic, possibly sexist'. His girlfriend, Tit (short for Titia), was cramming the trolley with pulses and rice. She had a long skirt on but now and again I caught a glimpse of her hairy ankles. My father said he preferred a nice shaven leg any day. My father likes stockings, suspenders, mini-skirts and low necklines! He is dead old-fashioned.

Sunday September 13th
Thirteenth after Trinity

Went to see Blossom. Pandora doesn't ride her now because her feet drag on the ground. Pandora is having a proper horse delivered next week. It is called Ian Smith. The people who are selling it used to live in Africa, in Zimbabwe.

Tomorrow is my mother's birthday. She is thirty-seven.

Monday September 14th
Full Moon

Phoned my mother before school. There was no answer. I expect she was lying in bed with that stinking rat Lucas.

School dinners are complete crap now. Gravy seems to have been phased out along with custard and hot puddings. A typical menu is: hamburger, baked beans, chips, carton of yoghurt, or a doughnut. It's not enough to build healthy bone and sinew. I am considering making a protest to Mrs Thatcher. It won't be our fault if we grow up apathetic and lacking in moral fibre. Perhaps Mrs Thatcher wants us to be too weak to demonstrate in years to come.

Tuesday September 15th

Barry Kent has been late three times in one week. So it is my unfortunate duty to report him to Mr Scruton.

Unpunctuality is the sign of a disordered brain. So he cannot go unpunished.

Wednesday September 16th

Our form is going to the British Museum on Friday. Pandora and I are going to sit together on the coach.

She is bringing her *Guardian* from home so that we can have some privacy.

Thursday September 17th

Had a lecture on the British Museum from Ms Fossington-Gore. She said it was a 'fascinating treasure house of personkind's achievements'. Nobody listened to the lecture. Everyone was watching the way she felt her left breast whenever she got excited.

Friday September 18th

2 a.m. Just got back from London. Coach driver suffered from motorway madness on the motorway. I am too shaken by the experience to be able to give a lucid or intelligent account of the day.

Saturday September 19th

The school may well want a clear account by an unprejudiced observer of what happened on the way to, during and coming back from our trip to London. I am the only person qualified. Pandora, for all her qualities, does not possess my nerves of steel.

Class Four-D's Trip to the British Museum

7 a.m.	Boarded coach.
7.05	Ate packed lunch, drank low-calorie drink.
7.10	Coach stopped for Barry Kent to be sick.
7.20	Coach stopped for Claire Neilson to go to the Ladies.
7.30	Coach left school drive.
7.35	Coach returned to school for Ms Fossington-Gore's handbag.
7.40	Coach driver observed to be behaving oddly.
7.45	Coach stopped for Barry Kent to be sick again.
7.55	Approached motorway.
8.00	Coach driver stopped coach and asked everyone to stop giving 'V' signs to lorry drivers.
8.10	Coach driver loses temper, refuses to drive on motorway until 'bloody teachers control kids'.
8.20	Ms Fossington-Gore gets everyone sitting down.
8.25	Drive on to motorway.
8.30	Everyone singing 'Ten Green Bottles'.
8.35	Everyone singing 'Ten Green Snotrags'.
8.45	Coach driver stops singing by shouting very loudly.
9.15	Coach driver pulls in at service station and is observed to drink heavily from hip-flask.
9.30	Barry Kent hands round bars of chocolate stolen from self-service shop at service station. Ms Fossington-Gore chooses Bounty bar.
9.40	Barry Kent sick in coach.
9.50	Two girls sitting near Barry Kent are sick.
9.51	Coach driver refuses to stop on motorway.
9.55	Ms Fossington-Gore covers sick in sand.

9.56	Ms Fossington-Gore sick as a dog.
10.30	Coach crawls along on hard shoulder, all other lanes closed for repairs.
11.30	Fight breaks out on back seat as coach approaches end of motorway.
11.45	Fight ends. Ms Fossington-Gore finds first-aid kit and sees to wounds. Barry Kent is punished by sitting next to driver.
11.50	Coach breaks down at Swiss Cottage.
11.55	Coach driver breaks down in front of AA man.
12.30	Class Four-D catch London bus to St Pancras.
1 p.m.	Class Four-D walk from St Pancras through Bloomsbury.
1.15	Ms Fossington-Gore knocks on door of Tavistock House, asks if Dr Laing will give Barry Kent a quick going-over. Dr Laing in America on lecture tour.
1.30	Enter British Museum. Adrian Mole and Pandora Braithwaite awestruck by evidence of heritage of World Culture. Rest of class Four-D run berserk, laughing at nude statues and dodging curators.
2.15	Ms Fossington-Gore in state of collapse. Adrian Mole makes reverse-charge phone call to headmaster. Headmaster in dinner lady strike-meeting, can't be disturbed.
3 p.m.	Curators round up class Four-D and make them sit on steps of museum.
3.05	American tourists photograph Adrian Mole saying he is a 'cute English schoolboy'.
3.15	Ms Fossington-Gore recovers and leads class Four-D on sightseeing tour of London.

4 p.m.	Barry Kent jumps in fountain at Trafalgar Square, as predicted by Adrian Mole.
4.30	Barry Kent disappears, last seen heading towards Soho.
4.35	Police arrive, take Four-D to mobile police unit, arrange coach back. Phone parents about new arrival time. Phone headmaster at home. Claire Neilson has hysterical fit. Pandora Braithwaite tells Ms Fossington-Gore she is a disgrace to teaching profession. Ms Fossington-Gore agrees to resign.
6 p.m.	Barry Kent found in sex shop. Charged with theft of 'grow-it-big' cream and two 'ticklers'.
7 p.m.	Coach leaves police station with police escort.
7.30	Police escort waves goodbye.
7.35	Coach driver begs Pandora Braithwaite to keep order.
7.36	Pandora Braithwaite keeps order.
8 p.m.	Ms Fossington-Gore drafts resignation.
8.30	Coach driver afflicted by motorway madness.
8.40	Arrive back. Tyres burning. Class Four-D struck dumb with terror. Ms Fossington-Gore led off by Mr Scruton. Parents up in arms. Coach driver charged by police.

Sunday September 20th
Fourteenth after Trinity. Moon's Last Quarter

Keep having anxiety attacks every time I think about London, culture or the M1. Pandora's parents are lodging an official complaint to everyone they can think of.

Monday September 21st

Mr Scruton complimented Pandora and I on our leadership qualities. Ms Fossington-Gore is on sick leave. All future school trips have been cancelled.

Tuesday September 22nd

The police have dropped charges against coach driver because there is 'evidence of severe provocation'. The sex shop are not pressing charges either because officially Barry Kent is a child. A child! Barry Kent has never been a child.

Wednesday September 23rd

Mr Scruton has now read my report on the trip to London. He gave me two merit marks for it!

It was on the news today that the British Museum is thinking of banning school parties.

Thursday September 24th

Pandora and I are enjoying the last of the autumn together by walking through leaves and sniffing bonfires. This is the first year I have been able to pass a horse-chestnut tree without throwing a stick at it.

Pandora says I am maturing very quickly.

Friday September 25th

Went out conkering with Nigel tonight. I found five big beauties and smashed Nigel's into pulp. Ha! Ha! Ha!

Saturday September 26th

Took Blossom to see Bert. He can't walk far these days.

Blossom is being sold to a rich family, a girl called Camilla is going to learn to ride on her. Pandora says Camilla is so posh as to be unintelligible. Bert was dead sad, he said, 'You and me will both end up in the knacker's yard, gel'.

Sunday September 27th
Fifteenth after Trinity

Blossom went off at 10.30 a.m. I gave her a sixteen-pence apple to take her mind off the heartbreak. Pandora ran after the little horse-box shouting, 'I've changed my mind', but it carried on.

Pandora has also changed her mind about Ian Smith. She never wants to see another pony or horse again. She is guilt-ridden about selling Blossom.

Ian Smith turned up at 2.30 p.m. and was turned away. There was an evil look on his black face as he stood in his horse-box and was driven away. Pandora's father is going to his bank early tomorrow to cancel the cheque he wrote out last Thursday. There was an evil look on his face as well.

Monday September 28th
New Moon

Bert has got something wrong with his legs. The doctor says he needs daily nursing. I went in today but he is too heavy for me to lug about. The district nurse thinks that Bert will be better off in the Alderman Cooper Sunshine Home. But I don't think he will. I pass by it on my way to school. It looks like a museum. The old people look like the exhibits.

Bert, you are dead old.
Fond of Sabre, beetroot and Woodbines.
We have nothing in common,
I am fourteen and a half,
You are eighty-nine.
You smell, I don't.
Why we are friends
Is a mystery to me.

Tuesday September 29th

Bert doesn't get on with his district nurse. He says he doesn't like having his privates mauled about by a woman. Personally, I wouldn't mind it.

Wednesday September 30th

I am glad September is nearly over, it has been nothing but trouble. Blossom gone. Pandora sad. Bert on his last legs. My father still out of work. My mother still besotted with creep Lucas.

Autumn

Thursday October 1st

7.30 a.m. Just woke up to find chin covered in spots! How can I face Pandora?
10 p.m. Avoided Pandora all day but she caught up with me in school dinners. I tried to eat with my hand over my chin but it proved very difficult. I confessed to her during the yoghurt. She accepted my disability very calmly. She said it made no difference to our love but I couldn't help thinking that her kisses lacked their usual passion as we were saying goodnight after youth club.

Friday October 2nd

6 p.m. I am very unhappy and have once again turned to great literature for solace. It's no surprise to me that intellectuals commit suicide, go mad or die from drink. We feel things more than other people. We know the world is rotten and that chins are ruined by spots. I am reading *Progress, Coexistence and Intellectual Freedom*, by Andrei D. Sakharov.

It is 'an inestimably important document' according to the cover.

11.30 p.m. Progress, Coexistence and Intellectual Freedom is inestimably *boring*, according to me, Adrian Mole.

I disagree with Sakharov's analysis of the causes of the revivalism of Stalinism. We are doing Russia at school so I speak from knowledge.

Saturday October 3rd

Pandora is cooling off. She didn't turn up at Bert's today. I had to do his cleaning on my own.

Went to Sainsbury's as usual in the afternoon; they are selling Christmas cakes. I feel that my life is slipping away.

I am reading *Wuthering Heights*. It is brilliant. If I could get Pandora up somewhere high, I'm sure we could regain our old passion.

Sunday October 4th
Sixteenth after Trinity

Persuaded Pandora to put her name down for the youth club's mountain survival course in Derbyshire. Rick Lemon is sending an equipment list and permission form to our parents. Or in my case to my parent. I have only got two weeks to reach peak condition. I try to do fifty press-ups a night. I try to do them but fail. Seventeen is my best so far.

Monday October 5th

Bert has been kidnapped by Social Services! They are keeping him at the Alderman Cooper Sunshine Home. I have been to see him. He shares a room with an old man called Thomas Bell. They have both got their names on their ashtrays. Sabre has got a place in the RSPCA hostel.

Our dog has gone missing. It is a portent of doom.

Tuesday October 6th
Moon's First Quarter

Pandora and I went to visit Bert, but it was a waste of time really.

His room had a strange effect on us, it made us not want to talk about anything. Bert says he is going to sue Social Services, for depriving him of his rights. He says he has to go to bed at nine-thirty! It is not fair because he is used to staying up until after *The Epilogue*. We passed the lounge on our way out. The old people sat around the walls in high chairs. The television was on but nobody was watching it, the old people looked as though they were thinking.

Social Services have painted the walls orange to try to cheer the old people up. It doesn't seem to have worked.

Wednesday October 7th

Thomas Bell died in the night. Bert says that nobody leaves the home alive. Bert is the oldest inmate. He is dead worried about dying. He is now the only man in the entire home. Pandora says that women outlive men. She says it is a sort of bonus because women have to suffer more earlier on.

Our dog is still missing. I have put an advert in Mr Cherry's shop.

Thursday October 8th

Bert is still alive so I took Sabre to visit him today. We propped Bert up at the window of his room and he waved to Sabre who was on the lawn outside. Dogs are not allowed inside the home. It is another of their poxy rules.

Our dog is still missing, now presumed dead.

Friday October 9th

The matron of the home says that if Bert is dead good he can come out for the day on Sunday. He is coming to our house for Sunday dinner and tea. The phone bill has come. I have hidden it under my mattress. It is for £289.19p.

Saturday October 10th

I am really worried about our dog. It has vanished off the face of our suburb. Nigel, Pandora and I have walked the cul-de-sacs looking for it.

Another worry is my father. He lies in bed until noon, then fries a mess in a pan, eats it, opens a can or bottle, then sits and watches *After Noon Plus*. He is making no attempt to find another job. He needs a bath, a haircut and a shave. It is Parents' Night at school next Tuesday. I have taken his best suit to the cleaner's.

I bought a book from W. H. Smith's, it was only five pence. It was written by an unsuccessful writer called Drake Fairclough; it is called *Cordon Bleu for the Elderly*. Bert is coming tomorrow. Pandora's father has ordered their phone to be taken out. He has found out about the reverse-charge calls.

Sunday October 11th
Seventeenth after Trinity

BERT'S VISIT

I got up early this morning and cleared the furniture out of the hall so that Bert's wheelchair had room for manoeuvre. I made my father a cup of coffee and took it up to him in bed, then I started cooking geriatric *coq au vin*. I left it on to boil whilst I went back upstairs to reawaken my father. When I got downstairs I knew that I'd made a mess of the *coq au vin*. All the vinegar had boiled away and left burnt chicken. I was most disappointed because I was thinking of making my debut as a cook today. I wanted to impress Pandora with my multi talents, I think she is getting a bit bored with my conversation about great literature and the Norwegian leather industry.

Bert insisted on bringing a big trunk with him when Pandora's father picked him up at the home. So what with that and his wheelchair and Bert sprawling all over the back seat I was forced to crouch in the hatch of the hatchback car. It took ages to get Bert out of the car and into his wheelchair. Almost as long as it took me to get my father out of bed.

Pandora's father stayed for a quick drink, then a pre-lunch one, then a chaser, then one for the road. Then he had one to prove that he never got drunk during the day. Pandora's lips started to go thin (women must teach young girls to do this). Then she confiscated her father's car keys and phoned her mother to come and collect the car. I had to endure watching my father do his imitation of some bloke called Frank Sinatra singing 'One for my baby and one more for the road'. Pandora's father pretended to be the bartender with our Tupperware custard jug. They were both drunkenly singing when Pandora's mother came in. Her lips were so thin they had practically disappeared. She ordered Pandora and Pandora's father out into the car, then she said that it was about time my father pulled himself together. She said she knew my father felt humiliated, alienated and bitter because he was unemployed, but that he was setting a bad example to an impressionable adolescent. Then she drove off at 10 mph. Pandora blew me a kiss through the rear windscreen.

I object strongly! Nothing my father does impresses me any more. Had Vesta curry and rice for dinner, during which Mrs Singh came round and talked Hindi to Bert. She seemed to find our curry very funny, she kept pointing to it and laughing. Sometimes I think I am the only person in the world who still has manners.

Bert told my father that he is convinced the matron is trying to poison him (Bert, not my father), but my father said that all institutional food is the same. When it was time to go home, Bert started crying. He said, 'Don't make me go back there', and other sad things. My father explained that we didn't have the skill to look after him at our house, so Bert was wheeled to the car (although he kept putting the brake of the wheelchair on). He asked us to keep his trunk at our house. He said it was to be opened on his death. The key is round his neck on a bit of string.

Dog is still AWOL.

Monday October 12th
Columbus Day, USA. Thanksgiving Day, Canada

Went to the 'off-the-streets' youth club tonight. Rick Lemon gave us a lecture on survival techniques. He said that the best thing to do if you are suffering from hypothermia is to climb into a plastic bag with a naked woman. Pandora made a formal objection, and Rick Lemon's girlfriend, Tit, got up and walked away. It is just my luck to be on the mountain with a frigid woman!

RIP Dog.

Tuesday October 13th
Full Moon

Had an angry phone call from my grandma to ask when we were coming round to collect the dog! The stupid dog turned up at her house on the 6th October. I went round immediately and was shocked at the dog's condition: it looks old and grey. In human years it is eleven years old. In dog years it should be drawing a pension. I have never seen a dog age so quickly. Those eight days with grandma must have been hell. My grandma is very strict.

Wednesday October 14th

I have nearly got used to the old ladies in the home now. I call in every afternoon on my way home from school. They seem pleased to see me. One of them is knitting me a balaclava for my survival weekend. She is called Queenie.

Did thirty-six and a half press-ups tonight.

Thursday October 15th

Went to the youth club to try yukky, lousy old walking boots for size. Rick Lemon has hired them from a mountaineering shop. To make mine fit I have to wear three pairs of socks. Six of us are going. Rick is leading us.

He is unqualified but experienced in surviving bad conditions. He was born and brought up in Kirby New Town. I went to Sainsbury's and bought my survival food. We have got to carry our food and equipment in our rucksacks, so weight is an important factor. I bought:

1 box cornflakes
2 pints milk
box tea-bags
tin rhubarb
5 lb spuds
½ lb lard
½ lb butter
2 loaves bread
1 lb cheese
2 packets biscuits
2 lb sugar
toilet roll
washing-up liquid
2 tins tuna
1 tin stewed steak
1 tin carrots

I could hardly carry my survival food home from Sainsbury's, so how I will manage it on a march across the hills I don't know! My father suggested leaving something out. So I have not packed the toilet roll or cornflakes.

Friday October 16th

Have decided not to take my diary to Derbyshire. I cannot guarantee that it will not be read by hostile eyes. Besides it won't fit into my rucksack.

Must finish now, the mini-bus is outside papping its hooter.

Saturday October 17th

Sunday October 18th
Eighteenth after Trinity

8 p.m. It is wonderful to be back in civilization!

I have lived like an ignoble savage for the past two days! Sleeping on rough ground with only a sleeping-bag between me and the elements! Trying to cook chips over a tiny primus stove! Trudging through streams in my torturous boots! Having to perform my natural functions out in the open! Wiping my bum on leaves! Not being able to have a bath or clean my teeth! No television or radio or anything! Rick Lemon wouldn't even let us sit in the mini-bus when it started to rain! He said we ought to make a shelter out of nature's bounty! Pandora found a plastic animal-food sack so we took it in turns sitting under it.

How I survived I don't know. My eggs broke, my bread got saturated, my biscuits got crushed and nobody had a tin-opener. I nearly starved. Thank God cheese doesn't leak, break, soak up water or come in a tin. I was glad when we were found and taken to the Mountain Rescue headquarters. Rick Lemon was told off for not having a map or compass. Rick said he knew the hills like the back of his hand. The chief mountain rescuer said that Rick must have been wearing gloves because we were seven miles from our mini-bus and heading in the wrong direction!

I shall now sleep in a bed for the first time in two days. No school tomorrow because of blisters.

Monday October 19th

I have got to rest my feet for two days. Doctor Gray was very unpleasant: he said that he resented being called out for a few foot blisters.

I was very surprised at his attitude. It is a well-known fact that mountaineers get gangrene of the toes.

Tuesday October 20th
Moon's Last Quarter

Here I am lying in bed unable to walk because of excruciating pain and my father carries out his parental responsibilities by throwing a few bacon sandwiches at me three times a day!

If my mother doesn't come home soon I will end up deprived and maladjusted. I am already neglected.

Wednesday October 21st

Hobbled to school. All the teachers were wearing their best clothes because it is Parents' Evening tonight. My father got cleaned up and put his best suit on. He looked OK, Thank God! Nobody could tell he was unemployed. My teachers all told him that I was a credit to the school.

Barry Kent's father was looking as sick as a pig. Ha! Ha! Ha!

Thursday October 22nd

Limped half-way to school. Dog followed me. Limped back home. Shut dog in coal shed. Limped all the way to school. Fifteen minutes late. Mr Scruton said it was not setting a good example for the late prefect to be late. It is all right for him to talk! He can ride to school in a Ford Cortina and then all he has to do is be in charge of a school. I have got a lot of problems and no car.

Friday October 23rd

I have had a letter from the hospital to say that I have got to have my tonsils out on Tuesday the twenty-seventh. This has come as a complete shock to me! My father says I have been on the waiting list since I was five years old! So I have had to endure an annual bout of tonsillitis for nine years just because the National Health Service is starved of finance!

Why can't midwives remove babies' tonsils at birth? It would save a lot of trouble, pain and money.

Saturday October 24th
United Nations' Day

Went shopping for new dressing gown, slippers, pyjamas, and toiletries. My father was moaning as usual. He said he didn't see why I couldn't just wear my old night-clothes in hospital. I told him that I would look ridiculous in my Peter Pan dressing gown and Winnie the Pooh pyjamas. Apart from the yukky design they are too small and covered in patches. He said that when he was a lad he slept in a nightshirt made out of two coal sacks stitched together. I phoned my grandma to check this suspicious statement and my father was forced to repeat it down the phone. My grandma said that they were not coal sacks but flour sacks, so I now know that my father is a pathological liar!

My hospital rig came to fifty-four pounds nineteen; this is before fruit, chocolates and Lucozade. Pandora said I looked like Noël Coward in my new bri-nylon dressing gown. I said, 'Thanks, Pandora', although to be honest I don't know who Noël Coward is or was. I hope he's not a mass murderer or anything.

Sunday October 25th
Nineteenth after Trinity. British Summer Time ends

Phoned my mother to tell her about my coming surgical ordeal. No reply. This is typical. She would sooner be out having fun with creep Lucas than comforting her only child!

Grandma rang and said that she knew somebody who knew somebody who knew somebody who had their tonsils out and bled to death on the operating theatre table. She ended up by saying, 'Don't worry Adrian, I'm sure everything will be all right for you'.

Thanks a million, grandma!

Monday October 26th
Bank Holiday in the Rep. of Ireland

11 a.m. I did my packing, then went to see Bert. He is sinking fast so it could be the last time we see each other. Bert also knows somebody who bled to death after a tonsils' extraction. I hope it's the same person.

Said goodbye to Pandora: she wept very touchingly. She brought me one of Blossom's old horseshoes to take into hospital. She said a friend of her father had a cyst removed and didn't come out of the anaesthetic. I'm being admitted to Ivy Swallow Ward at 2 p.m. Greenwich Mean Time.

6 p.m. My father has just left my bedside after four hours of waiting around for permission to leave. I have had every part of my body examined. Liquid substances have been taken from me, I have been weighed and bathed, measured and prodded and poked, but nobody has looked in my throat!

I have put our family medical dictionary on my bedside table so that the doctors see it and are impressed. I can't tell what the rest of the ward is like yet because the nurses have forgotten to remove the screens. A notice has been hung over my bed; it says 'Liquids Only'. I am dead scared.

10. p.m. I am starving! A black nurse has taken all my food and drink away. I am supposed to go to sleep but it is like bedlam in here. Old men keep falling out of bed.

Midnight. There is a new notice over my bed; it says

'Nil by Mouth'. I am dying of thirst! I would give my right arm for a can of Low Cal.

Tuesday October 27th
New Moon

4 a.m. I am dehydrated!

6 a.m. Just been woken up! Operation is not until 10 a.m. So why couldn't they let me sleep? I have got to have another bath. I told them that it is the *inside* of my body that is being operated on, but they don't listen.

7 a.m. A Chinese nurse stayed in the bathroom to make sure I didn't drink any water. She kept staring so I had to put a hospital sponge over my thing.

7.30 a.m. I am dressed like a lunatic, ready for the operation. I have had an injection, it is supposed to make you sleepy but I'm wide awake listening to a row about a patient's lost notes.

8 a.m. My mouth is completely dry, I shall go mad from thirst, I haven't had a drink since nine forty-five last night. I feel very floaty, the cracks in the ceiling are very interesting. I have got to find somewhere to hide my diary. I don't want prying Nosy Parkers reading it.

8.30 a.m. My mother is at my bedside! She is going to put my diary in her organizer-handbag. She has promised (on the dog's life) not to read it.

8.45 a.m. My mother is in the hospital grounds

smoking a cigarette. She is looking old and haggard. All the debauchery is catching up with her.

9 a.m. The operating trolley keeps coming into the ward and dumping unconscious men into beds. The trolley-pushers are wearing green overalls and wellingtons. There must be loads of blood on the floor of the theatre!

9.15 a.m. The trolley is coming in my direction!

Midnight. I am devoid of tonsils. I am in a torrent of pain. It took my mother thirteen minutes to find my diary. She doesn't know her way round her organizer-handbag yet. It has got seventeen compartments.

Wednesday October 28th

I am unable to speak. Even groaning causes agony.

Thursday October 29th

I have been moved to a side ward. My suffering is too much for the other patients to bear.

Had a 'get well' card from Bert and Sabre.

Friday October 30th

I was able to sip a little of grandma's broth today. She brought it in her Thermos flask. My father brought me a family pack of crisps; he might just as well have brought me razor blades!

Pandora came at visiting time, I had little to whisper to her. Conversation palls when one is hovering between life and death.

Saturday October 31st
Hallowe'en

3 a.m. I have been forced to complain about the noise coming from the nurses' home. I am sick of listening to (and watching) drunken nurses and off-duty policemen cavorting around the grounds dressed as witches and wizards. Nurse Boldry was doing something particularly unpleasant with a pumpkin.

I am joining BUPA as soon as they'll have me.

Sunday November 1st
Twentieth after Trinity

The nurses have been very cold towards me. They say that I am taking up a bed that could be used by an ill person! I have got to eat a bowl of cornflakes before they let me out. So far I have refused: I cannot bear the pain.

Monday November 2nd

Nurse Boldry forced a spoon of cornflakes down my damaged throat, then, before I could digest it, she started stripping my bed. She offered to pay for a taxi, but I told her that I would wait for my father to come and carry me out to the car.

Tuesday November 3rd
Election Day, USA

I am in my own bed. Pandora is a tower of strength. She and I communicate without words. My voice has been damaged by the operation.

Wednesday November 4th

Today I croaked my first words for a week. I said, 'Dad, phone mum and tell her that I am over the worst'. My father was overcome with relief and emotion. His laughter was close to hysteria.

Thursday November 5th
Moon's First Quarter

Dr Gray says my malfunctioning voice is 'only adolescent wobble'. He is always in a bad mood!

He expected me to stagger to his surgery and queue in a germ-filled waiting room! He said I ought to be outside with other lads of my age building a bonfire. I told him that I was too old for such paganistic rituals. He said he was forty-seven and he still enjoyed a good burn-up.

Forty-seven! It explains a lot, he should be pensioned off.

Friday November 6th

My father is taking me to an organized bonfire party tomorrow (providing I am up to it, of course). It is being held to raise funds for Marriage Guidance Councillors' expenses.

Pandora's mother is cooking the food and Pandora's father is in charge of the fireworks. My father is going to be in charge of lighting the bonfire so I'm going to stand at least a hundred metres away. I have seen him singe his eyebrows many times.

Last night some irresponsible people down our street had bonfire parties in their own back gardens!

Yes!

In spite of being warned of all the dangers by the radio, television, *Blue Peter* and the media they went selfishly ahead. There were no accidents, but surely this was only luck.

Saturday November 7th

The Marriage Guidance Council bonfire was massive. It was a good community effort. Mr Cherry donated hundreds of copies of a magazine called *Now*! He said they had been cluttering up the back room of his shop for over a year.

Pandora burnt her collection of *Jackie* comics, she said that they 'don't bear feminist analysis' and she 'wouldn't like them to get into young girls' hands'.

Mr Singh and all the little Singhs brought along Indian firecrackers. They are much louder than English ones. I was glad our dog was locked in the coal shed with cotton wool in its ears.

Nobody was seriously burnt, but I think it was a mistake to hand out fireworks at the same time the food was being served.

I burnt the red phone bill that came this morning.

Sunday November 8th
Twenty-first after Trinity. Remembrance Sunday

Our street is full of acrid smoke. I went to see the bonfire, the *Now* magazines are still in the hot ashes, they are refusing to burn properly. (Our red phone bill has disappeared, thank God!)

Mr Cherry is going to have to dig a big pit and pour

quicklime over the *Now* magazines before they choke the whole suburb.

Went to see Bert. He was out with Queenie.

Monday November 9th

Back to school. The dog is at the vet's having the cotton wool surgically removed.

Tuesday November 10th

My nipples have swollen! I am turning into a girl!!!

Wednesday November 11th
Veterans' Day, USA. Remembrance Day, Canada.
Full Moon

Dr Gray has struck me off his list! He said nipple-swelling is common in boys. Usually they get it when they are twelve and a half. Dr Gray said I was emotion-ally and physically immature! How can I be immature? I have had a rejection letter from the BBC! And how could I have walked to the surgery with swollen nipples?

I don't know why he calls it a surgery anyway; he never does any surgery in it.

Thursday November 12th

Told Mr Jones I couldn't do PE because of swollen nipples. He was extremely crude in his attitude. I don't know what they teach them at teacher-training college.

Friday November 13th

Pandora and I had a frank talk about our relationship tonight. She doesn't want to marry me in two years' time!

She wants to have a career instead!

Naturally I am devastated by this blow. I told her I wouldn't mind her having a little job in a cake shop or something after our wedding, but she said she intended to go to university and that the only time she would enter a cake shop would be to buy a large crusty.

Harsh words were exchanged between us. (Hers were harsher than mine.)

Saturday November 14th

Charred *Now!* magazines are blowing all over our cul-de-sac. They seem to have special powers of survival. The council have sent a special cleaning squad to try and trap them all.

The dog's ears are now clear of cotton wool. It only pretends not to hear.

Went to see B. B. but he is out with Queenie. She is pushing him around the leisure centre.

Sunday November 15th
Twenty-second after Trinity

Read *A Town Like Alice*, by Nevil Shute, it is dead brill. I wish I had an intellectual friend whom I could discuss great literature with. My father thinks *A Town Like Alice* was written by Lewis Carroll.

Monday November 16th

I came home from school with a headache. All the noise and shouting and bullying is getting me down! Surely teachers should be better behaved!

Tuesday November 17th

My father is a serious worry to me. Even the continuing news of Princess Diana's conception does not cheer him up.

Grandma has already knitted three pairs of bootees and sent them off care of Buckingham Palace. She is a true patriot.

Wednesday November 18th
Moon's Last Quarter

> The trees are stark naked.
> Their autumnal clothes
> Litter the pavements.
> Council sweepers apply fire
> Thus creating municipal pyres.
> I, Adrian Mole,
> Kick them
> And burn my Hush Puppies.

I have copied it out carefully and sent it to John Tydeman at the BBC. He strikes me as a man who might like poems about autumn leaves.

I have got to get something broadcast or printed soon else Pandora will lose all respect for me.

Thursday November 19th

Pandora has suggested I start a literary magazine using the school duplicator. I wrote the first edition during dinner-time. It is called *The Voice of Youth*.

Friday November 20th

Pandora looked at *The Voice of Youth*. She suggested that instead of writing the whole magazine myself, I invite contributions from other talented scribblers.

She said she would do a piece about window-box gardening. Claire Neilson has submitted a punk poem, it is very avant garde, but I am not afraid to break new ground.

> *Punk Poem*
> Society is puke,
> Soiled vomit.
> On the Union Jack
> Sid was vicious
> Johnnie's rotten,
> Dead, dead, dead.
> Killed by greyness.
> England stinks.
> Sewer of the world.
> Cess-pit of Europe.
> Hail punks,
> Kings and Queens
> Of the street.

She wants it put in under an assumed name, her father is a Conservative councillor.

Nigel has written a short piece about racing-bike maintenance. It is very boring but I can't tell him because he is my best friend.

We go to press on Wednesday.

Pandora is typing the stencils over the weekend. *Here is my first editorial:*

Hi Kids,

Well here's your very own school magazine. Yes! Written and produced entirely using child labour. I have tried to break new ground in our first edition. Many of you will be unaware of the miracles of window-box gardening and the joys of racing-bike maintenance. If so, hang on to your hats, you're in for a magic surprise!

ADRIAN MOLE, EDITOR

We are going to charge twenty-five pence a copy.

Saturday November 21st

Pandora's father has stolen a box of stencils from his office. As I write, Pandora is typing the first pages of *The Voice of Youth*. I am half-way through writing an exposé about Barry Kent. It is called 'Barry Kent: The Truth!' He hasn't dared to lay a finger on me since grandma's dramatic intervention, so I know I shall be safe.

Too busy to go and see Bert, I will go tomorrow.

Sunday November 22nd
Last after Trinity

Finished the exposé on Barry Kent. It will rock the school to its foundations. I have mentioned Barry Kent's sexual perversions – all about his disgusting practice of showing his thing for five pence a look.

Monday November 23rd

Had a Christmas card from grandma, and a letter from the post office to say that they are cutting the phone off!

Forgot to call round and see Bert. Pandora and I were too busy putting the paper to bed. How I wish I was putting Pandora to bed.

2 a.m. What am I going to do about the phone bill?

Tuesday November 24th

Nigel has just gone off in a sulk. He objected to the editing I did on his article. I tried to point out to him that one thousand five hundred words on bicycle spokes was pure self-indulgence, but he wouldn't listen. He has withdrawn his article. Thank God! Two pages less to fold.

The Voice of Youth hits the classrooms tomorrow.

Must go and see Bert tomorrow.

Wednesday November 25th

We have been hit by a wildcat strike! Mrs Claricoates, the school secretary, has refused to handle *The Voice of Youth*. She says there is nothing in her job description to say she has to mess about with school magazines.

The editorial team offered to duplicate copies ourselves, but Mrs Claricoates says that she alone knows how to 'work the wretched thing'. I am in despair. A whole six hours' work wasted!

Thursday November 26th
Thanksgiving Day, USA. New Moon

Pandora's father is photocopying *The Voice of Youth* on his office machine. He didn't want to, but Pandora sulked in her room and refused to eat until he agreed.

Friday November 27th

Five hundred copies of *The Voice of Youth* were on sale in the dinner hall today.

Five hundred copies were locked in the games cupboard by the end of the afternoon. Not one copy was sold! Not one! My fellow pupils are nothing but Philistines and Morons!

We are dropping the price to twenty pence on Monday.

My mother phoned and wanted to speak to my father. I told her that he is on a fishing weekend with the Society of Redundant Electric Storage Heater Salesmen.

A postcard from the post office to say that unless my father phones the post office before five-thirty our phone will be disconnected.

Saturday November 28th

A telegram! Addressed to me! The BBC? No, from my mother:

ADRIAN STOP COMING HOME STOP

What does she mean 'Stop coming home'? How can I 'stop coming home'? I live here.

The phone has been cut off! I am considering running away from home.

Sunday November 29th
Advent Sunday

My mother has just turned up with no warning! She had all her suitcases with her. She has thrown herself on the mercy of my father. My father has just thrown himself on the body of my mother. I tactfully withdrew to my bedroom where I am now trying to work out how I feel about my mother's return. On the whole I am over the moon, but I'm dreading her looking around our squalid house. She will go mad when she finds out that I have lent Pandora her fox-fur coat.

Monday November 30th
St Andrew's Day

My mother and father were still in bed when I left for school.

Sold one copy of *The Voice of Youth*, to Barry Kent. He wanted to discover the truth about himself. He is a slow reader so it will probably take him until Friday to find out. We are going to try dropping the price to fifteen pence to try to stimulate demand. There are now four hundred and ninety-nine copies to be sold!

My mother and father are in bed again and it's only 9 p.m.!

The dog is very pleased my mother is back. It has been going about smiling all day.

Tuesday December 1st

I called the post office and pretended to be my father. I spoke in a very deep voice and told a lot of lies. I said that I, George Mole, had been in a lunatic asylum for three months and I needed the phone to ring up the Samaritans, etc. The woman sounded dead horrible, she said she was fed up with hearing lame excuses from irresponsible non-payers. She said that the phone would only be reconnected when £289.19 had been paid, plus £40 reconnection fee, plus a deposit of £40!

Three hundred and sixty-nine pounds! When my parents get out of bed and discover the lack of dialling tone, I will be done for!

Wednesday December 2nd

My father tried to phone up after a job today! He has gone berserk.

My mother cleaned my bedroom, she turned up my mattress and found the *Big and Bouncys* and the blue phone bill.

I sat on the kitchen stool while they interrogated me and shouted abuse. My father wanted to give me a 'to-within-an-inch-of-his-life thrashing', but my mother stopped him. She said, 'It would be more of a punishment to make the tight-fisted sod cough up some of his building-society savings'. So that is what I'm being forced to do.

Now I will never be an owner-occupier.

Thursday December 3rd

Drew out two hundred pounds from my building-society account. I don't mind admitting that there were tears in my eyes. It will take another fourteen years before I can replace it.

Friday December 4th
Moon's First Quarter

I am suffering from severe depression. It is all Pandora's father's fault. He should have had a holiday in England.

Saturday December 5th
Had a letter from grandma to ask why I hadn't sent her a Christmas card yet.

Sunday December 6th
Second in Advent

I am still being treated like a criminal. My mother and father are not speaking to me, and I'm not allowed out. I might just as well turn to delinquency.

Monday December 7th

Stole a Kevin Keegan key ring from Mr Cherry's shop. It will do for Nigel's Christmas present.

Tuesday December 8th

I am dead worried about the key ring; we did Morals and Ethics at school today.

Wednesday December 9th

Can't sleep for worrying about the key ring. The papers are full of stories about old ladies getting done for shoplifting. I tried to overpay Mr Cherry for my Mars bar, but he called me back and gave me my change.

Thursday December 10th

Had a dream about a jailer locking me in a prison cell. The big iron key was attached to the Kevin Keegan key ring.

The lousy, stinking, sodding phone is reconnected!

Friday December 11th
Full Moon

Phoned the Samaritans and confessed my crime. The man said, 'Put it back then, lad'. I will do it tomorrow.

Saturday December 12th

Mr Cherry caught me in the act of replacing the key ring. He has written a letter to my parents. I might as well do myself in.

Sunday December 13th
Third in Advent

Thank God there is no post on Sundays.

My mother and father had a festive time decorating the Christmas tree. I watched them hanging the baubles with a heavy heart.

I am reading *Crime and Punishment*. It is the most true book I have ever read.

Monday December 14th

Got up at 5 a.m. to intercept the postman. Took the dog for a walk in the drizzle. (It wanted to stay asleep, but I wouldn't let it.) The dog moaned and complained all the way round the block so in the end I let it climb back into its cardboard box. I wish I was a dog; they haven't got any ethics or morals.

The postman delivered the letters at seven-thirty when I was sitting on the toilet. This is just my luck!

My father collected the letters and put them behind the clock. I had a quick look through them while he was coughing on his first cigarette of the day. Sure enough there was one addressed to my parents in Mr Cherry's uneducated handwriting!

My mother and father slopped over each other for a few minutes and then opened the letters whilst their Rice Krispies were going soggy. There were seven lousy Christmas cards, which they put up on a string over the fireplace. My eyes were focused on Mr Cherry's letter. My mother opened it, read it and said, 'George, that old git Cherry's sent his bloody paper bill in'. Then they ate their Rice Krispies and that was that. I wasted a lot of adrenalin worrying. I won't have enough left if I'm not careful.

Tuesday December 15th

My mother has told me why she left creep Lucas and returned to my father. She said, 'Bimbo treated me like a sex object, Adrian, and he expected his evening meal cooked for him, and he cut his toe-nails in the living room, and besides I'm very fond of your father'. She didn't mention me.

Wednesday December 16th

I am in an experimental Nativity play at school. It is called *Manger to Star*. I am playing Joseph. Pandora is playing Mary. Jesus is played by the smallest first-year. He is called Peter Brown. He is on drugs to make him taller.

Thursday December 17th

Another letter from the BBC!

Dear Adrian Mole,

Thank you for submitting your latest poem. I understood it perfectly well once it had been typed. However, Adrian, understanding is not all. Our Poetry Department is inundated with autumnal poems. The smell of bonfires and the crackling of leaves pervade the very corridors. Good try, but try again, eh?

Yours with best wishes,

John Tydeman

'Try again'! He is almost giving me a commission. I have written back to him:

Dear Mr Tydeman,

How much will I get if you broadcast one of my poems on the radio? When do you want me to send it? What do you want it to be about? Can I read it out myself? Will you pay my train fare in advance? What time will it go out on the airways? I have to be in bed by ten.

Yours faithfully,

A. Mole

P.S. I hope you have a dead good Christmas.

Friday December 18th
Moon's Last Quarter

Today's rehearsal of *Manger to Star* was a fiasco. Peter Brown has grown too big for the crib, so Mr Animba, the Woodwork teacher, has got to make another one.

Mr Scruton sat at the back of the gym and watched rehearsals. He had a face like the north face of the Eiger by the time we'd got to the bit where the three wise men were reviled as capitalist pigs.

He took Miss Elf into the showers and had a 'Quiet Word'. We all heard every word he shouted. He said he wanted to see a traditional Nativity play, with a Tiny Tears doll playing Jesus and three wise men dressed in dressing gowns and tea towels. He threatened to cancel the play if Mary, alias Pandora, continued to go into simulated labour in the manger. This is typical of Scruton, he is nothing but a small-minded, provincial, sexually-inhibited fascist pig. How he rose to become a headmaster I do not know. He has been wearing the same hairy green suit for three years. How can we change it all now? The play is being performed on Tuesday afternoon.

My mother has had a Christmas card from creep Lucas! Inside he had written, 'Paulie, Have you got the dry-cleaning ticket for my best white suit? Sketchley's are being very difficult'. My mother was very upset. My father rang Sheffield and ordered Lucas to cease communications, or risk getting a bit of Sheffield steel in between his porky shoulder blades. My father looked dead good on the telephone. He had a cigarette stuck between his lips. My mother was leaning on the corner of the fridge. She had a cigarette in her hand. They looked a bit like the Humphrey Bogart and Lauren Bacall postcard on my wall. I wish I was a *real* gangster's son, at least you would see a bit of life.

Saturday December 19th

I've got no money for Christmas presents. But I have made my Christmas list in case I find ten pounds in the street.

Pandora – Big bottle of Chanel No. 5 (£1.50)
Mother – Egg-timer (75p)
Father – Bookmark (38p)
Grandma – Packet of J cloths (45p)
Dog – Dog chocolates (45p)
Bert – 20 Woodbines (95p)
Auntie Susan – Tin of Nivea (60p)
Sabre – Box of Bob Martins, small (39p)
Nigel – Family box of Maltesers (34p)
Miss Elf – Oven-glove (home-made)

Sunday December 20th
Fourth in Advent

Pandora and I had a private Mary and Joseph rehearsal in my bedroom. We improvised a great scene where Mary gets back from the Family Planning Clinic and tells Joseph she's pregnant. I played Joseph like Marlon Brando in *A Streetcar Named Desire*. Pandora played Mary a bit like Blanche Dubois; it was dead good until my father complained about the shouting. The dog was supposed to be the lowly cattle, but it wouldn't keep still long enough to make a tableau.

After tea my mother casually mentioned that she was going to wear her fox-fur coat to the school concert tomorrow. Shock! Horror! I immediately went round to Pandora's house to get the mangy coat, only to find that Pandora's mother has borrowed it to go to the Marriage Guidance Christmas dinner and dance! Pandora said that she hadn't realized that the coat was only on loan; she thought it was a lover's gift! How can a $14^3/_4$-year-old schoolboy afford to give a fox-fur coat as a gift? Who does Pandora think I am, a millionaire like Freddie Laker?

Pandora's mother won't be back until the early hours so I will have to go round before school and sneak the coat into its plastic cover. It's going to be difficult, but then nothing in my life is simple or straightforward any more. I feel like a character in a Russian novel half the time.

Monday December 21st

Woke up with a panic attack to see that it was eight-fifty by my bedside digital! My black walls looked unusually light and sparkly; one glance outside confirmed my suspicions that indeed the snow lay outside like a white carpet.

I stumbled through the snow to Pandora's house in my father's fishing boots but found that the house was devoid of humans. I looked through the letterbox and saw my mother's fur coat being mauled about by Pandora's ginger cat. I shouted swear-words at it but the lousy stinking cat just looked sarcastic and carried on dragging the coat around the hall. I had no choice but to shoulder-charge the laundry-room door and rush into the hall and rescue my mother's coat. I left quickly (as quickly as anyone can wearing thigh-length fishing boots, four sizes too big). I put the fur coat on to keep me warm on my hazardous journey home. I nearly lost my bearings at the corner of Ploughman's Avenue and Shepherd's Crook Drive, but I fought my way through the blizzard until I saw the familiar sight of the prefabricated garages on the corner of our cul-de-sac.

I fell into our kitchen in a state of hypothermia and severe exhaustion; my mother was smoking a cigarette and making mince pies. She screamed, 'What the bloody hell are you doing wearing my fox-fur coat?' She was not kind or concerned or anything that mothers are supposed to be. She fussed about, wiping snow off the coat and drying the fur with a hair dryer. She didn't even offer to make me a hot drink or anything. She said, 'It's been on the radio that the school is closed because of the snow, so you can make yourself useful and check the camp beds for rust. The Sugdens are staying over Christmas.' The Sugdens! My mother's relations from Norfolk! Yuk, Yuk. They are all inbred and can't speak properly!

Phoned Pandora to explain about the fox-fur and the damage, etc., but she had gone skiing on the slope behind the Co-op bakery. Pandora's father asked me to get off the line, he had to make an urgent phone call to the police station. He said he had just come home and discovered a break-in! He said the place was a shambles (the cat must have done it, I was very careful), but fortunately the only thing that was missing was an old fox-fur coat that Pandora had lined the cat's basket with.

Sorry Pandora, but this is the final straw that broke the donkey's back! You can find yourself another Joseph, I refuse to share the stage with a girl who puts her cat's comfort before her boyfriend's dilemma.

Tuesday December 22nd

School was closed this morning because the teachers couldn't manage to get in on time because of the snow. That will teach them to live in old mill houses and windmills out in the country! Miss Elf lives with a West Indian in a terraced house in the town, so she bravely turned out to prepare for the school concert in the afternoon. I decided to forgive Pandora for the fox-fur in the cat's basket incident after she had pointed out that the cat was an expectant mother.

The school concert was not a success. The bell ringing from class One-G went on too long, my father said 'The Bells! The Bells!' and my mother laughed too loudly and made Mr Scruton look at her.

The school orchestra was a disaster! My mother said, 'When are they going to stop tuning-up and start playing?' I told her that they had just played a Mozart horn concerto. That made my mother and father and Pandora's mother and father start laughing in a very unmannerly fashion. When ten-stone Alice Bernard from Three-C came on stage in a tutu and did the dying swan I thought my mother would explode. Alice Bernard's mother led the applause, but not many people followed.

The Dumbo class got up and sang a few boring old carols. Barry Kent sang all the vulgar versions (I know because I was watching his lips) then they sat down cross-legged, and brainbox Henderson from Five-K played a trumpet, Jew's harp, piano and guitar. The smarmy git looked dead superior when he was bowing during his applause. Then it was the interval and time for me to change into my white T-shirt-and-Wranglers Joseph costume. The tension backstage was electric. I stood in the wings (a theatrical term – it means the side of the stage) and watched the audience filing back into their places. Then the music from *Close Encounters* boomed out over the stereo speakers, and the curtains opened on an abstract manger and I just had time to whisper to Pandora 'Break a leg, darling', before Miss Elf pushed us out into the lights. My performance was brilliant! I really got under the skin of Joseph but Pandora was less good, she forgot to look tenderly at Jesus/Peter Brown.

The three punks/wise men made too much noise with their chains and spoiled my speech about the Middle East situation, and the angels representing Mrs Thatcher got hissed by the audience so loudly that their spoken chorus about unemployment was wasted.

Still, all in all, it was well received by the audience. Mr Scruton got up and made a hypocritical speech about 'a brave experiment' and 'Miss Elf's tireless work behind the scenes', and then we all sang 'We wish you a Merry Christmas'!

Driving home in the car my father said, 'That was the funniest Nativity play I have ever seen. Whose idea was it to turn it into a comedy?' I didn't reply. It wasn't a comedy.

Wednesday December 23rd

9 a.m. Only two shopping days left for Christmas and I am still penniless. I have made a *Blue Peter* oven-glove for Miss Elf, but in order to give it to her in time for Christmas I will have to go into the ghetto and risk getting mugged.

I will have to go out carol singing, there is nothing else I can do to raise finance.

10 p.m. Just got back from carol singing. The suburban houses were a dead loss. People shouted, 'Come back at Christmas', without even opening the door. My most appreciative audience were the drunks staggering in and out of the Black Bull. Some of them wept openly at the beauty of my solo rendition of 'Silent Night'. I must say that I presented a touching picture as I stood in the snow with my young face lifted to the heavens ignoring the scenes of drunken revelry around me.

I made £3.13½ plus an Irish tenpence and Guinness bottle-top. I'm going out again tomorrow. I will wear my school uniform, it should be worth a few extra quid.

Thursday December 24th

Took Bert's Woodbines round to the home. Bert is hurt because I haven't been to see him. He said he didn't want to spend Christmas with a lot of malicious old women. Him and Queenie are causing a scandal. They are unofficially engaged. They have got their names on the same ashtray. I have invited Bert and Queenie for Christmas Day. My mother doesn't know yet but I'm sure she won't mind, we have got a big turkey. I sang a few carols for the old ladies. I made two pounds eleven pence out of them so I went to Woolworth's to buy Pandora's Chanel No. 5. They hadn't got any so I bought her an underarm deodorant instead.

The house looks dead clean and sparkling, there is a magic smell of cooking and satsumas in the air. I have searched around for my presents but they are not in the usual places. I want a racing bike, nothing else will please me. It's time I was independently mobile.
11 p.m. Just got back from the Black Bull. Pandora came with me, we wore our school uniforms and reminded all the drunks of their own children. They coughed up conscience money to the tune of twelve pounds fifty-seven! So we are going to see a pantomime on Boxing Day and we will have a family bar of Cadbury's Dairy Milk each!

Friday December 25th
Christmas Day

Got up at 5 a.m. to have a ride on my racing bike. My father paid for it with American Express. I couldn't ride it far because of the snow, but it didn't matter. I just like looking at it. My father had written on the gift tag attached to the handlebars, 'Don't leave it out in the rain this time' – as if I would!

My parents had severe hangovers, so I took them breakfast in bed and gave them my presents at the same time. My mother was overjoyed with her egg-timer and my father was equally delighted with his bookmark, in fact everything was going OK until I casually mentioned that Bert and Queenie were my guests for the day, and would my father mind getting out of bed and picking them up in his car.

The row went on until the lousy Sugdens arrived. My grandma and grandad Sugden and Uncle Dennis and his wife Marcia and their son Maurice all look the same, as if they went to funerals every day of their lives. I can hardly believe that my mother is related to them. The Sugdens refused a drink and had a cup of tea whilst my mother defrosted the turkey in the bath. I helped my father carry Queenie (fifteen stone) and Bert (fourteen stone) out of our car. Queenie is one of those loud types of old ladies who dye their hair and try to look young. Bert is in love with her. He told me when I was helping him into the toilet.

Grandma Mole and Auntie Susan came at twelve-thirty and pretended to like the Sugdens. Auntie Susan told some amusing stories about life in prison but nobody but me and my father and Bert and Queenie laughed.

I went up to the bathroom and found my mother crying and running the turkey under the hot tap. She said, 'The bloody thing won't thaw out, Adrian. What am I going to do?' I said, 'Just bung it in the oven'. So she did.

We sat down to eat Christmas dinner four hours late. By then my father was too drunk to eat anything. The Sugdens enjoyed the Queen's Speech but nothing else seemed to please them. Grandma Sugden gave me a book called *Bible Stories for Boys*. I could hardly tell her that I had lost my faith, so I said thank-you and wore a false smile for so long that it hurt.

The Sugdens went to their camp beds at ten o'clock. Bert, Queenie and my mother and father played cards while I polished my bike. We all had a good time making jokes about the Sugdens. Then my father drove Bert and Queenie back to the home and I phoned Pandora up and told her that I loved her more than life itself.

I am going round to her house tomorrow to give her the deodorant and escort her to the pantomime.

Saturday December 26th
Bank Holiday in UK and Rep. of Ireland (a day may be given in lieu). New Moon

The Sugdens got up at 7 a.m. and sat around in their best clothes looking respectable. I went out on my bike. When I got back my mother was still in bed, and my father was arguing with Grandad Sugden about our dog's behaviour, so I went for another ride.

I called in on Grandma Mole, ate four mince pies, then rode back home. I got up to 30 mph on the dual carriageway, it was dead good. I put my new suede jacket and corduroy trousers on (courtesy of my father's Barclaycard) and called for Pandora; she gave me a bottle of after-shave for my Christmas present. It was a proud moment, it signified the *End of Childhood*.

We quite enjoyed the pantomime but it was rather childish for our taste. Bill Ash and Carole Hayman were good as Aladdin and the Princess, but the robbers played by Jeff Teare and Ian Giles were best. Sue Pomeroy gave a hilarious performance as Widow Twankey. In this she was greatly helped by her cow, played by Chris Martin and Lou Wakefield.

Sunday December 27th
First after Christmas

The Sugdens have gone back to Norfolk, thank God!
The house is back to its usual mess. My parents

took a bottle of vodka and two glasses to bed with them last night. I haven't seen them since.

Went to Melton Mowbray on my bike, did it in five hours.

Monday December 28th

I am in trouble for leaving my bike outside last night. My parents are not speaking to me. I don't care, I have just had a shave and I feel magic.

Tuesday December 29th

My father is in a bad mood because there is only a bottle of V. P. sherry left to drink. He has gone round Pandora's house to borrow a bottle of spirits.

The dog has pulled the Christmas tree down and made all the pine needles stick in the shag-pile.

I have finished all my Christmas books and the library is still shut. I am reduced to reading my father's *Reader's Digests* and testing my word power.

Wednesday December 30th

All the balloons have shrivelled up. They look like old women's breasts shown on television documentaries about the Third World.

Thursday December 31st

The last day of the year! A lot has happened. I have fallen in love. Been a one-parent child. Gone Intellectual. And had two letters from the BBC. Not bad going for a 14³/₄-year-old!

My mother and father have been to a New Year's Eve dance at the Grand Hotel. My mother actually wore a dress! It is over a year since she showed her legs in public.

Pandora and I saw the New Year in together, we had a dead passionate session accompanied by Andy Stewart and a bagpiper.

My father came crashing through the front door at 1 a.m. carrying a lump of coal in his hand. Drunk as usual.

My mother started going on about what a wonderful son I was and how much she loved me. It's a pity she never says anything like that when she is sober.

Winter

Friday January 1st
Bank Holiday in UK, Rep. of Ireland, USA and Canada

These are my New Year's resolutions:

1. I will be true to Pandora.
2. I will bring my bike in at night.
3. I will not read unworthy books.
4. I will study hard for my O levels, and get Grade 'A's.
5. I will try to be more kind to the dog.
6. I will try to find it in my heart to forgive Barry Kent his multiple sins.
7. I will clean the bath after use.
8. I will stop worrying about the size of my thing.
9. I will do my back-stretching exercises every night without fail.
10. I will learn a new word and use it every day.

Saturday January 2nd
Bank Holiday in Scotland (a day may be given in lieu)

How interesting it is that Aabec should be an Australian bark used for making sweat.

Sunday January 3rd
Second after Christmas. Moon's First Quarter

I wouldn't mind going to Africa and hunting an Aardvark.

Monday January 4th

Whilst in Africa I would go south and look out for an Aardwolf.

Tuesday January 5th

And I would avoid tangling with an Aasvogel.

Wednesday January 6th
Epiphany

I keep having nightmares about the bomb. I hope it isn't dropped before I get my GCE results in August 1983. I wouldn't like to die an unqualified virgin.

Thursday January 7th

Nigel came round to look at my racing bike. He said that it was mass produced, unlike his bike that was 'made by a craftsman in Nottingham'. I have gone off Nigel, and I have also gone off my bike a bit.

Friday January 8th

Got a wedding invitation from Bert and Queenie, they are getting married on January 16th at Pocklington Street Register Office.

In my opinion it is a waste of time. Bert is nearly ninety and Queenie is nearly eighty. I will leave it until the last minute before I buy a wedding present.

It has started snowing again. I asked my mother to buy me some green wellingtons like the Queen's but she came back with dead common black ones. I only need them to walk Pandora to our gate. I am staying in until the snow melts. Unlike most youths of my age, I dislike frolicking in the snow.

Saturday January 9th
Full Moon

Nigel said the end of the world is coming tonight. He said the moon is having a total collapse. (Nigel should read *Reader's Digest* and increase his word power.) True enough it did go dark, I held my breath and feared the worst but then the moon recovered and life went on as usual, except in York where fate has flooded the town centre.

Sunday January 10th
First after Epiphany

I can't understand why my father looks so old at forty-one compared to President Reagan at seventy. My father has got no work or worries yet he looks dead haggard. Poor President Reagan has to carry the world's safety on his shoulders yet he is always smiling and looking cheerful. It doesn't make sense.

Monday January 11th

I've been looking through last year's diary and have been reminded that Malcolm Muggeridge never did reply to my letter about what to do if you are an intellectual. That is a first-class stamp wasted! I should have written to the British Museum, that's where all the intellectuals hang out.

Tuesday January 12th

Pandora and I went to the youth club tonight. It was quite good. Rick Lemon led a discussion on sex. Nobody said anything, but he showed some interesting slides of wombs cut in half.

Wednesday January 13th

Pandora's parents have had a massive row. They are sleeping in separate bedrooms. Pandora's mother has joined the SDP and Pandora's father is staying loyal to the Labour Party.

Pandora is a Liberal, so she gets on all right with them both.

Thursday January 14th

Pandora's father has come out of the closet and admitted that he is a Bennite. Pandora is staying loyal to him, but if the Co-op Dairy find out he will be finished.

Friday January 15th

Thank God the snow is melting! At last I can walk the streets in safety, secure in the knowledge that no one is going to ram a snowball down the back of my anorak.

Saturday January 16th
Moon's Last Quarter

Bert got married today.

The Alderman Cooper Sunshine Home hired a coach and took the old ladies to form a guard of honour with their walking-frames.

Bert looked dead good. He cashed his life insurance in and spent the money on a new suit. Queenie was wearing a hat made of flowers and fruit. She had a lot of orange make-up on her face to try and cover the wrinkles. Even Sabre had a red bow round his neck. I think it was kind of the RSPCA to let Sabre out for his master's wedding. My father and Pandora's father carried Bert's wheelchair up the steps with Bert a single man and then down again with Bert a married man. The old ladies threw rice and confetti and my mother and Pandora's mother gave Queenie a kiss and a lucky horseshoe.

A newspaper reporter and photographer made everyone pose for photographs. I was asked my name, but I said I didn't want publicity for my acts of charity to Bert.

The reception took place back at the home. Matron made a cake with 'B' and 'Q' written in Jellytots.

Bert and Queenie are moving into a bungalow on Monday, after they have had their honeymoon in the home.

Honeymoon! Ha! Ha! Ha!

Sunday January 17th
Second after Epiphany

Last night I dreamed about a boy like me collecting pebbles in the rain. It was a dead strange dream.

I am reading *The Black Prince*, by Iris Murdoch. I can only understand one word in ten. It is now my ambition to actually enjoy one of her books. Then I will know I am above the common herd.

Monday January 18th

School. First day of term. Loads of GCE homework. I will never cope. I am an intellectual but at the same time I am not very clever.

Tuesday January 19th

Brought four hundred and eighty-three copies of *The Voice of Youth* home in my satchel and Adidas bag. Mr Jones needs the games cupboard.

Wednesday January 20th

Two-and-a-half hours of homework! I will crack under the strain.

Thursday January 21st

My brain is hurting. I have just had two pages of *Macbeth* to translate into English.

Friday January 22nd

I am destined to become a manual worker. I can't keep working under this pressure. Miss Elf said my work is perfectly satisfactory, but that isn't good enough when Pandora keeps getting 'Excellent' in red pen on everything she does.

Saturday January 23rd

Stayed in bed until five-thirty to make sure I missed Sainsbury's. Listened to Radio Four play about domestic unhappiness. Phoned Pandora. Did Geography homework. Teased dog. Went to sleep. Woke up. Worried for ten minutes. Got up. Made cocoa.
     I am a nervous wreck.

Sunday January 24th
Third after Epiphany

My mother blames my bad nerves on Iris Murdoch.

She says painful adolescence shouldn't be read about when one is studying for O levels.

Monday January 25th
New Moon

Couldn't do my Maths homework. Phoned the Samaritans. The nice man on the end of the phone told me the answer was nine-eighths. He was dead kind to someone in despair.

Tuesday January 26th

The stupid Samaritan got the answer wrong! It's only seven-fifths. I only got six out of twenty. Pandora got them all right. In fact she got a hundred per cent.

Wednesday January 27th

My mother is holding her women's rights meetings in our lounge. I can't concentrate on my homework properly with women laughing and shouting and stamping up the stairs. They are not a bit ladylike.

Thursday January 28th

Got fifteen out of twenty for History. Pandora got twenty-one out of twenty. She got an extra mark for knowing Hitler's father's name.

Friday January 29th

Came home from school early with a severe migraine (missed the Comparative Religion test). Found my father watching *Play School* and pretending to be an acorn growing into an oak.

Went to bed too shocked to speak.

Saturday January 30th

Migraine. Too ill to write.

Sunday January 31st
Fourth after Epiphany

Pandora came round. I copied her homework. Feel better.

Monday February 1st
Moon's First Quarter

My mother has given my father an ultimatum: either he finds a job, or starts doing housework, or leaves.

He is looking for a job.

Tuesday February 2nd
Candlemas (Scottish Quarter-Day)

Grandma Mole came to tell me that the end of the world was announced at her Spiritualist church last week. She said it should have all ended yesterday.

She would have come round sooner only she was washing her curtains.

Wednesday February 3rd

My father has had his credit cards taken off him! Barclays, Nat West and American Express have got fed up with his reckless spending. Time is running out for us. He has only got a few quid's redundancy money left in his sock drawer.

My mother is looking for a job.

I have got a sense of *déjà vu*.

Thursday February 4th

Went round to see Bert and Queenie. Their bungalow is so full of knick-knacks that there is hardly room for a person to move. Sabre knocks at least ten things over every time he wags his tail. They both seem happy enough, though their sex life can't be up to much.

Friday February 5th

I've got to write an essay on the causes of the Second World War. What a waste of time! Everyone knows the causes. You can't go anywhere without seeing Hitler's photo.

Saturday February 6th

Finished essay; copied it out of *Pear's Encyclopedia*.

My mother has gone to a women's workshop on self-defence. So if my father moans at her for burning the toast she will be able to karate-chop him in the windpipe.

Sunday February 7th
Septuagesima

Bored stiff all day. My parents never do anything on Sundays but read the Sunday papers. Other families go out to safari parks, etc. But we never do.

When I am a parent I will fill my children with stimulation at weekends.

Monday February 8th
Full Moon

My mother has found a job. She collects money from Space Invader machines. She started today in response to an urgent phone call from the job agency that she is registered with.

She said that the fullest machines are those in unrespectable cafés and university common rooms.

I think my mother is betraying her principles. She is pandering to an obsession of weak minds.

Tuesday February 9th

My mother has given up her job. She said she is sexually harassed during her work and she is also allergic to ten-pence pieces.

Wednesday February 10th

My father is going to start his own business making spice-racks. He has spent the last of his redundancy money on buying pine and glue. Our spare bedroom has been turned into a workshop. Sawdust is all over the house.

I am very proud of my father. He is now a company director, and I am a company director's son!

Thursday February 11th

Delivered Mrs Singh's massive spice-rack after school. It took two of us to carry it round and install it on her kitchen wall. We had a cup of sickly Indian tea and Mrs Singh paid my father and then started to fill up her shelves with exotic Indian spices. They looked a lot more interesting than my mother's boring parsley and thyme.

My father bought a bottle of champagne to celebrate his first sale! He has got no respect for capital investment.

Friday February 12th

Pandora has gone to London with her father to hear Tony Benn speak. Pandora's mother has gone to a

SDP rally in Loughborough. It is a sad day when families are split by politics.

I'm not sure how I will vote. Sometimes I think Mrs Thatcher is a nice kind sort of woman. Then the next day I see her on television and she frightens me rigid. She has got eyes like a psychotic killer, but a voice like a gentle person. It is a bit confusing.

Saturday February 13th

Pandora has got a crush on Tony Benn, just like the one she had on Adam Ant. She says that older men are exciting.

I am trying to grow my moustache. Valentine's Day tomorrow. A big card came today, it had a Sheffield postmark.

Sunday February 14th
Sexagesima. St Valentine's Day

At last I have had a valentine from somebody who is not a blood relation! Pandora's card was charming, she had written a simple message of love:

Adrian, it is you alone.

I gave Pandora a false Victorian card, inside I wrote:

My young love,
Treacle hair and knee-socks
Give my system deep shocks.
You've got a magic figure:
I'm Roy Rogers, you are Trigger.

It doesn't scan very well, but I was in a hurry. Pandora didn't get the literary reference to Roy Rogers, so I have lent her my father's old Roy Rogers annuals.

My father threw the Sheffield card in the waste-bin. My mother took it out when my father had gone to the pub. Inside it said:

Pauline, I am in anguish.

My mother smiled and ripped it up.

Monday February 15th
Washington's Birthday, USA. Moon's Last Quarter

Came home from school to hear my mother talking to creep Lucas on the phone. She was using a yukky voice and saying things like: 'Don't ask me to do it, Bimbo', and 'It's all over between us now, darling. We must try to forget'.

I can't stand much more emotional stress. I am up to my ears in it already what with studying hard and vying with Tony Benn for Pandora's attention.

Tuesday February 16th

Pandora's mother came round last night to complain about her spice-rack. It fell off the wall and spilt rosemary and tumeric all over her cork tiles. My mother apologized on behalf of my father who was hiding in the coal shed.

I am seriously thinking of giving everything up and running away to be a tramp. I would quite enjoy the life, providing I could have a daily bath.

Wednesday February 17th

Miss Elf told us about her boyfriend today. He is called Winston Johnson. He is a Master of Arts and can't get a job! So what chance do I stand?

Miss Elf said that school-leavers are despairing all over the country. She said that Mr Scruton should be ashamed to have a portrait of Mrs Thatcher over his desk.

I think I am turning radical.

Thursday February 18th

This morning the whole school was ordered to go to the assembly hall. Mr Scruton got up on the stage and acted like the films of Hitler. He said in all his long years of teaching he had never come across an act of such serious vandalism. Everybody went dead quiet and wondered what had happened. Scruton said that somebody had entered his office and drawn a moustache on Margaret Thatcher and written 'Three million unemployed' in her cleavage.

He said that defiling the greatest leader this country has ever known was a crime against humanity. It was tantamount to treason and that when the culprit was found they would be immediately expelled. Scruton's eyes bulged out so far that a few of the first-years started to cry. Miss Elf led them outside to safety.

The whole school has got to have handwriting tests.

Friday February 19th

Miss Elf has resigned. I will miss her, she was responsible for my political development. I am a committed radical. I am against nearly everything.

Saturday February 20th

Pandora, Nigel, Claire Neilson and myself have formed a radical group. We are the 'Pink Brigade'. We discuss things like war (we are against it); peace (we are for it); and the ultimate destruction of capitalist society.

Claire Neilson's father is a capitalist; he owns a greengrocer's shop. Claire is trying to get her father to give cheap food to the unwaged but he refuses. He waxes fat on their starvation!

Sunday February 21st
Quinquagesima

Had an argument with my father over the *Sunday Express*. He can't see that he is a willing tool of the reactionary right. He refuses to change to the *Morning Star*. My mother reads anything; she is prostituting her literacy.

Monday February 22nd

Once again I am spotty. I am also extremely sexually frustrated. I'm sure a session of passionate lovemaking would improve my skin.

Pandora says she is not going to risk being a single parent just for the sake of a few spots. So I will have to fall back on self-indulgence.

Tuesday February 23rd
Shrove Tuesday. New Moon

Ate nine pancakes at home, three at Pandora's and four at Bert and Queenie's. Grandma was very hurt when I refused her kind offer to whip me a batter, but I was full up.

It is disgusting when the Third World is living on a few grains of rice.

I feel dead guilty.

Wednesday February 24th
Ash Wednesday

Our school dinner-ladies have got the sack! The dinners now come in hot boxes from a central kitchen. I would have staged a protest but I have got a Geography test tomorrow.

Mrs Leech was presented with a microwave oven for her thirty years of toil over the custard jug.

Thursday February 25th

Got fifteen out of twenty for Geography. I lost points for saying that the Falkland Islands belonged to Argentina.

Friday February 26th

My thing is now thirteen centimetres long when it is extended. When it is contracted it is hardly worth measuring. My general physique is improving. I think the back-stretching exercises are paying off. I used to be the sort of boy who had sand kicked in his face, now I'm the sort of boy who watches somebody else have it kicked in their face.

Saturday February 27th

My father hasn't made or sold a single spice-rack all week. We are now living on Social Security and dole money.

My mother has stopped smoking. The dog is down to half a tin of Chum a day.

Sunday February 28th
Quadragesima (First in Lent)

Had egg and chips and peas for Sunday dinner! No pudding! Not even a proper serviette.

My mother says we are the *nouveau poor.*

Monday March 1st
St David's Day (Wales)

My father has stopped smoking. He is going around with a white face finding fault with everything I do.

My mother and him had their first row since she came back. The dog caused it by eating the Spam for tea. It couldn't help it, the poor thing was half crazed with hunger. It is back on a full tin of Chum a day.

Tuesday March 2nd
Moon's First Quarter

My parents are suffering severe nicotine withdrawal symptoms. It is quite amusing to a non-smoker like me.

Wednesday March 3rd

I had to lend my father enough money for a gallon of petrol, he had an interview for a job. My mother cut his hair and gave him a shave and told him what to say and how to behave. It is pathetic to see how unemployment has reduced my father to childish dependence on others.

He is waiting to hear from Manpower Services.

He is still ill from not smoking. His temper has reached new peaks of explosion.

Thursday March 4th

No news yet about the job. I spend as much time as I can out of the house. My parents are unbearable. I almost wish they would start smoking again.

Friday March 5th

He got it!!!

He starts on Monday as a Canal Bank Renovation Supervisor. He is in charge of a gang of school-leavers. To celebrate he bought my mother sixty Benson and Hedges and himself sixty Players. I got a family pack of Mars bars.

Everybody is dead happy for once. Even the dog has cheered up a bit. Grandma is knitting my father a woolly hat for work.

Saturday March 6th

Pandora and I went to see the bit of canal bank that my father is now in charge of. If he worked for a thousand years he will never get it cleaned of all the old bikes and prams and weeds and Coca-Cola tins! I told my father that he was in a no-win situation, but he said, 'On the contrary, in one year's time it will be a beauty spot'. Yes! And I am Nancy Reagan, Dad!

Sunday March 7th
Second in Lent

My father went to see his canal bank this morning. He came home and shut himself in his bedroom. He is still there, I can hear my mother saying encouraging words to him.

It is uncertain whether or not he will turn up for work tomorrow. On the whole I think not.

Monday March 8th

He went to work.

After school I walked home along the canal bank. I found him bossing a gang of skinheads and punks about. They were looking surly and unco-operative. None of them wanted to get their clothes dirty. My father seemed to be the only one doing any work. He was covered in mud. I attempted to exchange a few civilities with the lads, but they spurned my overtures. I pointed out that the lads are alienated by a cruel, uncaring society, but my father said, 'Bugger off home, Adrian. You're talking a load of lefty crap'. He will have a mutiny on his hands soon if he's not careful.

Tuesday March 9th
Full Moon

My schoolwork is plummeting down to new depths. I only got five out of twenty for spelling. I think I might be anorexic.

Wednesday March 10th

My father has asked me not to bring Pandora to the canal after school. He says he can't do anything with the lads after she has gone. It's true that she is stunningly beautiful, but the lads will just have to learn self-control. I have had to learn it. She has refused to consummate our relationship. Sometimes I wonder what she sees in me. I live in daily terror of our relationship ending.

Thursday March 11th

Pandora and Pandora's mother have joined my mother's women's group. No men or boys are allowed in our front room. My father had to be in charge of the crèche in our dining room.

Rick Lemon's baby daughter Herod was crawling under the table shouting: 'Tit! Tit!' My father kept telling Herod to shut up until I explained that Tit was Herod's mother's name. Herod is a very radical baby who never eats sweets and stays up until 2 a.m.

My father says that women ought to be at home cooking. He said it in a whisper so that he wouldn't be karate-chopped to death.

Friday March 12th

My father had a good day on the canal bank. He is almost through to the grass now. To celebrate he brought the skinheads and punks round to our house for a glass of home-made beer. Mrs Singh and my mother looked shocked when the lads trooped into our kitchen, but my father introduced Baz, Daz, Maz, Kev, Melv and Boz and my mother and Mrs Singh relaxed a bit.

Boz is going to help me fix the brakes on my bike, he is an expert bike-fixer. He has been stealing them since he was six.

Saturday March 13th

Boz offered me a sniff of his glue today, but I declined it with thanks.

Sunday March 14th
Third in Lent

All the women I know have gone to a rally to protest about a woman's right to work. Mrs Singh has gone wearing a disguise.

Saw Rick Lemon in the park, he was pushing Herod too high on a swing. Herod was shouting: 'Tit! Tit!'

Monday March 15th

I am loved by two women! Elizabeth Sally Broadway gave Victoria Louise Thomson a note in Science. It said: 'Ask Adrian Mole if he wants to go out with me.'

Victoria Louise Thomson (hereafter known as V.L.T.) passed on the message. I replied to V.L.T. in the negative.

Elizabeth Sally Broadway (hereafter known as E.S.B.) looked dead sad and started to cry into her bunsen burner.

It is really wonderful to know that Pandora and Elizabeth are both in love with me.

Perhaps I am not so ugly after all.

Tuesday March 16th

Pandora and E.S.B. have had a fight in the playground. I am disgusted with Pandora. At the last meeting of the Pink Brigade she swore to be a pacifist all her life. Pandora won! Ha! Ha! Ha!

Wednesday March 17th
St Patrick's Day. Bank Holiday (Ireland). Moon's Last Quarter

Mr O'Leary was brought home by a police car at 10.30 p.m. Mrs O'Leary came over to ask my father if he would help her to get Mr O'Leary upstairs to bed. My father is still over there. I can hear the music and singing through the double-glazing.

It is no joke when you need your sleep for school.

Thursday March 18th

I am reading *How Children Fail*, by John Holt. It is dead good. If I fail my O levels it will be all my parents' fault.

Friday March 19th

My creative English essay:

Spring, by A Mole

The trees explode into bud, indeed some of them are in leaf. Their branches thrust to the sky like drunken scarecrows. Their trunks writhe and twist into the earth and form a plethora of roots. The brilliant sky hovers uncertainly like a shy bride at the door of her nuptial chamber. Birds wing and scrape their erratic way into the cotton-wool clouds like drunken scarecrows. The translucent brook gurgles majestically towards its journey's end. 'To the sea!' it cries, 'to the sea!' it endlessly repeats.

A lonely boy, his loins afire, sits and watches his calm reflection in the torrential brook. His heart is indeed heavy. His eyes fall on to the ground and rest on a wondrous majestic many-hued butterfly. The winged insect takes flight and the boy's eyes are carried far away until they are but a speck on the red-hued sunset. He senses on the zephyr a hope for mankind.

Pandora thinks this is the best thing I have ever written, but I know I have got a long way to go until I have learned my craft.

Saturday March 20th
Vernal Equinox

My mother has had all her hair cut off. She looks like one of Auntie Susan's inmates. She doesn't look a bit maternal any more. I don't know whether to get her anything for Mother's Day or not. She was going on about it last night, saying it was a commercial racket fed by gullible fools.

Sunday March 21st
Fourth in Lent. Mothering Sunday

11.30 a.m. Didn't get my mother anything so she has been in a bad mood all morning.
1 p.m. My father said, 'If I were you, lad, I'd nip round Cherry's and get your mother a card and present'. He gave me two pounds so I got a card saying 'Mummy I love you' (it was the only one left, just my luck), and five boxes of liquorice allsorts (going cheap because the boxes were squashed). She cheered up and didn't

even mind when my father took a bunch of tulips round to grandma's and came back five hours later smelling of drink.

Pandora's mother was taken out and spoilt in a restaurant. I will do the same for my mother when I am famous.

Monday March 22nd

I have catalogued my bedroom library. I have got a hundred and fifty-one books, not counting the Enid Blytons.

Tuesday March 23rd

I will be fifteen in eleven days. So I have only got to wait one year and eleven days to get married, should I want to.

Wednesday March 24th

The only thing that really worries me about my appearance now is my ears. They stick out at an angle of ninety degrees. I have checked them with my geometry set so I know it is a scientific fact.

Thursday March 25th
Lady Day (Quarter Day). New Moon

I have had a spiritual awakening. Two nice men representing a religious group called the Sunshine People called at the house. They talked about how they alone could bring peace to the world. It is twenty pounds to join. I will get the money somehow. Nothing is too expensive where peace is concerned.

Friday March 26th

Tried to persuade Pandora to join the Sunshine People. She was not swayed by my arguments. They are calling round tomorrow to meet my parents and sign the agreement.

Saturday March 27th

The Sunshine People came at six o'clock. My father made them stand on the doorstep in the rain. Their robes got wet through. My father said they were trying to brainwash a simple child. When they left my mother watched them walk up the cul-de-sac. She said, 'They don't look very charismatic now, they just look bloody wet'. I wept a few tears. I think I was weeping out of relief – twenty quid is a lot of money.

Sunday March 28th
Passion Sunday. British Summer Time begins

My father forgot to change the clocks last night so I was late for the Pink Brigade's meeting in Pandora's lounge. We voted to exclude Pandora's father from the meeting on the grounds of his extreme left-wing views. We have decided to back Roy Hattersley in the expected fight for the leadership.

Pandora has gone off Tony Benn since she found out that he is a lapsed aristocrat.

Claire Neilson introduced a new member, her name is Barbara Boyer. She is dead good-looking and also dead intelligent. She disagreed with Pandora over NATO's nuclear arms policy. Pandora had to concede that China was an unknown factor. Pandora asked Claire Neilson not to bring Barbara again.

Monday March 29th

I ate my school dinner sitting next to Barbara Boyer. She is a truly wonderful girl. She pointed out that Pandora has got a lot of faults. I was forced to agree with her.

Tuesday March 30th

I am committing non-sexual adultery with Barbara. I am at the centre of an eternal triangle. Nigel is the only one to know: he has been sworn to secrecy.

Wednesday March 31st

Nigel has blabbed it all over the school. Pandora spent the afternoon in matron's office.

Thursday April 1st
All Fools' Day. Moon's First Quarter

Barbara Boyer has ended our brief *affaire*. I rang her up at the pet shop where she works part time cleaning the cages out. She said she couldn't bear to see the pain in Pandora's eyes. I asked her if it was an April Fools' joke, she said no and pointed out that it was after 12 a.m.

I have learnt an important lesson, because of lust I am without love.

I am fifteen tomorrow.

Had a shave to cheer myself up.

Friday April 2nd

I am fifteen, but legally I am still a child. There is nothing I can do today that I couldn't do yesterday. Worse luck!

Had seven cards from relations and three from friends. My presents were the usual load of Japanese rubbish, though I did get a model aeroplane from Bert that was made in West Germany.

Pandora has ignored my birthday. I don't blame her. I betrayed her trust.

Boz, Baz, Daz, Maz, Kev and Melv came back from the canal and gave me the bumps. Boz gave me a tube of glue for my model aeroplane.

Saturday April 3rd

8 a.m. Britain is at war with Argentina!!! Radio Four has just announced it. I am overcome with excitement. Half of me thinks it is tragic and the other half of me thinks it is dead exciting.

10 a.m. Woke my father up to tell him Argentina has invaded the Falklands. He shot out of bed because he thought the Falklands lay off the coast of Scotland. When I pointed out that they were eight thousand miles away he got back into bed and pulled the covers over his head.

4 p.m. I have just had the most humiliating experience of my life. It started when I began to assemble my model aeroplane. I had nearly finished it when I thought I would try an experimental sniff of glue. I put my nose to the undercarriage and sniffed for five seconds, nothing spiritual happened but my nose stuck to the plane! My father took me to Casualty to have it removed, how I endured the laughing and sniggering I don't know.

The Casualty doctor wrote 'Glue Sniffer' on my outpatient's card.

I rang Pandora; she is coming round after her viola lesson. Love is the only thing that keeps me sane . . .

CELEBRATING 30 YEARS
OF ADRIAN MOLE

'One of literature's most endearing figures'
OBSERVER

In eight books, two TV series, a stage play and on radio, Adrian Mole has delighted millions of people young and old across the world over the last thirty years.

Whether you have grown up with Mole or have only recently become acquainted with his diaries, you will find on the following pages the full story about Adrian's literary birth as well as plenty of information about his creator Sue Townsend and her other works.

To find out even more about
Sue and Adrian don't forget to visit
www.suetownsend.co.uk

Turn the page and read on, starting with an extract from Sue's latest Top 10 bestseller ...

Sue Townsend

The WOMAN WHO WENT TO BED FOR A YEAR

Chapter 1

After they'd gone Eva slid the bolt across the door and disconnected the telephone. She liked having the house to herself. She went from room to room tidying, straightening and collecting the cups and plates that her husband and children had left on various surfaces. Somebody had left a soup spoon on the arm of her special chair – the one she had upholstered at night school. She immediately went to the kitchen and examined the contents of her Kleeneze cleaning products box.

'What would remove a Heinz tomato soup stain from embroidered silk damask?'

As she searched, she remonstrated with herself. 'It's your own fault. You should have kept the chair in your bedroom. It was pure vanity on your part to have it on display in the sitting room. You wanted visitors to notice the chair and to tell you how beautiful it was, so that you could tell them that it had taken two years to complete the embroidery, and that you had been inspired by Claude Monet's "Water-Lily Pond and Weeping Willow".'

The trees alone had taken a year.

There was a small pool of tomato soup on the kitchen floor that she hadn't noticed until she stepped in it and left orange footprints. The little non-stick saucepan containing half a can of tomato soup was still simmering on the hob. 'Too lazy to take a pan off the stove,' she thought. Then she remembered that the twins were Leeds University's problem now.

She caught her reflection in the smoky glass of the wall-mounted oven. She looked away quickly. If she had taken a while to look she would have seen a woman of fifty with a lovely, fine-boned face, pale inquisitive eyes and a Clara Bow mouth that always looked as though she were about to speak. Nobody – not even Brian, her husband – had seen her without lipstick. Eva thought that red lips complemented the black clothes she habitually wore. Sometimes she allowed herself a little grey.

Once, Brian had come home from work to find Eva in the garden, in her black wellingtons, having just pulled up a bunch of turnips. He'd said to her, 'For Christ's sake, Eva! You look like post-war Poland.'

Her face was currently fashionable. 'Vintage' according to the girl on the Chanel counter where she bought her lipstick (always remembering to throw the receipt away – her husband would not understand the outrageous expense).

She picked up the saucepan, walked from the kitchen into the sitting room and threw the soup all over her precious chair. She then went upstairs, into her bedroom and, without removing her clothes or her shoes, got into bed and stayed there for a year.

She didn't know it would be a year. She climbed into bed thinking she would leave it again after half an hour, but the comfort of the bed was exquisite, the white sheets were fresh and smelled of new snow. She turned on her side towards the open window and watched the sycamore in the garden shed its blazing leaves.

She had always loved September.

She woke when it was getting dark, and she heard her husband shouting outside. Her mobile rang. The display showed that it was her daughter, Brianne. She ignored it. She pulled the duvet over her head and sang the words of Johnny Cash's 'I Walk The Line'.

When she next poked her head out from under the duvet, she heard her next-door neighbour Julie's excited voice saying, 'It's not right, Brian.'

They were in the front garden.

Her husband said, 'I mean, I've been to Leeds and back, I need a shower.'

'Of course you do.'

Eva thought about this exchange. Why would driving to Leeds and back necessitate having a shower? Was the northern air full of grit? Or had he been sweating on the M1? Cursing the lorries? Screaming at tailgaters? Angrily denouncing whatever the weather was doing?

She switched on the bedside lamp.

This provoked another episode of shouting outside, and demands that she, 'Stop playing silly buggers and unbolt the door!'

She realised that, although she wanted to go

downstairs and let him in, she couldn't actually leave the bed. She felt as though she had fallen into a vat of warm quick-setting concrete, and that she was powerless to move. She felt an exquisite languor spread throughout her body, and thought, 'I would have to be mad to leave this bed.'

There was the sound of breaking glass. Soon after, she heard Brian on the stairs.

He shouted her name.

She didn't answer.

He opened the bedroom door. 'There you are,' he said.

' Yes, here I am.'

'Are you ill?'

'No.'

'Why are you in bed in your clothes and shoes? What are you playing at?'

'I don't know.'

'It's empty-nest syndrome. I heard it on *Woman's Hour*.'

When she didn't speak, he said, 'Well, are you going to get up?'

'No, I'm not.'

He asked, 'What about dinner?'

'No thanks, I'm not hungry.'

'I meant what about *my* dinner? Is there anything?'

She said, 'I don't know, look in the fridge.'

He stomped downstairs. She heard his footsteps on the laminate floor he'd laid so ineptly the year before. She knew by the squeak of the floorboards that he'd gone into the sitting room. Soon he was stomping back up the stairs.

'What the bloody hell has happened to your chair?' he asked.

'Somebody left a soup spoon on the arm.'

'There's soup all over the bloody thing.'

'I know. I did it myself.'

'What – threw the soup?'

Eva nodded.

' You're having a nervous breakdown, Eva. I'm ringing your mum.'

'No!'

He flinched at the ferocity in her voice.

She saw from the stricken look in his eyes that after twenty-five years of marriage his familiar domestic world had come to an end. He went downstairs. She heard him cursing at the disconnected phone then, after a moment, stabbing at the keys. As she picked up the bedroom extension her mother was laboriously giving her phone number down the line, '0116 2 444 333, Mrs Ruby Brown-Bird speaking.'

Brian said, 'Ruby, it's Brian. I need you to come over straight away.'

'No can do, Brian. I'm in the middle of having a perm. What's up?'

'It's Eva –' he lowered his voice '– I think she must be ill.'

'Send for an ambulance then,' said Ruby irritably.

'There's nothing wrong with her physically.'

'Well, that's all right then.'

'I'll come and pick you up and bring you back so you can see for yourself.'

'Brian, I can't. I'm hosting a perm party and I've got to have my own personal solution rinsed off in half an hour. If I don't, I shall look like Harpo Marx. 'Ere, talk to Michelle.'

After a few muffled noises a young woman came on the line.

'Hello . . . Brian, is it? I'm Michelle. Can I talk you through what would happen if Mrs Bird abandoned the perm at this stage? I *am* insured, but it would be extremely inconvenient for me if I had to appear in court. I'm booked up until New Year's Eve.'

The phone was handed back to Ruby. 'Brian, are you still there?'

'Ruby, she's in bed wearing her clothes and shoes.'

'I *did* warn you, Brian. We were in the church porch about to go in, and I turned round and said to you, "Our Eva's a dark horse. She doesn't say much, and you'll never know what she's thinking . . ." ' There was a long pause, then Ruby said, 'Phone your own mam.'

The phone was disconnected.

Eva was astounded that her mother had made a lastminute attempt to sabotage her wedding. She picked up her handbag from the side of the bed and rooted through the contents, looking for something to eat. She always kept food in her bag. It was a habit from when the twins were young and hungry, and would open their mouths like the beaks of fledgling birds. Eva found a squashed packet of crisps, a flattened Bounty bar and half a packet of Polos.

She heard Brian stabbing at the keys again.

Brian was always slightly apprehensive when he called his mother. His tongue couldn't form words properly. She had a way of making him feel guilty, whatever the subject of the conversation.

His mother answered promptly with a snappy, ' Yes?'

Brian said, 'Is that you, Mummy?'

Eva picked up the extension again, being careful to muffle the mouthpiece with her hand.

'Who else would it be? Nobody else phones this house. I'm on my own seven days a week.'

Brian said, 'But . . . er . . . you . . . er . . . don't like visitors.'

'No, I don't like visitors but it would be nice to have to turn them away. Anyway, what is it? I'm halfway through *Emmerdale*.'

Brian said, 'Sorry, Mummy. Do you want to ring me back when the adverts come on?'

'No,' she said. 'Let's get it over with, whatever it is.'

'It's Eva.'

'Ha! Why am I not surprised? Has she left you? The first time I clapped eyes on that girl I knew she'd break your heart.'

Brian wondered if his heart had ever been broken. He had always had difficulty in recognising an emotion. When he had brought his First Class Bachelor of Science degree home to show his mother, her current boyfriend had said, ' You must be very happy, Brian.'

Brian had nodded his head and forced a smile, but the truth was that he didn't feel any happier than he had felt the day before, when nothing remarkable had happened.

His mother had taken the embossed certificate, examined it carefully and said, 'You'll struggle to find an astronomy job. There are men with more superior qualifications than you've got who can't find work.'

Now Brian said, mournfully, 'Eva's gone to bed in her clothes and shoes.'

His mother said, 'I can't say I'm surprised, Brian. She's always brought attention to herself. Do you remember when we all went to the caravan that Easter in 1986? She took a suitcase full of her ridiculous beatnik clothes. You don't wear beatnik clothes at Wells-Next-The-Sea. Everybody was staring at her.'

Eva screamed from upstairs, ' You shouldn't have thrown my lovely black clothes into the sea!'

Brian hadn't heard his wife scream before.

Yvonne Beaver asked, 'What's that screaming?'

Brian lied. 'It's the television. Somebody's just won a lot of money on

Eggheads.'

His mother said, 'She looked very presentable in the holiday wear I bought her.'

As Eva listened, she remembered taking the hideous clothes out of the carrier bag. They had smelled as if they had been in a damp warehouse in the Far East for years, and the colours were lurid mauves, pinks and yellows. There had been a pair of what Eva thought looked like men's sandals and a beige, pensioner-style anorak. When she tried them on, she looked twenty years older.

Brian said to his mother, 'I don't know what to do, Mummy.'

Yvonne said, 'She's probably drunk. Leave her to sleep it off.'

Eva threw the phone across the room and screamed, 'They were men's sandals she bought me in Wells-Next-The-Sea! I saw men wearing them with white socks! You should have protected me from her, Brian! You should have said, "My wife would not be seen dead in these hideous sandals!" '

She had screamed so loudly that her throat hurt. She shouted downstairs and asked Brian to bring her a glass of water.

Brian said, 'Hang on, Mummy. Eva wants a glass of water.'

His mother hissed down the phone, 'Don't you dare fetch her that water, Brian! You'll be making a rod for your own back if you do. Tell her to get her own water!'

Brian didn't know what to do. While he dithered in the hallway his mother said, 'I could do without this trouble. My knee has been playing me up. I was on the verge of ringing my consultant and asking him to chop my leg off.'

He took the phone into the kitchen with him and ran the cold tap.

His mother asked, 'Is that water I can hear running?'

Brian lied again. 'Just topping up a vase of flowers.'

'Flowers! You're lucky you can afford flowers.'

'They're out of the garden, Mummy. Eva grew them from seed.'

' You're lucky to have the space for a garden.'

The phone went dead. His mother never said goodbye.

He went upstairs with the glass of cold water. When he handed it to Eva, she took a small sip, then put it on the crowded bedside table. Brian hovered at the end of the bed. There was nobody to tell him what to do.

She almost felt sorry for him, but not enough to get out of bed. Instead, she said, 'Why don't you go downstairs and watch your programmes?'

Brian was a devotee of property programmes. His heroes were Kirstie and Phil. Unbeknown to Eva he had written to Kirstie, saying that she always looked nice, and was she married to Phil or was their partnership purely a business arrangement? He had received a reply three months later, saying 'Thank you for your interest' and signed ' Yours, Kirstie'. Enclosed was a photograph of Kirstie. She was wearing a red dress and showing an alarming amount of bosom. Brian kept the photograph inside an old Bible. He knew it would be safe there. Nobody ever opened it.

Later that night, a full bladder forced Eva out of bed. She changed from her day clothes into a pair of pyjamas that she had been keeping for emergency hospital admittance. This was on her mother's advice. Her mother believed that if your dressing gown, pyjamas and sponge bag were good quality, the nurses and doctors treated you better than the scruffs who came into hospital with their shoddy things in a Tesco's carrier bag.

Eva got back into bed and wondered what her children were doing on their first night at university. She imagined them sitting in a room together, weeping and homesick, as they had done when they first went to nursery school.

Chapter 2

Brianne was in the communal kitchen and lounge of the accommodation block. So far she had met a boy dressed like a girl, and a woman dressed like a man. They were both talking about clubs and musicians she'd never heard of.

Brianne had a short attention span and soon stopped listening, but she nodded her head and said 'Cool' when it seemed appropriate. She was a tall girl with broad shoulders, long legs and big feet. Her face was mostly hidden behind a long straggly black fringe which she pushed out of her eyes only when she actually wanted to see something.

A waiflike girl in a leopard-print maxi dress and tan Ugg boots came in with a bulging bag from Holland & Barrett which she stuffed into the fridge. Half her head had been shaved and a broken heart tattooed on to her scalp. The other half was a badly dyed lopsided green curtain.

Brianne said, 'Amazing hair. Did you do it yourself ?'

'I got my brother to help me,' the girl said. 'He's a poofter.'

The girl's sentences had a rising inflection as though she were permanently questioning the validity of her own statements.

Brianne asked, 'Are you Australian?'

The girl shouted, 'God! No!'

Brianne said, 'I'm Brianne.'

The girl said, 'I'm Poppy. Brianne? I haven't heard that before.'

'My dad's called Brian,' said Brianne tonelessly. 'Is it hard to walk in a maxi?'

'No', said Poppy. 'Try it on if you like. It might stretch to fit you.'

She pulled the maxi dress over her head and stood revealed in a wispy bra and knickers. They both looked as though they had been made from scarlet cobwebs. She seemed to have no inhibitions whatsoever. Brianne had many inhibitions. She hated everything about herself: face, neck, hair, shoulders, arms, hands, fingernails, belly, breasts, nipples, waist, hips, thighs, knees, calves, ankles, feet, toenails and voice.

She said, 'I'll try it on in my room.'

' Your eyes are amazing,' said Poppy.

'Are they?'

'Are you wearing green contacts?' asked Poppy.

She stared into Brianne's face and pushed the fringe away.

'No.'

'They're an amazing green.'

'Are they?'

'Awesome.'

'I need to lose some weight.'

' Yeah, you do. I'm a weight loss expert. I'll teach you how to be sick after every meal.'

'I don't want to be bulimic.'

'It was good enough for Lily Allen.'

'I hate being sick.'

'Isn't it worth it to be thin? Remember the saying: "You can't be too rich or too thin." '

'Who said that?'

'I think it was Winnie Mandela.'

Poppy followed Brianne to her room, still in her underwear. They met Brian Junior in the corridor as he was locking the door to his room. He stared at Poppy and she stared back. He was the most beautiful man she had ever seen. She threw her arms above her head and affected a glamour girl pose, hoping that Brian Junior would admire her C cup breasts.

He said under his breath, but loud enough to be heard, 'Gross.'

Poppy said, 'Gross? It would be really useful to me if you would elaborate. I need to know which bits of me are particularly repellent.'

Brian Junior shifted uncomfortably.

Poppy walked up and down past him, did a twirl and rested one hand on a bony hip. She then looked at him expectantly but he did not speak. Instead, he unlocked the door to his room and went back inside.

Poppy said, 'He's a baby. A rude, mindblowingly awesome-looking baby.'

Brianne said, 'We're both seventeen. We took our A levels early.'

'I would have taken mine early but I had a personal tragedy . . .' Poppy paused, waiting for Brianne to ask about the nature of the tragedy. When Brianne remained silent, she said, 'I can't talk about it. I still managed to get four A*s. Oxbridge wanted me. I went for an interview, but quite honestly I couldn't live and study somewhere so old-fashioned.'

Brianne asked, 'Where was your interview – Oxford or Cambridge?'

Poppy said, 'Do you have auditory defects? I told you, I was interviewed in *Oxbridge*.'

'And you were offered a place to study at *Oxbridge* University?' Brianne checked, 'Remind me, where is Oxbridge?'

Poppy mumbled, 'It's in the middle of the country,' and went out.

Brianne and Brian Junior had been interviewed at Cambridge University, and both of them had been offered a place. The Beaver twins' small fame had gone before them. At Trinity College they were given what looked like an impossibly difficult maths problem to solve. Brian Junior went to a separate room with an invigilator. When they each put down their pencil after fifty-five minutes of frenzied workings-out on the A4 paper supplied, the chair of the interviewing panel read their workings as if they were a chapter of a racy novel. Brianne had meticulously, if unimaginatively, worked her way straight to the solution. Brian Junior had reached it by a more mysterious path. The panel declined to ask the twins about hobbies or pastimes. It was easy to tell that they did nothing outside of their chosen field.

After the twins had turned the offer down, Brianne explained that she and her brother would follow the famous professor of mathematics Lenya Nikitanova to Leeds.

'Ah, Leeds,' said the chairperson. 'It has a remarkable mathematical faculty, world class. We tried to tempt the lovely Nikitanova here by offering her disgracefully extravagant inducements, but she emailed that she preferred to teach the children of the workers – an expression I have not heard since Brezhnev was in office – and was taking up the post of lecturer at Leeds University! Typically quixotic of her!'

Now, in Sentinel Towers student residence, Brianne said, 'I'd sooner try the dress on in private. I'm shy about my body.'

Poppy said, 'No, I'm coming in with you. I can help you.'

Brianne felt suffocated by Poppy. She did not want to let her inside her room. She did not want her as a friend but, despite her feelings, she unlocked the door and let Poppy inside.

Brianne's suitcase was open on the narrow bed. Poppy immediately began to unpack and put Brianne's clothes and shoes away in the wardrobe. Brianne sat helplessly on the end of the bed, saying, 'No, Poppy. I can do it.' She thought that when Poppy had gone, she would arrange her clothes to her own satisfaction.

Poppy opened a jewellery box decorated in tiny pearlised shells and began to try on various pieces. She pulled out the silver bracelet with the three charms: a moon, a sun and a star.

The bracelet had been bought by Eva in late August to celebrate Brianne's five A*s at A level. Brian Junior had already lost the cufflinks his mother had given him to commemorate his six A*s.

'I'll borrow this,' Poppy said.

'No!' Brianne shouted. 'Not that! It's precious to me.'

She took it from Poppy and slipped it on to her own wrist.

Poppy said, 'Omigod, you're such a materialist. Chill out.'

Meanwhile, Brian Junior paced up and down in his shockingly tiny room. It took only three steps to move from the door to the window. He wondered why his mother had not rung as she had promised.

He had unpacked earlier and everything had been neatly put away. His pens and pencils were lined up in colour order, starting with yellow and finishing with black. It was important to Brian Junior that a red pen came exactly at the centre of the line.

Earlier that day, once the twins' belongings had been brought up from the car, their laptops were being charged, and the new Ikea kettles, toasters and lamps had been plugged in, Brian, Brianne and Brian Junior had sat in a line on Brianne's bed with nothing to say to each other.

Brian had said, 'So,' several times.

The twins were expecting him to go on to speak, but he had relapsed into silence.

Eventually, he cleared his throat and said, 'So, the day has come, eh? Daunting for me and Mum, and even more so for you two – standing on your own two feet, meeting new people.'

He stood up and faced them. 'Kids, make a bit of an effort to be friendly to the other students. Brianne, introduce yourself, try to smile. They won't be as clever as you and Brian Junior, but being clever isn't everything.'

Brian Junior said, in a flat tone, 'We're here to work, Dad. If we needed "friends" we'd be on Facebook.'

Brianne took her brother's hand and said, 'It might be good to have a friend, Bri. Y'know, like, somebody I could talk to about . . .' She hesitated.

Brian supplied, 'Clothes and boys and hairdos.'

Brianne thought, 'Ugh! Hairdos? No, I'd want to talk about the wonders of the world, the mysteries of the universe.'

Brian Junior said, 'We can make friends once we've obtained our doctorates.'

Brian laughed, 'Loosen up, BJ. Get drunk, get laid, hand an essay in late, for once. You're a student, steal a traffic cone!'

Brianne looked at her brother. She could no more imagine him roaring drunk with a traffic cone on his head than she could see him on that stupid programme *Strictly Come Dancing*, clad in lime-green Lycra, dancing the rumba.

Before Brian left, there were some badly executed hugs and backslaps. Noses were kissed instead of lips and cheeks. They trod on each other's toes in their haste to leave the cramped room and get to the lift. Once there, they waited an interminable time for the lift to travel up six floors. They could hear it wheezing and grinding its way towards them.

When the doors opened, Brian almost ran inside. He waved goodbye to the twins and they waved back. After a few seconds, Brian stabbed at the Ground Floor button, the doors closed and the twins did a high five.

Then the lift returned with Brian its captive.

The twins were horrified to see that their father was crying. They were about to step in when the doors crushed shut, and the lift jerked and groaned itself downstairs.

'Why is Dad *crying*?' asked Brian Junior.

Brianne said, 'I think it's because he's sad we've left home.'

Brian Junior was amazed. 'And is that a normal response?'

'I think so.'

'Mum didn't cry when we said goodbye.'

'No, Mum thinks tears should be reserved for nothing less than tragedy.'

They had waited by the lift for a few moments to see if it would return their father again. When it did not, they went to their rooms and tried, but failed, to contact their mother.

Sue Townsend

Sue Townsend was born in Leicester in 1946 and left school at 15 years of age. She married at 18, and by 23 was a single parent with three children. She worked in a variety of jobs including factory worker, shop assistant, and as a youth worker on adventure playgrounds. She wrote in secret for twenty years, eventually joining a writers' group at the Phoenix Theatre, Leicester, in her thirties.

At the age of 35, she won the Thames Television Playwright Award for her first play, *Womberang*, and started her writing career. Other plays followed including *The Great Celestial Cow* (1984), *Ten Tiny Fingers, Nine Tiny Toes* (1990), and most recently *You, me and Wii* (2010), but she has become most well-known for her series of books about Adrian Mole, which she originally began writing in 1975.

The first of these, *The Secret Diary of Adrian Mole aged 13¾* was published in 1982 and was followed by *The Growing Pains of Adrian Mole* (1984). These two books made her the best-selling novelist of the 1980s. They have been followed by several more in the same series including *Adrian Mole: The Wilderness Years* (1993); *Adrian Mole and the Weapons of Mass Destruction* (2004); and most recently *Adrian Mole: The Prostrate Years* (2009). The books have been adapted for radio, television and theatre; the first being broadcast on radio in 1982. Townsend also wrote the screenplays for television adaptations of the first and second books, and *Adrian Mole: The Cappuccino Years* (published 1993, BBC television adaptation 2001).

Several of her books have been adapted for the stage, including *The Secret Diary of Adrian Mole aged 13¾: the Play* (1985) and *The Queen and I: a Play with Songs* (1994), which was performed by the Out of Joint Touring Company at the Vaudeville Theatre and toured Australia. The latter is based on another of her books, in which the Royal Family become deposed and take up residence on a council estate in Leicester. Other books include *Rebuilding Coventry* (1988) and *Ghost Children* (1997).

She is an honorary MA of Leicester University, and in 2008 she was made a Distinguished Honorary Fellow, the highest award the University can give. She is an Honorary Doctor of Letters at Loughborough University, and a Fellow of the Royal Society of Literature. Her other awards include the James Joyce Award of the Literary and Historical Society of University College Dublin, and the Frink Award at the Women of the Year Awards. In 2009 she was given the Honorary Freedom of Leicester, where she still lives and works.

Sue Townsend was registered blind in 2001, and had a kidney transplant in 2009. She writes using a mixture of longhand and dictation.

Sue Townsend

Does the thirtieth anniversary of the first publication of the Secret Diary feel like a milestone or a millstone?

A milestone. He's certainly not a millstone. I think that authors who complain about the success of their most well-known characters are fools; although they mostly do this in private.

How did you spend your thirtieth birthday?

Nursing a month-old baby called Elizabeth; she was the last of my four children.

How has Adrian changed over the last 30 years?

In *The Prostrate Years* Mole has become more physically attractive, and is a much more sympathetic character.

Which is your favourite Adrian Mole book?

The Prostrate Years. I've had a lot of health problems and wanted to write about serious illness, yet still write in a comic form.

Do you have a favourite diary entry from the last thirty years?

Saturday April 3 1982 – The last line in the last entry of *The Secret Diary of Adrian Mole, aged 13¾*. Written after he had tried glue sniffing and accidentally stuck a model aeroplane to his nose: '*I rang Pandora, she is coming round after her viola lesson. Love is the only thing that keeps me sane...*'

I also like the sequence of entries in the same book made when Mole was trying to paint his bedroom black to cover the Noddy wallpaper; only to be repeatedly thwarted by the bell on Noddy's hat.

What has been Adrian's biggest mistake?

To ignore the many persons who have told him that his serial killer comedy, 'The White Van', and his memoir 'Lo, the Flat Hills of my Homeland', are unpublishable. Mole does not suffer from a lack of self-belief in this regard. Also at the Dept of the Environment when he misplaced a decimal point, and erroneously stated that the projection of live newt births for Newport Pagnall was 120,000.

And his greatest triumph?

He still believes his awful novels will be published one day.
That he is still a decent, kind person.

If Adrian Mole was a teenager today, what would he be doing and writing about?

He would be exactly the same, but he wouldn't be using Twitter to memorialize his life. He would keep a secret diary. Mole's privacy is still intact.
He would not use social networking.
There are still Mole types everywhere, watching the absurdities of the world from the sidelines.

Are there any plot decisions that you made that you subsequently regretted?

I should not have made Bert Baxter so old. I hated it when I had to kill him off at the age of 105.

Sue Townsend

I regret Mole's marriage to Jo Jo, and the subsequent birth of William. It was tiresome (as it is in life) to have the child constantly there, or having to account for his whereabouts. It restricted Adrian's movements. He always had to be at the nursery at 3.15 p.m. every weekday. I solved this for myself by sending William to live with his mother in Nigeria, and then forgot about him.

Are any of the characters in the books, such as Adrian, Pandora or Pauline, based on anyone in particular?

All those characters have elements of the author within them.

Before you put pen to paper, was there any point where Adrian might have been a girl? If so, did she have a name?

No, girls are more sociable, they talk to each other about their emotional lives; boys don't.

I once wrote a column for the *London Evening Standard*, which took the form of a diary written by a teenage girl called Christabel Fox. It didn't work for me and after eighteen months it didn't work for the *Evening Standard* either.

What does the future hold for Adrian?

I don't know, but hopefully he will go onward, ever onward.

What limitations/opportunities are there to writing in diary form?

There are no limitations. The diary is one voice talking to you about people, places, events, high emotion, low spirits and the minutiae of everyday life. Diaries have a simple structure. You just plod on, day by day, week by week, month by month, until you've written a book.

What do you enjoy/dislike about the process of writing?

With each writing project I have a different type of nervous breakdown. I am convinced that I have chosen wrong words and placed them in the wrong order. Once published, I never read my own work.

There are sometimes a few exhilarating moments when the words come easily, when the tone and rhythm feel right.

It's great that writers don't have to leave the house and struggle through the rain to their place of work. They can lie in bed all day with a pen and notebook, which are the minimum requirements. Unfortunately I cannot allow myself to loll about in bed for longer than about six hours, as I am still brainwashed by the Calvinist work ethic.

Which authors have most influenced you as a writer?

In rough chronological order:

Richmal Crompton, Charlotte Brontë, Alfred E. Nuemann (*Mad* comic), Harriet Beecher Stowe, Mark Twain, Dickens, George Elliot, Oscar Wilde, Chekov, Dostoevsky, Tolstoy, Kingsley Amis, Evelyn Waugh, George Orwell, Stella Gibbons, Iris Murdoch, Flaubert, John Updike, Richard North.

Do you get much opportunity to meet or interact with your readers?

I have become a recluse lately as a result of ill health and late-onset shyness, but on rare outings I like to meet readers.

Is there any truth to the rumour put about by one A. Mole that you stole and profited from his life?

Yes. I ruthlessly exploited him. But he can't afford to sue me due to the new egislation on legal aid. Mole no longer qualifies. He should have taken me to court years ago.

THE MOLE STORY

Adrian Mole is one of the most memorable and enduring comic creations of recent decades. Long before Bridget Jones we had the diaries of the neglected intellectual of Ashby de la Zouch: neurotic, acne ridden and hopelessly devoted to Pandora Braithwaite. Mole's is a particularly British story: that of continued, almost heroic, failure. Despite his best intentions he never quite gets what he wants. Like Basil Fawlty and, more recently, David Brent, much of the comedy in these books derives from self-delusion. It is the repetition of the same errors which invests these characters with a kind of tragic grandeur. We identify with them not because they are grotesque caricatures but because we know there is something of all of us within them.

Throughout the Mole books, Townsend has offered a caustic evaluation of contemporary Britain. There is an underlying seriousness to her work, a political consciousness, the desire to attack injustice and intolerance. Townsend is able to say in a couple of sentences what it would take many political journalists a thousand words to convey. Mole is an unknowingly subversive character and that is why he causes such delight. Laugh-out-loud funny, yet often painfully sad and poignant, the Mole books reveal Townsend's natural sense of comic timing and empathetic gifts.

Garan Holcombe, British Council Contemporary Writers

1946 - 1953

Sue Townsend is born in Leicester and brought up in a semi-rural suburb, where she lives in a prefabricated bungalow on an unadopted mud road. Most of her free time is spent playing in the surrounding fields and woods of a country estate.

1953

At eight, she is frightened of her violent teacher, can't read, and has had the same book on her desk for three years. While Townsend is absent from school with mumps, her mother buys a stack of Richmal Crompton's *Just William* books, and teaches her to read in three weeks. It begins a life-long addiction to print. She reads three books a day until local librarians accuse her of attention seeking.

1960

By fourteen she excels at English, writes for the school magazine and has toured various churches and mental institutions as Jesus in the Passion of Christ. Her book addiction is sated by second-hand orange Penguin classics bought from market stalls. 'I would ponce about Leicester with the spines of the books pointing to the public. A very indifferent public.' After a school visit to Rome, Capri and Naples, returning to the dour greyness of 1950s Leicester badly affects the young Townsend. After this trauma, and heavily influenced by a recent reading of Dostoevsky: 'I took to the black. White face, white lips, black eyes, black clothing. Juliette Greco bohemian.'

Entering the only coffee bar in town, copy of *The Idiot* in hand, and asking a man who looks intelligent how to pronounce Dostoevsky, she is immediately accepted as a part of Leicester bohemian society. There are few suitable careers in Leicester for a black-clad aesthete with no qualifications. As school leaving day approaches Townsend is urged by her Drama and English teachers to transfer to the Grammar School and take some exams; but the uniform would cost her parents a month's wages, and she leaves school a week before her fifteenth birthday. She works in a shoe factory, sells encyclopaedias door to door, and is sacked from the best and most pretentious dress shop in Leicestershire for reading Oscar Wilde in a changing cubicle. She works as a petrol attendant, with a paperback stuffed into the BP standard-issue duffle coat. She misses writing and carries on in secret.

1964

At eighteen she marries a sheet metal-worker; the marriage doesn't last, and at twenty-three she is on her own with three young children and three jobs. Always tired and always worried, she writes semi-autobiographical prose and poetry when the children are asleep and hides it.

The only good job is at the youth club on her estate, where she works for eleven years, overhearing the conversations adults are not meant to hear. It leads to building and running an adventure playground on the tougher estate next-door. She writes pantomimes and plays for the children, receiving regular deputations of young men requesting knife-fight scenes.

1975 Summer

'I was living in a council house at the time, on my own with three kids and three part-time jobs to keep us going. So Sunday was a total collapse; I was exhausted. My eldest son said, 'Why can't we go to safari parks like other families do?' The answer is that they have no money, no car and she feels sorry for the animals, but his martyred tone triggers the memory of her own harsh criticism of the adult world as a powerless child: 'That adolescent, self-pitying voice. Mole's voice. I just heard it. He descended with his family in the space of an afternoon.' She writes it down in diary form, completing the opening two and a half months in one burst, files it in a box and forgets it.

1978

She meets Colin Broadway, who will become her second husband.

Three weeks after the birth of their daughter she admits to him that she writes secretly, and has done for twenty years. It fills a fridge-box stuffed into the under-stairs cupboard. He has heard of a writers' group at the Phoenix Theatre, and encourages her to join.

The Phoenix is Leicester's 300-seat 'second' theatre, with a writers group which uses actors to perform new plays. She attends two meetings without speaking. At the third, director Ian Giles asks her to bring some work that they can read and discuss. She has never written a play, but returns two weeks later with *Womberang*, a comedy set in a gynaecological waiting room. It has ten female parts, one male, and lasts thirty minutes. The structure is 'unorthodox', but as soon as the actors begin to read they are laughing out loud.

1979

Ian Giles puts *Womberang* forward for the 1979 Thames Television Playwright Award. John Mortimer is chair of the panel; he likes the play, reads it aloud and makes his fellow judges laugh. Townsend wins the prize, a £2,000 bursary to work for a year as writer in residence at the sponsoring theatre. She is terrified, and her training as a professional dramatist begins.

1980
July

Phoenix actor Nigel Bennett is auditioning for *Huckleberry Finn* and asks Townsend if she has anything he can use. She remembers the Mole diary and digs out the handwritten script. Bennett is the first to perform the Mole character, in a writers' group meeting. He types the script up and works on adapting it for a one-man show.

October

Townsend rewrites part of the original diary for a new local arts publication, edited by Leicester playwright David Campton, and put together on her kitchen table. Mole is published for the first time in the October 1980 edition of *the arts journal magazine*, under the title *Excerpts From the Secret Diary of Nigel Mole, aged 14 ¾*.

November

On a visit to Townsend's home, her theatrical agent Janet Fillingham sees a file of Mole material.

Fillingham thinks it would make a good radio script and sends a Nigel Mole monologue to Vanessa Whitburn at BBC Radio Birmingham. Ms Whitburn turns it down.

1981
February

A version of 'The Diary of Nigel Mole' is sent to the Assistant Head of Radio Drama for Radio 4, John Tydeman. It sit on his desk for a month, but 'When I finally read it, I thought it was marvellous.' He decides to produce it as a thirty-minute monologue.

March 10th

John Tydeman officially commissions 'The Diary of Nigel Mole' for Radio Four, and promises more episodes will be considered 'if it is as successful as it ought to be'.

April

There are concerns at the BBC that the character's name is too similar to the public schoolboy Nigel Molesworth, from the *Down with Skool!* books by Geoffrey Willans. Tydeman writes to Townsend that the character is established as Nigel Mole and will be broadcast under that title. He advises her that there 'is a lot of mileage in Mole' and that she should try to get a diary published.

September

Janet Fillingham sends the radio script to Geoffrey Strachan at Methuen, who is responsible for the Monty Python books and Simon Bond's hugely successful *101 Uses of a Dead Cat*. He is, in the words of Fillingham's colleague Giles Gordon, later Townsend's agent – 'the greatest publisher of the humour book'.

November/December

Geoffrey Strachan is keen on the script and the writer. 'I met Sue soon after and was immediately impressed. She was very funny and had a tremendous sense of what she was doing.' He requests a treatment for the book that he can sell to the Methuen board, but is unhappy with the similarity to 'Nigel Molesworth' and asks for a name change. Townsend sends him a typescript treatment using 'Malcolm Mole'. A contract is signed with Methuen.

'Malcolm' reminds Townsend of blocked sinuses and she looks for an alternative. A handwritten sheet shows her working through some unlikely variations; wisely putting a cross next to the name of her second son, who would have been very unhappy with 'Daniel Mole'. She is looking for something 'upper working class', unthreatening, with a soft, feminine quality. After the low point of 'Darius' and 'Marius', 'Adrian' appears twice at the right-hand side of the page.

Townsend is not convinced and writes to Strachan, asking him to reconsider. 'Are you absolutely dead set against "Nigel Mole"? I am suffering severe withdrawal symptoms. I have lived closely with Nigel for a couple of years and Adrian can't take his place. I've tried to accommodate him but failed.' Strachan's long experience as a publisher tells him that the two characters would always be confused, and he is not persuaded. It is a bad moment for university lecturer Adrian Mole, who in an interview in a Sunday broadsheet, claimed that his life has been ruined by sniggering students.

1982
January 2nd
The Diary of Nigel Mole, aged 13¾ is broadcast on Radio Four's Thirty Minute Theatre, read by Nicholas Barnes. *The Times* calls it 'a delightful original', and within days five publishers have contacted John Tydeman.

April/May
The book is sent to Strachan in instalments. He commissions Caroline Holden to provide the illustrations. A number of people at Methuen are in favour of printing 3,000 copies, but Strachan thinks the book is 'a bit special' and decides on a first edition of 7,500, at the accessible price of £4.95.

Townsend asks Strachan if her name can be removed from the cover, arguing that 'It was supposed to be written by a 13¾-year-old boy. It seemed stupid to have my name on it. But he said gravely it was a wonderful thing to write a book, and that I should take the credit.' She has an advance of £1,500 and is worried about covering it.

'I thought Methuen were mad to print 7,500. I thought it would be remaindered by Christmas'.

June
The Methuen sales team are selling the book before it even exists. Often the booksellers have heard the radio production and are enthusing about the character to the reps.

July 30th
In the first mention of an Adrian Mole book in print media, Leo Cooper in *Publishing News* praises 'The funniest book I have read for ages...I welcome a genuine new talent.'

September
Pre-publicity is limited, with very few author interviews. There are serializations in the *Evening Standard* and *Woman's Realm*, and Radio Four puts out seven 15-minute episodes to a hugely positive response. Tom Sharpe reads an advance copy and is reduced to tears of laughter. The most successful comic novelist of the time gives a rave review for the jacket.

October 7th
The Secret Diary of Adrian Mole, aged 13¾ is published by Methuen. The initial run sells out before publication. The book is reprinted and continues to sell quickly through word of mouth; helped by a Jilly Cooper review which calls it 'touching and screamingly funny', and comparing it to *Catcher in the Rye*. Strachan commissions a sequel.

October 31st

The book enters the *Sunday Times* bestseller charts at number six. Townsend idly scans the book charts as usual and is amazed, delighted and relieved.

November

The *Secret Diary* tops the best-seller list.
It will remain in the charts for twenty weeks.
Thames buy the TV rights for ITV.

1983

By the end of January hardback sales are over 60,000.

October 27th

The paperback edition of the *Secret Diary* is published. The book
reaches the widest possible audience and sales explode. According to
David Ross, marketing director of Methuen, 'it started with the parent
generation and filtered downwards. The paperback put Adrian Mole
into the school playground.' Adrian Mole is one of the rare popular
classics that was originally written for adults and eventually appealed
to every generation.

November 7th

The paperback hits number one in the *Sunday Times* bestseller charts, with
275,000 copies in print. More than two years later it is still at number two,
kept from the top spot by its sequel.

1984

At the end of March sales have exceeded 600,000. Strachan estimates it is
selling 10,000 copies per week. Townsend has spent the winter and spring
working on the sequel, and by April Methuen have the complete manuscript
of *The Growing Pains of Adrian Mole*.

August 2nd

The Growing Pains of Adrian Mole is published. On publication day
100,000 hardback copies are in print, supplied in a 56-copy
string-vest display box.

September

250,000 hardback copies of *Growing Pains* have been sold.
Sue Townsend has the number one book in both hardback and
paperback charts. After the Frankfurt book fair Paul Marsh has
sold translation rights to every country in Western Europe.

November

The paperback edition of the *Secret Diary* has sold more than one million copies.

Adrian Mole: The Play, premiered at the Phoenix Theatre in Leicester, begins a run of two years in the West End.

1985

In January hardback sales of *Growing Pains* stand at 450,000.

1st August

The paperback of *The Growing Pains of Adrian Mole* is published, enters the bestseller chart at number one, and stays there for over a year.

September

The Secret Diary of Adrian Mole is premiered on ITV, written by Townsend and Trevor Waite, starring Gian Sammarco as Adrian Mole, Julie Walters as Pauline and Beryl Reid as Grandma Mole. Sammarco has been chosen from 6,000 applicants. *Mole* runs for two series, with Lulu taking over as Pauline Mole for season two, *The Growing Pains of Adrian Mole*, written by Patrick Barlow. The theme song by Ian Dury, 'Profoundly in Love with Pandora', reaches 45 in the singles charts.

November

The paperback editions of the Mole books remain at the top of the bestseller chart two years after the original paperback publication of the *Secret Diary*. Total paperback sales are approaching four million.

1986

The two original Mole books are published in the US by Grove, as a one volume edition, *The Adrian Mole Diaries*. The reviews are characterized as 'simply extraordinary' by the publisher. The great American comedienne Phyllis Diller is an early fan: 'A wonderfully touching, hilarious book. It goes beyond *Catcher in the Rye*. You must read it. Trust me!' *Newsweek* pronounces that 'Adrian Mole, superstar, has become one of the biggest successes in the history of British publishing'. The *New York Times* raves: 'Part Woody Allen, part a kindred spirit to Philip Roth's early novellas...as sad and devastating as it is laugh-out-loud funny!

1990

In an end-of-the-decade survey in the *Guardian*, headlined 'Mole triumphant over Archer', *The Secret Diary of Adrian Mole* is the top paperback of the eighties, with three million copies sold, beating *Kane and Abel* by Jeffrey Archer into second place. Jackie Collins and Barbara Taylor Bradford trail behind. *The Growing Pains of Adrian Mole* is the top hardback. Total Mole sales in English alone total six million and Sue Townsend is the best-selling author of the eighties in terms of individual books. Later, through a third party, Archer lets it be known that he would like to speak to her. Townsend has little to discuss with the ex-Deputy Chairman of the Conservative Party, and a meeting doesn't take place.

1993
August 31st

Adrian Mole: The Wilderness Years is published with a 'New Adult Adrian Mole!' sticker on the front. Mole begins the book wearing a blazer and ends it swimming naked in the Aegean.

1999

Following consolidation within the publishing industry and the loss of key staff at Methuen, Townsend moves to Penguin, who acquire the rights to her future books and the Adrian Mole backlist.

Michael Joseph publish *Adrian Mole: The Cappuccino Years*. It is a number one bestseller and remains in the top three for four months.

2000

Penguin publish the paperback edition of *Adrian Mole: The Cappuccino Years*. The original audio-book is read by Nigel Planer, a later issue by Paul Daintry.

2001

Adrian Mole: the Cappuccino Years is produced as a six-part series for BBC1, written by Townsend, with Stephen Mangan as Adrian Mole, Alison Steadman as Pauline Mole, Helen Baxendale as Pandora, Zoe Wanamaker as Tania Braithewaite, Alun Armstrong as George Mole, and Keith Allen as Peter Savage.

Mole fan Steven Mangan also reads the audio book re-recording of *The Secret Diary of Adrian Mole*.

2004

Adrian Mole and The Weapons of Mass Destruction is published to wide acclaim, spends three months in the top ten, and is one of *The Village Voice*'s books of the year.

2007

Adrian Mole and The Weapons of Mass Destruction is re-released in the classic Penguin three-pane orange cover as one of the 'Celebrations' series.

2009
Autumn

As Townsend's health suffers she is drawn to the subject of serious illness, and gives Adrian prostate 'trouble'. He is maddened by the mispronunciation of prostate to 'prostrate' by his family and friends. *Adrian Mole – The Prostrate Years* is published by Michael Joseph in early November.

Sue Townsend's papers, including the original Adrian Mole manuscripts, are held in the Special Collections archives at the University of Leicester, where she is a Distinguished Honorary Fellow, the highest award the University can give. She is an Honorary Doctor of Letters at Loughborough University and a Fellow of the Royal Society of Literature. Her awards include the Frink Award at the Women of the Year Awards, and a James Joyce Award of the Literary and Historical Society of University College Dublin. In 2009 she was given the Honorary Freedom of Leicester.

ADRIAN'S CV

Name: Adrian Albert Mole

DOB: 2nd April 1967

Place of Birth: Leicester, England

Address: 1 The Old Pigsty
The Piggeries
Bottom Field
Lower Lane
Mangold Parva
Leicestershire

Height: 5 feet seven inches

Weight: 10 Stones eight pounds *in 1989*

Marital Status: Married *but only just*

Next of kin: Mr and Mrs George Mole
2 The Old Pigsty
The Piggeries *etc. etc. an alarming proximity*

Key Skills:
— Novelist *(unpublished: see enclosed literary CV for explanation)*
— Poet *(ditto)*
— Playwright *(unperformed)*
— Fluent in Antiquarian Book Phraseology
— Offal Cheffing
— Parenting
— Proficient in cycling *(major village-town commute)*

Current Employment:
— Senior Bookseller and Assistant Manager, Carlton-Hayes'
Second-hand and Antiquarian Books; High Street, Leicester
takings last week: £132.69

Employment History and Reasons for Leaving:

— Catering Manager - Eddie's Tea Bar

Two months frying burgers and changing the Calor-gas cylinder in an A46 lay-by. I couldn't forget Eddie's warning words on my first day: 'You'll never shake off the stink of the fat, lad. It makes it hard to get a woman outside the trade.'

— Turkey Operative (Seasonal) — Mr Nobby Brown, Poulterer

plucking recently deceased birds with six cackling women in an ill-lit shed

— Presenter of *Offaly Good!* (Pie Crust Productions)
  Millennium Channel, Wednesdays, 10.30 a.m
  (Co-presenter Dev Singh)
  I realised that cooking offal and/or television presenting
  was not my forte.

It was the review from A.A. Gill in *The Times*:
'Offally Good! is offally bad. A wooden presenter, Adrian Mole, stumbles and bumbles his way through twenty minutes of Cross-roads-quality TV. We watch with horrible fascination as he makes sheep's head broth. After twenty minutes Mole produces a pot of grey liquid, on the surface of which floats a layer of scum.'

And the G2 section of the *Guardian*:
'Dev's dazzling wit and uproarious physical comedy is in glorious contrast to the dour televisual presence of Adrian Mole, a pedant from Middle England.'

Employment History continued:

— Head Chef (Offal) at Hoi Polloi, Dean Street, London

I was reviewed in the national press: A.A. Gill in the Sunday Times
The memory still hurts:
'The sausage on my plate could have been a turd: it looked like a
turd, it tasted like a turd, it smelled like a turd, it had the texture
of a turd. In fact, thinking about it, it probably was a turd.'

— Assistant Chef at Savages, Dean Street, London

washer upper, vegetable chopper

— Security consultant — Bell Safe, Evington, Leicester

Three weeks selling alarms door to door for the alluring Bellinda
Bellingham. A low point in my life. My sales patter started: 'Don't
you think your family deserves more protection from the dark forces
of evil that are at large in our community?'

— Civil Service Scientific Officer Grade One
    Department of the Environment - Wildlife, Oxford

— Newt Development Officer,
    with later responsibility for Badgers and Natterjack toads

sacked due to bogus biology A level certificate

— Library Assistant — Leicester Central Lending Library

I left after a dispute over Jane Austen with Miss Froggatt, the
head librarian. I still maintain that her work is romantic fiction and
does not belong in the literary stacks

— Paper delivery boy — Mr Cherry's Newsagent

Resigned after Mr Cherry attempted to pervert me with free copies of
Big 'n' Bouncy

Voluntary Work:

— Writing/Directing/Producing/Training
  actor-dogs for the Mangold Parva Community Play

— Chairman of the Leicestershire and Rutland Writers' Group
Two members remaining

— I am perpetually surrounded by needy pensioners

Education:

inadequate due to parental indifference
and lack of Anglepoise lamp

Recreations:

— Writing

— Reading

— Purchasing Stationary

— Letter Writing

— Contemplating Nature
Depressingly, I am tempted to add bickering with wife, eating crab
paste sandwiches and satisfying mild addiction to both Starburst
(formerly Opal Fruits) and hardcore Nurofen. Is this the summation
of my life so far?

References:

Mr. Hugh Carlton-Hayes, Antiquarian Bookseller

Dr. Pandora Braithwaite MP (with whom I once shared a flat in Oxford)

ADRIAN'S LITERARY CV

I am attempting to write my literary CV. I feel the need to reassess my writing career and the inexplicably negative critical response to my work. What to include from the vast body of material I have accumulated over the years? This is my hesitant first draft; it lacks a certain Je ne sais quoi that only I can do.

LITERARY CURRICULUM VITAE (BREVIS)

Adrian A. Mole

Published Work:

— *Offally Good! – The Book!* (Stoat Books, 1991)
  Cookbook based on the cult Millennium Channel offal cookery show

Ghost-written in five days by Pauline Mole for 50% of all royalties and residuals. This explains chapter ten, 'The Future For Men Is Bleak', and the general over-emphasis on gender politics. My three-month struggle with the text tragically led to only one recipe - for pig's trotters. My foreword - a learned treatise on primitive man's experiments with the offal cut out of woolly mammoths etc. - which started so brilliantly, sadly came to nothing.

  Reviewed in the *Sunday Times* Book Section - 'Briefly' column:
  '100 ways with offal – a hoot.'

I bought six copies of the *Sunday Times*. My mother rang later to ask if I'd seen 'her' review

LITERARY CURRICULUM VITAE (BREVIS)

Unpublished Work: everything else

Novels

— *Lo! The Flat Hills of My Homeland*
Later to be titled: *Birdwatching*
A Lawrentian treatment of late twentieth-century man and his
dilemma, as Jake Westmoreland returns to the town of his birth after
experiencing The World

— *Sparg from Kronk*
Or *Krog of Gork*
Originally a novel by Jake Westmoreland, hero of *Lo!*
The novel without language within Jake Westmoreland's novels was
praised as 'a brilliant concept', by the renowned novelist and celebrity
Angela Hacker. Faxos – April 1992

Query: was Angela Hacker just being kind? She was drunk on Amstel
most of the time. Is a novel without language within the hero's
unfinished Stone Age novel without dialogue within my novel about
the dilemma of 20th century man worthy of the adjective 'brilliant'?
I wish I knew.

— *Sty*
The intellectual progress of a discontented pig

{My diary from Wednesday, April 12 1999 shows some early difficulties:

I embarked on a new novel, *Sty*, today. Progress was slow. I only
managed to write 104 words, including the title and my name.

LITERARY CURRICULUM VITAE (BREVIS)

Sty, by Adrian Mole

The pig grunted in its sty. It was deeply sad. Somehow it felt different from the other pigs with which it shared a home.

'Look at them,' thought the pig. 'They are oblivious to the fact that they are merely part of the food chain.' The pig had felt discontented since it had glimpsed Alain de Botton's TV programme, *Philosophy: A Guide to Life*, through a gap in the pig farmer's curtain. The wisdom of Socrates, Epicurus and Montaigne had brought home to the pig that it was completely uneducated and knew nothing of the world beyond the sty.

Notes on new novel:
1. Should the pig have a name?
2. Should the pig's thoughts be in quotes?
3. Has the story got legs? Or is the main protagonist (the pig) too restricting a character, ie., being (a) unable to communicate with the other pigs and (b) never leaving the sty?

Epic Poetry

— *The Restless Tadpole*
  A tadpole's journey from the early days of frogspawnhood to the dying moments of old frogdom

Prospectus for Monograph (Non-fiction)

— *Celebrity and Madness*
  (A work in progress)
  Charts the rise of celebritocracy and the subsequent demise of democracy in Britain today
  I present part of the original preface:

LITERARY CURRICULUM VITAE (BREVIS)

I have been working on a book called *Celebrity and Madness*, for some weeks. On many an occasion I have stayed up until almost midnight; honing the sentences, adding the adjectives and creating new verbs. (I distinctly remember, while watching the Olympics with my mother, asking her 'Has Britain medalled yet?')

But, I digress. *Celebrity and Madness* is a well-researched work – many copies of the *News of the World*, *Hello* and *Heat* magazines were read. Scores of letters were written, though it must be said that few celebrities had the courtesy to reply. I listened to countless anecdotes told by my dearest friend, the recently disgraced Dr. Pandora Braithwaite M.P., former junior minister in the Department of the Environment, whose own book, *Out of the Box* was published last year, and condemned by *Playboy*, who said, 'leaves a bad taste in the mouth'.

The book contains many examples of celebrities and their madness:

David Beckham has locked the keys inside his car on 91 different occasions!
Prince Charles tried to teach his favourite dog, Toby, to recite the Lord's Prayer!
Liz Hurley keeps a succession of lucky spiders in a customized, Gucci, matchbox!
Sven Goran-Eriksson has a photograph of a long-dead pet reindeer on his bedside table!

Professor Laurie Taylor, the eminent sociologist, was sent a rough first draft and returned a compliment slip acknowledging receipt

Situation Comedy

— *The White Van*
A serial killer comedy, hopefully starring Russell Brand as the serial killer and Kerry Katona as his wife.
(The performers have yet to be approached).

LITERARY CURRICULUM VITAE (BREVIS)

Plays

— *Plague!*

Writer/Dramaturg of a community play involving the total population of Mangold Parva (144 Souls plus intelligent animals), loosely based on the fact that the village was a centre for the Black Death. The animals are required to take part.

A typical stage direction would be: 'The dogs bow their heads in unison and the chicken goes to centre stage and lays an egg'. This coup de theatre may require the help of an animal trainer.
Difficult, but I think we can pull it off.

Agent : Brick Eagleburger at Brick Eagleburger Associates
brickeagleburger@yanklit.com

Tuesday, November 21, 2000:
Brick Eagleburger has sent my epic poem, The Restless Tadpole, to a certain Geoffrey Perkins at BBC TV Centre. I asked Brick which department Mr Perkins worked in. Brick said, 'The guy's head of fuckin' comedy.' I angrily pointed out that The Restless Tadpole is an entirely serious dramatic work written in the tradition of the Icelandic sagas. Brick said, 'Listen up, Adrian, I flicked through the fuckin' manuscript Tadpole and I godda tell ya I almost peed my fuckin' pants, it's so funny.' Brick carried on, 'My favourite scene is when the tadpole is lying in Marilyn Monroe's garden pond and it overhears Arthur Miller talking crap about Tolstoy.'

I have always known that Brick Eagleburger is a Philistine; however, he is now totally misrepresenting me and my work.

This is where Mr Eagleburger and myself parted company for a while.

ADRIAN'S FAMILY TREE

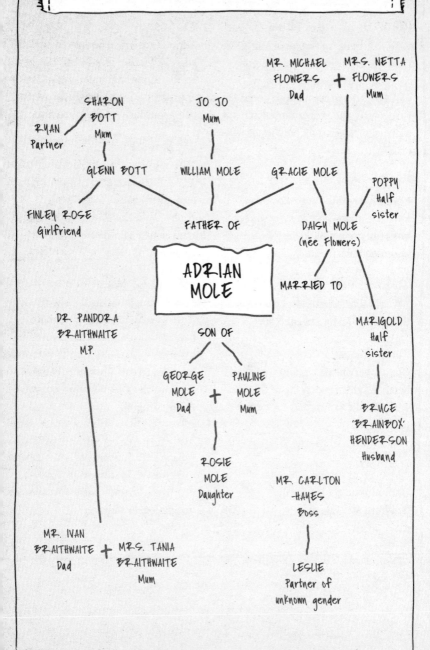

ADRIAN'S FAMILY TREE

MOLE, Daisy (née Flowers):
Wife of Adrian, half-sister of Marigold.
Dark, ravishing ex-PR to the famous
who claims to be 'author of my own
life'. Loathes the countryside, longs for
Dean Street and is not amused at being
reduced to flogging off her Jimmy Choos
on eBay.

MOLE, Gracie:
Adrian's daughter. A precocious
mini-Stalinist who hates her nursery
uniform, preferring to drag her little
mermaid tail to school.

BOTT, Glenn:
Adrian's illegitimate son by Sharon
Bott, in the Royal Logistics corp.

Finley Rose:
Glenn's very beautiful and well-
balanced girlfriend. A fan of *Silent
Witness*, she aspires to be a forensic
pathologist.

BOTT, Sharon:
Old flame of Adrian's. Mother of Glenn
Bott. Also mother of Kent,
Bradford and Caister.

Ryan:
Sharon Bott's partner, a youth of
27 years.

Jo Jo:
Adrian's ex-wife. Has moved back to
Nigeria. Mother of William. Has beauty
brains, money and talent, and frankly
was out of Adrian's league, as well as
being four inches taller than him.

MOLE, William:
Adrian's young son by African princess
Jo Jo. After his parents' separation,
brought up by the Mole family in
Ashby-de-la-Zouch. Unsurprisingly
returns to his mother in Nigeria,
changing his name to Wole Mole.

FLOWERS, Marigold:
Thirty-something on-the-shelf
depressive who once accidentally
became Adrian's girlfriend and is now
his sister-in-law. Now married to Brain
box Henderson, über-geek before it wa
fashionable. They regularly converse in
fluent Klingon.

HENDERSON, Bruce 'Brainbox':
Adrian's old schoolmate and husband
of Marigold. He also owns his own
company, Idiotech, who specialize in
'technology for idiots'.

FLOWERS, Michael:
Father of Marigold and Daisy, proprietor of Country Organics. Keen member of the Madrigal Society.

FLOWERS, Netta:
Wife of Michael and mother of Marigold and Daisy, another Madrigal.

FLOWERS, Poppy:
Sister of Marigold with extraordinarily long hair.

MOLE, George:
Adrian's father. Although his many episodes of hospitalization, depression, unemployment and erectile dysfunction have taken their toll, he is still chain smoking and has had an ashtray welded onto the arm of his wheelchair. Despite their various tribulations, he still loves Pauline Mole.

MOLE, Pauline:
Adrian's perennially unfulfilled mother. Living in a semi-detached converted pigsty with the stroke-ridden George Mole is not how she expected things to turn out. Still possessing a certain tawdry glamour, she is determined to have one last sexual fling before she dies.

MOLE, Rosie:
Adrian's much younger sister. Has adopted the 'rebel' persona, and is currently failing at Leeds University alongside her latest inelegantly wasted boyfriend. The doubts about her paternity are finally settled live on *The Jeremy Kyle Show*.

BRAITHWAITE, Ivan:
Father of Pandora. Supposedly freelance dairy management consultant and freethinker.

BRAITHWAITE, Dr. Pandora:
Adrian Mole's beautiful, treacle-haired first girlfriend and lifelong obsession. Now a Junior Minister in the Foreign Office. Willing to confide in Adrian as a trusted friend, but her autobiography *Out of the Box* has two entries under 'Mole, Adrian', and 112 under 'Lovers'.

BRAITHWAITE, Tania:
Mother of Pandora. Teaches Women's Studies at De Montford university.

CARLTON-HAYES, Mr:
Adrian's employer.

Leslie:
Mr Carlton-Hayes' partner of unknown gender.

THE ADRIAN MOLE DIARIES

The Secret Diary of Adrian Mole Aged 13 ¾ & The Growing Pains of Adrian Mole

(January 1981 – June 1983)

BAXTER, Bert

Belligerent and filthy 89-year-old communist who has sworn not to die until capitalism is destroyed; eventually becoming the oldest man in Leicester. Lives on beetroot sandwiches, Vesta curry and brown ale, and speaks fluent Hindi. After joining 'Good Samaritans' in a misguided attempt to avoid maths, Adrian becomes his toe-nail cutter, bottle washer and friend for the next sixteen years.

BRAITHWAITE, Pandora

Adrian Mole's beautiful, treacle-haired first girlfriend and lifelong obsession. In youth, a pony riding swot whose motto is 'get to Oxford or die'; she soon leaves Adrian and 'the wretched provinces' far behind. Academic stardom smoothes her way to Parliament, the edge of power and a love affair with the TV cameras. A political Helen of Troy, her ambitious path to become Labour's first woman Prime Minister is littered with strategic conquests. Although willing to confide in Adrian as a trusted friend, her autobiography *Out of the Box* has two entries under 'Mole, Adrian', and 112 under 'lovers'.

BRAITHWAITE, Ivan

Father of Pandora. In 1981 a self-satisfied, bourgeois-left dairy accountant. After transforming into a freelance information consultant he suffers several episodes of technology-induced mania and Choice Overload Syndrome. Involved in the great Mole family partner swap. A sartorial disaster area.

BRAITHWAITE, Tania

Mother of Pandora. A pretentious well-groomed bohemian who later loses her dress sense after a mild stroke. Also involved in the great Mole family partner swap. A fanatical devotee of Japanese gardening, she can often be seen raking the gravel.

Dog, The

The Mole dog, never given a proper name by family tradition. Follows Adrian to school, stands in front of the television and is always expensively at the vet's.

ELLIOT, Courtney

Erudite ex-academic postman with a red-spotted bow tie and ruffled shirt.

Will help with exam-coaching and lend a fiver when the giro fails to arrive.

KENT, Barry

Adrian's nemesis and tormenter. School bully and local yob leader. Taught to read in prison, he performs as 'Baz the skinhead poet' and fashions a career as a poet and novelist, delighting the intelligentsia with political rants in an exaggerated Leicester accent. His modern classic, 'Dork's Diary' featuring Aiden Vole' is still selling strongly. Adrian is constantly surprised by the extent of his hatred for Kent, which is undiminished after twenty years.

LEMON, Rick

Socially conscious leader of the 'Off the Streets' youth club, where he encourages Adrian to be an individual and throw off his petit-bourgeois shackles. Has since moved out of a squat and bought a new semi on the Badger's Copse Barrett estate.

LUCAS, Mr (Creep Lucas)

Next-door neighbour to the Mole family. A smarmy, self-assured insurance salesman. Embarks on a doomed affair with Pauline Mole which ends badly in a Sheffield bed-sit. Believes himself to be Rosie Mole's father.

LUCAS, Mrs

Estranged wife of Mr Lucas who left him for another woman.

MANCINI, Hamish

Adrian's American 'holiday friend' who becomes an unwanted pen pal and guest. Overenthusiastic and under analysis; his psychiatrist in New York is doing great things with his libido.

MOLE, George

Adrian's father. His many episodes of hospitalization, depression, unemployment and erectile dysfunction have taken their toll. A cynical persona hides a self-pitying, sentimental streak; will admit to crying over *Jonathan Livingston Seagull*, the only 'literature' he has ever read. Has made several attempts to join the middle-classes by pronouncing his aitches, but is sabotaged by his liking for HP sauce on toast and a lack-lustre employment history. In later life dresses to give the impression that he was once in the music business, but will always look like a retired storage heater salesman. Despite their many tribulations he still loves Pauline Mole, but yearns for pre-feminist times when she wore high heels in the house and women were not allowed to captain warships.

PRINCIPAL CHARACTERS

THE ADRIAN MOLE DIARIES

MOLE, Albert (Granddad Mole)

George Mole's father, Adrian's long-dead grandfather, whose memory is revered by May Mole. Shaved daily in the trenches at Ypres even though rats ate his soap. A rich source of inspiration for Adrian's various therapists.

MOLE, May (Grandma Mole)

George Mole's mother; Adrian's fearsome grandmother. The only real authority figure in the Mole family, the provider of proper Sunday dinners, constant electricity and unwanted religion. An enemy of Bert Baxter, whom she regards as a disruptive influence on Evergreen's coach trips.

MOLE, Pauline (née Sugden)

Adrian's mother is a mass of contradictions; an ardent feminist in the early eighties, she nevertheless still tends to define herself by the men in her life. She has a tawdry glamour and would not pick the milk up from the doorstep without first applying her lipstick. Pauline knows that she has not reached her full potential: 'I haven't got a single letter after my name and only Mrs in front.' She craves drama and excitement, which could explain why she has been married five times, (three to the same man, George Mole), and is very fond of litigation. Stumbling over a cracked paving slab, in Pauline's world, is a marvellous opportunity to make money and appear as a dramatic witness in the Small Claims court. As George Mole's health deteriorates, Pauline finds that she is not a natural nurse; the virtues of patience and constancy are foreign to her, as are the domestic arts — she was a pioneering and enthusiastic user of boil-in-the-bag convenience meals.

She has balsamic vinegar and HP sauce on the table, Barbara Taylor Bradford and Raymond Carver on her bookshelves and records *The Jeremy Kyle Show* and *Newsnight* on Sky Plus. She is determined to have one last sexual fling before she dies.

MOLE, Rosie

Adrian's much younger sister. Since the day he witnessed her birth she has been a worry to him. At three she was 'Rosemary' and followed him 'like a little shadow'; by fourteen a foul-mouthed vamp who regarded him with loathing. Although reconciled with Adrian, she has been known to spend Christmas day in Hull with a crack addicted boyfriend rather than endure the Mole family celebrations. There have always been doubts about her paternity.

MOLE, Susan

Adrian's aunt. A prison officer at Holloway, smokes Panama cigars and is partner to the glamorous and sexy Gloria

HETHERINGTON, Nigel

Adrian's life-long best friend, a cynical observer of his suffering over the years. Nigel's abundant consumer goods are a constant reminder to the young Adrian of his relative poverty and parental neglect. A seeker, Nigel flirts with various sexualities, religions and subcultures, finally escaping to London for 'music and sex' after being removed from NatWest counters for wearing Buddhist robes. Well connected in the Soho 'pink mafia', he is registered blind in 2002 and returns to Leicester embittered and unemployed.

Queenie

Bert Baxter's new wife, described by Adrian as 'one of those loud types of old lady that dyes her hair and tries to look young'. Their romance scandalizes the residents of the Alderman Cooper Sunshine Home.

SCRUTON, Mr (Pop-eyed Scruton)

Manic Headmaster of Neil Armstrong Comprehensive School who terrifies pupils and staff alike. His fanatical belief in dress standards is indirectly responsible for Adrian's Pandora Braithwaite fixation, via the 'red socks' protest movement. A devout admirer of Mrs Thatcher.

SINGH FAMILY

The Mole family's new next-door neighbours, temporary carers for Bert Baxter.

SLATER, Doreen (Stick Insect)

George Mole's anorexic lover, a single mother with 'no bust and no bum'. Mother of Adrian's half-brother Brett.

TYDEMAN, John

Kindly Assistant Head of Radio Drama for the BBC. The accidental recipient of Adrian's handwritten manuscripts, ensuring torment and large return postage bills for many years. Later Head of Radio Drama.

SABRE

Bert Baxter's irritable, vicious Alsatian. Fellow Alsatians cower as he passes by. Needs a four-mile daily walk or he chews the sink for entertainment.

SUGDEN, Mr & Mrs

Adrian's maternal grandparents. Norfolk potato farmers incapable of enjoying themselves unless something is being harvested or slaughtered. They have never understood why Pauline Mole abandoned the black fields for the bright lights of Leicester, but see it as their duty to spend every Christmas disapproving of her 'wanton' lifestyle.

PRINCIPAL CHARACTERS

THE ADRIAN MOLE DIARIES

True Confessions of Adrian Albert Mole, including Adrian Mole and the Small Amphibians

(October 1985 – January 1991)

BOTT, Sharon

Adrian's second girlfriend and the mother of his son, Glenn. 'A provincial dullard working in a laundry', in the harsh assessment of the 18-year-old Adrian. Since their disastrous first date at fourteen she has dramatically expanded and is now reminiscent of 'Moby Dick with a perm'. Adrian thinks their relationship was always doomed due to the class divide: he upper-working/lower-middle, she lower-working/underclass. A warm-hearted but ineffectual mother who lives in mild squalor.

BROWN, Mr

Adrian's boss in the Newt Section at the Department of the Environment in Oxford. A wildlife fanatic dressed by Man at C&A who claims to have not taken a day off in twenty-two years. Has spent Christmas Day classifying seaweed at Dungeness.

MUFFETT, Martin

Wilbur Smith-loving engineering student who holds Adrian and all intellectuals in contempt. A lodger in the Mole household who becomes Pauline Mole's second husband, ageing ten years in the process.

LIVINGSTONE, Rocky (Big Boy)

Pandora's live-in lover in Oxford. A 16-stone bodybuilder with a chain of gyms, he is happily unaware of the existence of the things Adrian worries about and 'lives in a world of sight and sound only'.

TWISLETON-FYFE, Julian

Pandora's horse-faced gay husband. Amiably studying Chinese at Oxford, but doesn't intend to sit his finals. A minor aristocrat who strives for eccentricity and fails to achieve it.

Adrian Mole: The Wilderness Years
(January 1991 – April 1992)

BELLINGHAM, Belinda

George Mole's glacial new partner/ employer, the managing director of a burglar alarm company with questionable sales tactics. A frightening blonde.

CAVENDISH, Jack (Bluebeard)

Pandora's lover. An aged professor of linguistics at Oxford. A three-times divorced, rumpled, womanizing alcoholic with ten children, many in therapy or rehab.

DARTINGTON, Bianca

A hydraulic-engineering graduate working at a newsagent's in Oxford. Quietly pretty, she is attracted to an oblivious Adrian, eventually drawing him to London despite his reservations over her profligate use of exclamation marks and love of Guns 'n' Roses. She gets him out of grey slip-on loafers and into Next and the 1990s.

De WITT, Leonora

Beautiful Gestalt psychotherapist, with long flowing 'midnight river' hair and no shortage of clients suffering from transference. Adrian is quite willing to pay her £30 and beat a chair with a stick. A boxing fan.

HACKER, Angela

Celebrity novelist and drinker, teaches Adrian 'Writing for Pleasure' at the Faxos Institute, Faxos. She 'facilitates Adrian's epiphany' and encourages him to swim naked in the Aegean.

HEDGE, Mrs

Adrian's mournful literary landlady. Slovenly.

MOLE, Jo Jo

African Princess. Heiress to her mother's Nigerian lorry tyre conglomerate. Tall, beautiful, dreadlocked, marries Adrian out of a mixture of pity and love. A talented artist and mother of William Mole. Out of Adrian's league in every way possible, the marriage can only be seen as a folie à deux.

PRINCIPAL CHARACTERS

THE ADRIAN MOLE DIARIES

PALMER, Christian
Adrian's live-in landlord/boss. An undercover popular-culture academic with three precocious children and a babysitting problem. Wears his hair in 'late-period Elvis' style, and laughs like a barking dog.

PALMER, Cassandra
Shaven-headed wife of Christian; absent directing a film on mutilation in LA, where she learns to function on the cutting edge of politically correct.

Her return is not joyfully celebrated by the Palmer household.

SAVAGE, Peter
Adrian's boss; a rotund celebrity alcoholic with a Bob Hoskins accent. Owner of Savage's and it's later perfection, Hoi Polloi, and winner of the 'Rudest Restauranteur of 1990' award. His arbitrary banning orders exclude most of the population of central London from his premises.

Adrian Mole: The Cappuccino Years
(April 1997 – May 1998)

BANKS, Les
A very unlucky builder contracted to work on the roof of Rampart Terrace.

BOTT-MOLE, Glenn
Adrian's long unidentified illegitimate son, by Sharon Bott. Semi-literate and a stranger to correct grammar, but with an optimistic and loving nature. Easily satisfied; the happiest time of his life was when Leicester City first won the Worthington Cup. Adrian cannot wait to get him out of gangsta clothes and into Junior Next.

FLOOD, Eleanor
Glenn's neurotic home-tutor, head of remedial studies at the Keith Joseph

Academy. Adrian's stalker, obsessed with phoenix symbolism and wears only black.

Justine
Adrian's Soho confidante, with all the latest gossip. An exotic dancer at Large Alan's with the dress sense expected of a woman who regularly embraces a python for cash.

KENT, Edna
Mother of Barry Kent. Toilet cleaner; later secretary to Pandora Braithwaite, courtesy of an access course and two degrees. One of which is in family law, where she has a good head start.

Luigi

The very Italian Maître d' of Hoi Polloi. Has been in the business twenty-seven years, and is a 'personal friend' of Sophia Loren and Tommy Steele.

Malcolm

Dishwasher at Hoi Polloi. Illiterate, but believes Tony Blair's new regime will teach him all he needs to know.

MOLE, William

Adrian's young son by Jo Jo. Obsessed with Teletubbies and 'motoring oaf' Jeremy Clarkson; living with the Mole family in Ashby-de-la-Zouch after his parents' separation. Spends most of his days sitting inside a cardboard box. Later moves to Nigeria, changing his name to Wole Mole.

MONTEFIORI, Zippo

Floppy-fringed producer of Adrian's daytime cookery show, *Offally Good!* Never seen without his black Armani overcoat, but doesn't sweat. There is rumoured to be a waiting list for potential girlfriends.

DOG, New

Replacement for the original Dog. Adrian is secretly less fond of it, believing it to lack character.

SINGH, Dev

Eye-rolling, double-entendre-loving Sikh co-presenter of *Offally Good!* A manufactured cult figure for students and the real star of the show, he is secretly scared by his own performance.

SAVAGE, Kim

Peter Savage's estranged wife, a former society florist from the East End with no intention of taking elocution lessons.

STOAT, Arthur

Head of Stoat Books, editor of *Offally Good! – The Book*. His record for turning a book around is three weeks, with *Diana at My Fingertips* by her personal manicurist. Adrian Mole presents more of a challenge.

TAIT, Archie

Ancient, ascetic revolutionary socialist, with one leg and one lung. Gravely ill and lives alone with his cat, Andrew. Adrian is compelled by conscience to help him, despite wondering if he will ever be free of pensioners with their 'liver-spotted hands circling my neck'.

PRINCIPAL CHARACTERS

THE ADRIAN MOLE DIARIES

Adrian Mole and The Weapons of Mass Destruction
(October 2002 – July 2004)

ANIMAL
Monstrously strong builder helping George and Pauline Mole to renovate The Piggeries. Communicates with Pauline in grunts and listens to the anecdotes George has told thirty times before. When asked his real name answers 'Animal'.

BLUNT, Ken
Long-serving member of the Leicestershire and Rutland Creative Writing Group, specializing in rabidly anti-American polemic. Not a natural diplomat, but a friend to Adrian.

BOND, Johnny
Travel agent at Latesun Ltd who steadfastly refuses to refund a £57.10 deposit for Adrian's cancelled holiday. The ability or otherwise of Saddam Hussein to deliver Weapons of Mass Destruction to Cyprus within 45 minutes is central to his case.

CARLTON-HAYES, Hugh
Adrian's elderly employer; one of the last of the provincial antiquarian booksellers. The person that Adrian most admires, despite knowing nothing about his private life. A refined and gentle man, but not averse to a punch-up; he is a life-long enemy of Michael Flowers after they came to blows over Tolkein's prose style in the car park of the Central Lending Library.

FLOWERS, Daisy
Half-sister of Marigold. Darkly fascinating London-based PR to the famous who claims to be 'the author of my own life'. Adrian is strangely attracted to her hedonism and complete disinterest in Dostoevsky; frightened by her passionate opposition to the Iraq war. Immaculate, but not as individualistic as she would like to believe, having recently undergone a full Nigella Lawson re-model. She lives in expensive disorder, with a growing pile of high-ticket designer goods flagged as potential returns.

FLOWERS, Marigold
A thirty-something on-the-shelf depressive who works at Country Organics and accidentally becomes Adrian's girlfriend. Builds miniature dolls' houses; performs Mary in a peripatetic Nativity with the Leicester Mummers, and is even less fun than this sounds. Fatally for Adrian, she has beautifully soft skin and fragile wrists.

A 'manipulative, hysterical hypochondriac', according to Daisy Flowers.

FLOWERS, Michael
Father of Marigold; the scratchy-sweatered proprietor of Country Organics and counter-tenor in the Madrigal Society. An English 'back to nature' fascist with plans for Adrian Mole, he is both repulsive and oddly persuasive. Has a severe aversion to Mexico and Mexicans.

FLOWERS, Netta
Mother of Marigold, uncommitted wife of Michael. Incredibly pink, she resembles a very pretty pig. Shows more affection for her compost heap than her family.

FLOWERS, Poppy
Sister of Marigold. Scientologist maths teacher whose distinguishing feature and main reason for living is her extraordinarily long hair. Not keen on her family's medievalism; she prefers the Romans, for their civilizing influence and 'amazing hair products'.

FORDINGBRIDGE, Gladys
Elderly member and regular host of the Leicestershire and Rutland Creative Writing Group. Her literary output consists entirely of sub-Pam Ayres cat poems; one of which, 'Naughty Paws', achieves the difficult task of rhyming 'Whiskas' with 'discus'.

Geilgud
Evil leader of a disruptive flock of swans at Rat Wharf, named after his resemblance to the classical English actor. Adrian believes Geilgud holds a personal grudge, claiming to see 'a sneer on his beak' during his attacks.

Graham
Nigel Hetherington's guide dog. The only living thing he has ever truly loved and a better friend to him than Adrian ever was. A creature with eerie intelligence.

Leslie
Mr Carlton-Hayes' partner, of whom Adrian knows absolutely nothing, except that she/he is reportedly not as keen on books as Mr Carlton-Hayes.

HENDERSON, Bruce ('Brainbox')
Adrian's old school 'friend', winner of 'geek of the year' at Neil Armstrong Comprehensive. Owns his own consultancy firm, Idiotech, supplier of non-threatening technology solutions to computerphobes. Has plenty of money and needs somebody to spend it on.

PRINCIPAL CHARACTERS

HOPKINS, Bernard

Very temporary assistant at Carlton-Hayes' Books. A hopelessly drunk ex-bookseller and one of the most politically incorrect men in Leicester; his standard term of address is 'cocker.' Disdains all 'bint' authors and anything written after Nabakov, although 'Salman' is supposedly a personal friend.

MILKSOP, Gary

Over-sensitive, tetchy member of the Leicestershire and Rutland Writing Group. The author of an epic experimental novel that has been worked on for fifteen years. The masterpiece spends two thousand words on Gary's first memory of eating a Hobnob and is unfinished.

Ivan

Tastelessly named replacement for the NEW DOG, which died on Christmas Day 2001, or was 'killed' by Adrian, according to his parents.

PARVEZ, Mohammed

Adrian's friend and financial adviser. A realist who lives within his means, choosing to work from a bedroom office with Postman Pat wallpaper. His concerned but pragmatic advice is generally ignored. Enjoys the drama of cutting up his clients' charge cards.

STAINFORTH, Robbie

Glenn Mole's best friend, a shy 18-year-old fellow soldier in the Royal Logistics Corps. According to Glenn, he knows 'a lot about everything'. Adrian sends him 'improving books' by BFPO and privately wishes Glenn was more like Robbie.

WONG, Wayne

Adrian's old school friend; the cynical owner of the best Chinese restaurant in town, the Imperial Dragon (Wong's), the only place Adrian really feels at home. A ten per cent discount and a good table near the fish tank are usually available. Not a fan of Marigold Flowers, whom he thinks resembles one of his 500-quid-per-throw carp.

Adrian Mole: The Prostrate Years
(June 2007 – May 2008)

DOCTOR PEARCE
An English lecturer with John Lennon glasses and 'overlarge breasts'. She enthusiastically pursues the possibility of an affair with Adrian, to his dismay. Overrun by her four children.

DR WOLFOWICZ
Adrian's Polish GP. A mournful giant who looks more like 'a Gdansk steelworker' than a doctor. Yearns for his wife and home.

FAIRFAX-LYCETT, Hugo
Heir of Fairfax Hall. A ravaged but handsome aristocrat and self-confessed establishment figure, who is building a safari park in his grounds. Employer of Daisy Mole, who is sourcing his giraffes.

LEWIS-MASTERS, Dorothea
Elderly upper-class world traveller and former camel-accessory importer. Frequently quotes the wisdom of the North African 'men of the desert'. She lives in a large Georgian house, stuffed full of animal skins and heads.

MOLE, Gracie
Adrian and Daisy's four-year-old daughter, who is already displaying 'alarmingly Stalinist tendencies'. Usually to be found wearing her little mermaid costume and being carried, as 'Fish can't walk.'

Sally
A 'small but sturdy', homely radiotherapist. Adrian is fascinated by her disastrous relationship with wolf-conservationist boyfriend, Anthony.

PRINCIPAL CHARACTERS

THE MOLE BOOKS

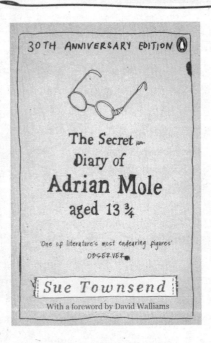

FRIDAY JANUARY 2ND

I felt rotten today. It's my mother's fault for singing 'My Way' at two o'clock in the morning at the top of the stairs. Just my luck to have a mother like her. There is a chance my parents could be alcoholic. Next year I could be in a children's home.

Meet Adrian Mole, a hapless teenager providing an unabashed, pimples-and-all glimpse into adolescent life.

'Townsend has held a mirror up to the nation and made us happy to laugh at what we see in it'
Sunday Telegraph

SUNDAY JULY 18TH

My father announced at breakfast that he is going to have a vasectomy. I pushed my sausages away untouched.

In this second instalment of teenager Adrian Mole's diaries, the Mole family is in crisis and the country is beating the drum of war. While his parents have reconciled after both embarked on disastrous affairs, Adrian is shocked to learn of his mother's pregnancy.

'The funniest, most bitter-sweet book you're likely to read this year'
Daily Mirror

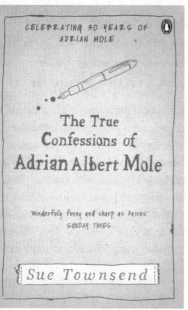

The True
Confessions of
Adrian Albert Mole

'Wonderfully funny and sharp as knives'
SUNDAY TIMES

Sue Townsend

MONDAY JUNE 13TH

I had a good, proper look at myself in the mirror tonight. I've always wanted to look clever, but at the age of twenty years and three months I have to admit that I look like a person who has never even *heard* of Jung or Updike.

Adrian Mole is an adult. At least that's what it says on his passport. But living at home, clinging to his threadbare cuddly rabbit 'Pinky', working as a paper pusher for the DoE and pining for the love of his life, Pandora, has proved to him that adulthood isn't quite what he expected. Still, without the slings and arrows of modern life what else would an intellectual poet have to write about . . .

'Essential reading for Mole followers' *Times Educational Supplement*

THURSDAY JANUARY 3RD

I have the most terrible problems with my sex life. It all boils down to the fact that I have no sex life. At least not with another person

Finally given the heave-ho by Pandora, Adrian Mole finds himself in the unenviable situation of living with the love-of-his-life as she goes about shacking up with other men. Worse, as he slides down the employment ladder, from deskbound civil servant in Oxford to part-time washer-upper in Soho, he finds that critical reception for his epic novel, *Lo! The Flat Hills of My Homeland*, is not quite as he might have hoped.

'A very, very funny book' *Sunday Times*

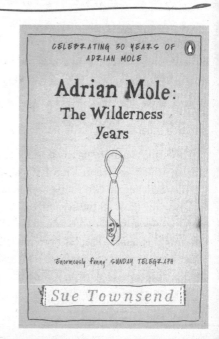

Adrian Mole:
The Wilderness
Years

'Enormously funny' SUNDAY TELEGRAPH

Sue Townsend

WEDNESDAY AUGUST 13TH

Here I am again – in my old bedroom. Older, wiser, but with less hair, unfortunately. The atmosphere in this house is very bad. The dog looks permanently exhausted. Every time the phone rings my mother snatches it up as though a kidnapper were on the line.

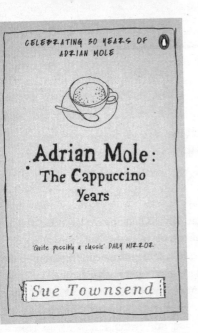

Adrian Mole: The Cappuccino Years

'Quite possibly a classic' DAILY MIRROR

Sue Townsend

Adrian Mole is thirty, single and a father. His cooking at a top London restaurant has been equally mocked ('the sausage on my plate could have been a turd' – AA Gill) and celebrated (will he be the nation's first celebrity offal chef?). And the love of his life, Pandora Braithwaite, is the newly elected MP for Ashby-de-la-Zouch – one of 'Blair's Babes'. He is frustrated, disappointed and undersexed.

'Three cheers for Mole's chaotic, non-achieving, dysfunctional family. We need him'
Evening Standard

MONDAY JANUARY 3, 2000

So how do I greet the New Millennium? In despair. I'm a single parent, I live with my mother . . . I have a bald spot the size of a jaffa cake on the back of my head . . . I can't go on like this, drifting into early middle-age. I need a Life Plan . . .

The 'same age as Jesus when he died', Adrian Mole has become a martyr: a single father bringing up two young boys in an uncaring world. With the ever-unattainable Pandora pursuing her ambition to become Labour's first female PM, his over-achieving half-brother Brett sponging off him, and literary success ever-elusive, Adrian tries to make ends meet and find a purpose.

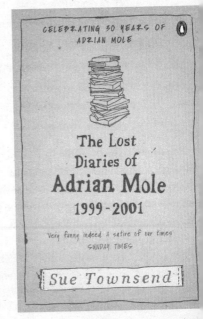

The Lost Diaries of Adrian Mole 1999-2001

'Very funny indeed A satire of our times'
SUNDAY TIMES

Sue Townsend

'One of the great comic creations of our time.' *Scotsman*

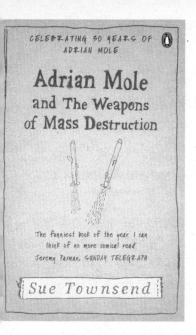

CELEBRATING 30 YEARS OF
ADRIAN MOLE

Adrian Mole
and The Weapons of Mass Destruction

'The funniest book of the year. I can think of no more comical read'
Jeremy Paxman, SUNDAY TELEGRAPH

Sue Townsend

WEDNESDAY APRIL 2ND
My birthday.
I am thirty-five today. I am officially middle-aged. It is all downhill from now. A pathetic slide towards gum disease, wheelchair ramps and death.

Adrian Mole is middle-aged but still scribbling. Working as a bookseller and living in Leicester's Rat Wharf; finding time to write letters of advice to Tim Henman and Tony Blair; locked in mortal combat with a vicious swan called Gielgud; measuring his expanding bald spot; and trying to win-over the voluptuous Daisy . . .

'Completely hilarious, laugh-out-loud, a joy' *Daily Mirror*

SUNDAY IST JULY
NO SMOKING DAY
A momentous day! Smoking in a public place or place of work is forbidden in England. Though if you're a lunatic, a prisoner, an MP or a member of the Royal Family you are exempt.

Adrian Mole is thirty-nine and a quarter. He lives in the country in a semi-detached converted pigsty with his wife Daisy and their daughter. His parents George and Pauline live in the adjoining pigsty. But all is not well.

The secondhand bookshop in which Adrian works is threatened with closure. The spark has fizzled out of his marriage. His mother is threatening to write her autobiography (*A Girl Called Shit*). And Adrian's nightly trips to the lavatory have become alarmingly frequent . . .

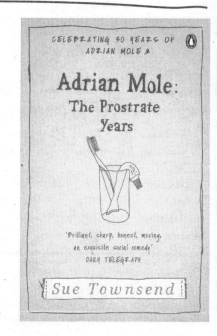

CELEBRATING 30 YEARS OF
ADRIAN MOLE

Adrian Mole:
The Prostrate Years

'Brilliant, sharp, honest, moving, an exquisite social comedy'
DAILY TELEGRAPH

Sue Townsend

'Unflinchingly funny' *Sunday Times*

'Laugh-out-loud . . . a teeming world of characters whose foibles and misunderstandings provide glorious amusement. Something deeper and darker than comedy' *Sunday Times*

The day her twins leave home, Eva climbs into bed and stays there. For seventeen years she's wanted to yell at the world, 'Stop! I want to get off!' Finally, this is her chance.

Her husband Brian, an astronomer having an unsatisfactory affair, is upset. Who will cook his dinner? Eva, he complains, is attention seeking. But word of Eva's defiance spreads.

Legions of fans, believing she is protesting, gather in the street, while her new friend Alexander the white-van man brings tea, toast and an unexpected sympathy. And from this odd but comforting place Eva begins to see both herself and the world very, very differently. . .

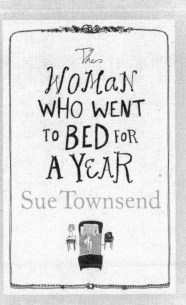

'She fills the pages with turmoil, anger, passion, love and big helpings of wit. It's full of colour and glows with life' *Independent*

'Touching and hilarious. Bursting with witty social commentary as well as humour' *Women's Weekly*

'A funny, poignant look at modern family life' *Daily Express*

'Touching and ridiculously funny . . . just genius' *Closer*

'Hilarious . . . will have you cheering Eva's one-woman war on everything' *Now*

THE MONARCHY HAS BEEN DISMANTLED

When a republican party wins the General Election, their first act in power is to strip the Royal Family of their assets and titles and send them to live on a housing estate in the Midlands.

Exchanging Buckingham Palace for a two-bedroomed semi in Hell Close (as the locals dub it), caviar for boiled eggs, servants for a social worker named Trish, the Queen and her family learn what it means to be poor among the great unwashed. But is their breeding sufficient to allow them to rise above their changed circumstance or deep down are they really just like everyone else?

'Kept me rolling about until the last page' *Daily Mail*

'There are two things that you should know about me immediately: the first is that I am beautiful, the second is that yesterday I killed a man. Both things were accidents . . .'

When Midlands housewife Coventry Dakin kills her neighbour in a wild bid to prevent him from strangling his wife, she goes on the run. Finding herself alone and friendless in London she tries to lose herself in the city's maze of streets.

There, she meets a bewildering cast of eccentric characters. From Professor Willoughby D'Eresby and his perpetually naked wife Letitia to Dodo, a care-in the-community inhabitant of Cardboard City, all of whom contrive to change Coventry in ways she could never have foreseen . . .

'Splendidly witty . . . the social observations sharp and imaginative' *Sunday Express*

What if being Royal was a crime?

The UK has come over all republican. The Royal Family has been exiled to an Exclusion Zone with the other villains and spongers. And to cap it all, the Queen has threatened to abdicate.

Yet Prince Charles is more interested in root vegetables than reigning . . . unless his wife Camilla can be Queen in a newly restored monarchy. But when a scoundrel who claims to be the couple's secret lovechild offers to take the crown off their hands, the stage is set for a right Royal showdown.

'Wickedly satirical, mad, ferociously farcical, subversive. Great stuff'
Daily Mail

Behind the doors of the most famous address in the country, all is not well.

Edward Clare was voted into Number Ten after a landslide election victory. But a few years later and it is all going wrong.
The love of the people is gone.
The nation is turning against him.

Panicking, Prime Minister Clare enlists the help of Jack Sprat, the policeman on the door of No 10, and sets out to discover what the country really thinks of him. In disguise, they venture into the great unknown:
the mean streets of Great Britain . . .

'A delight. Genuinely funny . . . compassion shines through the unashamedly ironic social commentary' *Guardian*

Enter the world of Sue Townsend . . .

This sparkling collection of Sue Townsend's hilarious non-fiction covers everything from hosepipe bans to Spanish restaurants, from writer's block to slug warfare, from slob holidays to the banning of beige.

These funny, perceptive and touching pieces reveal Sue, ourselves and the nation in an extraordinary new light. Sit back and chortle away as one of Britain's most popular and acclaimed writers takes a feather to your funny bone.

'Full of homely, hilarious asides on the absurdities of domestic existence . . . What a fantastic advertisement for middle-age – it can't be bad if it's this funny' *Heat*

'Gripping and disturbing. Utterly absorbing' *Independent*

Seventeen years ago Angela Carr aborted an unwanted child. The child's father, Christopher Moore, was devastated by the loss and he retreated from the world. Unable to accept what had happened between them, both went their separate ways.

However, when Christopher makes a horrifying discovery whilst out walking his dog on the heath he finds that he is compelled to confront Angela about the past. As they start seeing each other again can they avoid the mistakes of the past? And will their future together be eclipsed by those mistakes of yesterday?